Ernie and the Mage-Killer

JOOLS WARNER

Ernie
and the
Mage-Killer

JOOLS WARNER

ISBN (Hardcover) : 978-19159-525-78
ISBN (Perfectbound) : 978-19159-525-85
ISBN (EPUB) : 978-19159-525-92

This edition printed November, 2025
by Sphinx
(an imprint of Sul Books, LTD)
Lewes, UK / Rodenbourg, LUX

Cover and Interior Design: Sul Books

Find our books at SULBOOKS.COM

ONE

I was in my usual seat at the bar and settling into a Saturday afternoon whose passing I'd measure in pints. I'd just got to work on my second when I heard a voice I shouldn't have recognised.

"Hello, Ernie," it said, as though the last time I'd heard it had been five minutes, rather than five years, ago.

I sighed and closed my eyes, hoping I'd mistaken a stranger's voice for this one. Then, with a deep breath, I opened them again and risked a glance in its direction.

The chair beside mine was as empty as it had been since I'd sat down, and beyond it was everything you'd expect from a scruffy small-town pub with stained glass windows and walls yellowed with tobacco smoked many years earlier. I shook my head, exhaled. Just a ghost, then. Lucky escape. I shrugged, allowed myself a smirk of relief, and raised my glass to my lips.

There was a polite cough.

"I'm down here, Ernie," the voice said. It was well-spoken and had a softness so trustworthy it could get you into all kinds of bother. Uh-oh.

I put my glass down, and turned to look at the bit of floor behind the chair next to mine. Shitting hell. There he was. My best bloody mate, the cheeky bastard.

He leapt up onto the empty chair. It was rather clumsy; golden Labradors aren't renowned for their grace.

I held the chair steady while he tried out a range of sitting positions. My pint, I noticed with alarm, was in serious danger but, by some miracle, survived un-thwacked by a vigorously wagging tail.

He settled on his haunches, facing me, and grinned doggily, pleased with himself.

I let go of the chair, raised my eyebrows, folded my arms, unfolded them, and took a sip of beer. *Thank the Makers for beer, I* thought, and felt a tangle of emotions I would not allow my face to betray.

"I'll try again, then, shall I?" my best mate said, and politely coughed onto the back of a raised forepaw. It was adorable, but I wanted more than anything to be annoyed with him after five years of nothing. "Hello, Ernie, it's so nice to see you. "How're tricks?" he asked, with an emphasis that announced his expectation of a response.

"Y'alright, mate," I replied, rolling my eyes. "Didn't hear you sneak in."

Violet, for such was his name, looked at me through deep brown eyes ringed with honey-coloured fur. His muzzle had a smattering of paler hairs that reminded me of tiny splashes of emulsion from a decorator's paint roller.

"You're looking well," he said.

"Oh, give over." I snorted into my half-empty pint glass, causing a miniature storm. I wiped some drops of beer off the tip of my nose, took a long sip, then placed the glass down and smoothed the grimace from my face. "No offence, mate, but I hoped I'd never see you again. But time just flew by, and here you are, for some reason." My voice was low, and I tried to keep it taut, but a wobble crept in at the edges.

"It's a pleasure to be reacquainted with you too, my dear chum," Vi said. He looked around the room, inhaled deeply, and let out a satisfied sigh. "Ahh. I've missed this dusty old place. Missed you, more importantly." He nudged my arm gently and leaned in close. "We all have."

"Ah, piss off, mate," I said. I sniffed and wiped my nose with the back of my hand. "Anyway, I thought we were square. Debt paid. My adventuring days are over. They've been over for a long time." I rested my elbows on the bar and leaned forward over my glass. A couple of tears fell into the remaining inch-and-a-half of my pint.

Vi rested a concerned paw on my forearm. "Look at me, Ernie."

I turned my head, gritted my teeth, and regarded him through puffy, red-rimmed eyes.

The muscles in Vi's forehead tensed ever so slightly, then relaxed. He held my gaze for a moment. "Come back. You belong with us. We're your Clan."

I didn't like the smell of this. "Why now?" I said once I'd released the breath I'd been holding. "Why did it take you all this time to bother paying me a visit, if I mattered that much? Eh?"

Vi winced. "Well — there is something." He broke his gaze from mine, pretended to study one of the sticky patches on the bar for a moment, then glanced around to make sure no-one was in earshot. He needn't have worried; the place was virtually empty and would stay that way until happy hour started at five. "The Clan has need of your, ah, specialist skills," he said conspiratorially. "Well, all seven Clans do, really; it's just I was nominated for the errand since you and I are such good pals, you know." He brightened with this last statement, as though he'd been awarded a bloody medal. Probably deserved one, to be fair.

"I knew it. And there I was thinking you just wanted me back because of my boundless charm and fabulous looks." I huffed out air through my nose in a suitably disgruntled fashion. "Which skills is it you want, then?" I didn't mean to brag, but I'd been a formidable Earth-Mage in my day. I leaned back in my chair and folded my arms across my stomach.

"The ones you're best at, Ernie."

Arse. This could mean only one thing. "Escaped then, has he?"

"You, ah — you could say that, yes. In, ah, a manner of speaking. And, um, you know — sorry, *knew* — him better than the rest of us, not to mention your extraordinary grounding and resilience to attack." He gave another doggy grin, but this

one had an edge of sheepishness. It was a questionable juxta-
position and did not endear him to me at all.

My belly churned, and the skin of my face went hot and
clammy. This was too sudden. I wasn't ready. I unfolded my
arms and leaned forward over the bar. "Reg, mate?" I called to
the landlord, who was at the far end of the bar, drying glasses
with a greasy dishcloth while he chewed the fat with some old
codger. "Another, when you've got a sec, and one for my pal here.
And can you fetch us a bowl while you're at it?"

Reg lumbered into action immediately, picking up two of the
dry and freshly smeared glasses and filling one with my usual
and the other with the lager Vi used to favour back in the day. I
was impressed he remembered after all this time. He put the
full glasses down in front of me, picked up the empty one and
the money I'd left on the bar, and turned, wordlessly, to shuffle
to the till. I heard a few beeps, the clatter of coins, the drawer
sliding shut. He disappeared through the door that led to the
cellar, and came back with a chipped porcelain bowl, which he
liberated, using the same greasy dishcloth, from its coating of
cobwebs. He waddled over and plonked the bowl down next to
Vi's lager. I carefully did the honours and moved the lager-filled
receptacle to the edge of the bar with negligible spillage.

"Cheers," Vi said.

I gave a nod of acknowledgement that would have been im-
perceptible to the untrained eye, and downed a third of my
fresh pint in one go. When I put the glass down, I saw that my
hand was trembling. A flush of cold swept through my limbs
and migrated to my scalp, where it perched, tingling. I felt like
my hair might tear itself free and fly off into a corner somewhere to hang out with one of the frightening but amiable
spiders whose webs practically hold this dilapidated building
together. I sighed. "So," I said, "the infamous Mage-Killer's on
the loose. That's all I fuckin' need."

Vi unleashed a smile; a weirdly human grin formed around a fine set of pointed teeth. "What do you say, then? Coming back?" Claw-tips clacked on the edge of his bowl. His ears were pricked up, on guard. He never used to be this anxious.

I studied his face. He looked careworn around the eyes. Faint odours of muddy water and rotting leaves emanated from his coat. I'd smelt far worse, though, and my gut told me I would again, sooner rather than later.

"No, Vi," I said as I raised my fingers to air-quote position. "'No' is what I say, and 'no' is what I shall continue to say." I lowered my hands, shook my head slowly, and breathed: "Just: no."

"But—"

I raised my right hand, palm towards Vi to block any further attempts at persuasion. "Not after what happened the last time." My voice cracked, and I made that choked sound you make when you're trying not to cry and covered my face with my hands.

"Here." Vi nudged my arm.

I looked up to see him offering me a handkerchief. I almost asked him where he'd got it from, but thought better of it. It looked clean enough, though, and when I took it and brought the soft fabric close to my face it smelled of lavender. I blew my nose into it loudly. "Ta, mate," I mumbled.

"Please don't cry, Ernie," he said. "Come on, I don't like to see you upset."

"How could I not be? He's bloody dead." I wept again.

Vi sighed. "It's been five years, Ernie," he said, with a kindness in his voice that I found excruciating. "It's been a long time. You have to move on eventually. You can't live like this, weighed down by the past."

"I'm sorry my grief is so inconvenient for you."

"You know I didn't mean it like that."

"Like what?" I snapped. Christ on a bike, I wasn't making this easy. Poor Vi. He always did get the awkward jobs; that much hadn't changed.

He sighed again.

"It was all my fault," I continued. "It's my fault he died. I killed him."

"Elias was killed by — well, you're quite aware of his name. And you know as well as I do that he is the one solely responsible. We were both witnesses, after all."

Rage exploded in my chest. "That *fucker!*" I spat. "Aldrich the Great. That's not even his real name. It's his name for himself. You know Aldrich means 'wise leader,' right?" I sneered, unable to resist air-quoting again. "Pah! As if. He's neither. His name's Richard Grey, and he's from Whitby, for fuck's sake. I mean, nowt against the place personally, but it did produce that dickhead and therefore, by extension, has a lot to answer for." I took a few deep breaths, un-clenched my fists, and reached for my glass. My hand was trembling so much it was hard to raise it to my lips.

"Sorry," Vi said after a respectful pause. "Elias was killed by Richard ... of the Grey."

I sighed. "Ugh. Okay, I'll allow that. And yeah, that's true in a technical sense, but it was still my fault."

"No, Ernie."

"Yes! I hesitated. I was badly injured and scared shitless." I shook my head, and screwed my eyes up tight, trying not to cry again. "I fucked up. Couldn't protect him, and he died. I failed him, and I failed the Clans. All seven of 'em."

Vi's smooth brow furrowed again, but he kept his thoughts to himself.

I took the opportunity to carry on. "Haven't you lot considered the possibility that this could happen again? That's why I can't help you. I couldn't before, so it's ridiculous to assume I'd be any bloody good five years down the line when I'm out of practice." I flinched at a mental image: fur, and fangs, and red, red blood. I looked down at my hands, and momentarily saw it there, the stain that would never wear away or wash from my skin. An accusation. An execution. My shoulders slumped forward. "I said I can't help you, mate. I'm really sorry."

Vi glanced away, distracted by the rustle of a packet of crisps being handed over the bar. His lips pulled back, and a bead of drool escaped the corner of his mouth where it hung on a slender thread. My mouth watered, too, though I was more thirsty than hungry. I took another sip of beer.

He turned back to me, and the movement of his head flung the suspended bead of drool onto my sleeve. He smiled. I noticed how large and how sharp his teeth were. "You'll be handsomely compensated, of course," he said.

I pulled my left hand into my sleeve so I could wipe away the drool, but instead only rubbed it deeper into the fabric. I rolled my eyes. "That's what you said the last time. And I'm still waiting. Therefore, no offence, but my answer's still in the negative."

The door opened too quickly, creaking on its hinges. The hum and swoosh of traffic and the voices of smokers chatting and coughing outside intruded briefly upon the room before the door swung closed and thumped home. I thought of coffin lids. My heart rattled at the sound, and I placed a hand on my chest to soothe it. "Oof, steady on, love," I said.

There was no need to be startled; it was only an old bloke who'd stumbled in to occupy his usual position in the corner seat diagonally across the room from where me and Vi were. He collided with a table on the course of his clumsy orbit of the furniture; then, gripping the edge of the dark wood table top and leaning onto it with the heels of his hands, making the thing list alarmingly, he let out a chesty smokers' cackle any rogue celestial body would be proud of. He belched as he landed in his habitual spot, flinging his carrier bag of newspapers and cheap supermarket cider down onto the precariously up-holstered fire hazard of a seat beside him.

"Usual coming right up, squire," Reg called from beside the scrumpy cask that lurked on the back bar between the till and the glass wash. Not for the faint-hearted, that stuff; it's got life.

As I raised my glass to take another sip, the door opened again. Shards of yellow-white light refracted through its thick panes and swept across the wall, sharp and alien in the fusty gloom of the lounge bar. The old bloke across the room gave a start as a luminous beam scratched across his fleshless, desiccated cheek. A shadow filled the doorway. I gulped.

"Not just you who's been looking for me, then, is it mate?" I whispered in Vi's ear.

He didn't reply, but his fur bristled and he made a rumbling sound. It took me a second to realise he was growling; I'd never heard him do that before. I wasn't sure it suited him. Then, double-quick-sharp, his claws shortened and flattened into neatly clipped fingernails, his paws lost their fur and became broad, strong hands. The golden Lab's stocky physique became a solid, upright posture. Vi, now sitting beside me in human form, had sleek golden hair restrained in a plait that hung down between his shoulder blades and whose end was tied neatly with a white ribbon. He wore a yellow robe and hat with cute cream-coloured bones stitched all over them in a loose herringbone pattern. And, bless him, it didn't make him look like much of a warrior.

I hunkered down, using Vi as a temporarily human shield. Never let it be said that I'm not resourceful. I clutched my pint to my chest for safety.

A wave of energy rippled across the room as the shadow in the doorway cast a Shroud. Standard practice, this: shields all magic, malign or benign, from eyes and minds it's not meant for.

A shudder rippled through me when I realised that the shadow was one of the Heartless Ones. They're nowhere near as strong as their commander, the Grey Dickhead himself; but still, this was definitely not a Mage to trifle with. And I intended to do nothing of the sort. I couldn't have, in any case.

I leaned away, though my buttocks remained reluctant to give up their comfy position on the chair's cushion, and I moved only scant inches. Nowhere near enough to make a difference if any injurious incantations were directed my way. I prayed Vi wasn't hoping I'd do anything useful and hunkered down further, wanting to make myself small and inconsequential. Unfortunately, though I could remember all the mundane stuff like how the magic in our world works and who's a part of it, I had deliberately cast all my expertise regarding how to actually work said magic into oblivion. Now, for the first time in five years, I found myself regretting that decision.

As the Air-Mage billowed, cloud-formed, into the room, Vi executed a perfect back-flip off his chair and landed a few feet behind it, facing the enemy — who was of considerably taller stature than he — in a defensive stance. The impressiveness of this was slightly marred, however, by the fact that his crumpled hat had slid down to cover one eye. He righted it with haste, muttering an inoffensive curse that only added to the cuteness of the scene, then reached inside his cloak, pulled a staff from one of its interior pockets, cleared his throat, and barked some words that I fancied must come from the canine translation of the first stanza of the Standardised Invitation to Fisticuffs (Category B: Spontaneous Magics), or something.

At the sound of Vi's challenge, his adversary let out a tooth-shattering screech and surged forward into the centre of the room, where he stayed for a few seconds, drawing a palpable density into himself. Then, two protrusions snaked out like weird, misty arms from his centre — exactly where his heart should have been, had it not been ritually extracted from his body.

The air had grown thick and tarry. My breath caught in my throat as the tension packed the room like coils of razor wire. It was like watching a duel between brooding outlaws in the most surreal, hallucinogenic Western, thick air around them pulsing with life as they stood poised for action. I imagined a drug-addled visionary with a camera, about to give the order from behind the bar.

"Couldn't lend me a hand here could you, Ern?" the erstwhile dog stage-whispered from the corner of his mouth.

I pulled my best innocent expression, which, to be honest, was ineffective at the best of times, shook my head, and shrugged, my pre-arthritic shoulders rising and falling beneath the wool of my bright purple jumper. "Nah mate, looks like you've got it under control," I said. "Anyway, you know I'm no good for the scary stuff anymore." I slurped at my beer in a childish attempt to irritate him in the hopes that it might dissuade him from trying again to persuade me into this suicide match.

"You really can be the most obtuse of gits," he observed. Charming.

The tension finally broke. Vi and the Air-Mage flew toward each other, and clashed in mid-air in a roiling mass of magical words.

A well-timed utterance is the best way to a short, sharp fight by immobilising or vaporising the enemy before they can brandish a weapon. Such victories are rare, however, since Blocking Words are amongst the first knowledge any fledgling Mage acquires; the magical equivalent of nursery school. And so, Vi and his opponent launched successions of spells at each other, all of which were undone or snuffed out before any harm could be inflicted.

In a melee of guttural sounds, the duel gradually became a vortex, spinning in the middle of the pub. I wished I'd had some popcorn.

Vi's low growls were countered with venomous streamers of sound. He cut and thrust, spun and stabbed, and his attacking moves passed through dark vapour. As he stepped aside or leapt back between strikes, the Air-Mage fired out lightning bolts. Vi ducked and blocked, successfully at first, but a few hit home, making him yelp. I wrinkled my nose at the smell of singed hair. This put me firmly off the idea of snacks.

Slowly, Vi began to tire. The Air-Mage swelled by increments, and his poisoned words gained the narrowest edge over Vi's growls and snarls. I gritted my teeth. My old friend would be done for soon if he didn't pull something magnificent out of that hat which, against all reason, was still on his head, though smoke emanated from a scorched patch near its tip. They kept at it for what felt like ages in a tug-of-war that might last an aeon, but which, at the end of things, would still be a mere microcosm of the Eternal Battle in which we are all but tiny pawns being prodded with pointy things around the great gaming table of the Universe — without being allowed to roll the dice.

At one point, it looked as though Vi was in danger of being smothered in an asphyxiating embrace, but he used his staff and his free hand to pull his way out. I've seen an Air-Mage engulf someone before, and it isn't pretty. Vi was lucky to escape that fate. Sweat beaded on his forehead, and his sleeves were pushed up his arms. I squinted; I wasn't wearing my glasses and couldn't tell whether his skin was covered in scorch marks or he was a lot more tattooed than the last time I'd seen him.

At last, a succession of dog/human hybrid shouts was topped off with a great explosion as Vi deployed one of his Words, with a capital "W." To me it sounded like "GRAAAAAAARGGGHHHH!," though I'm sure the syllables were more nuanced to the canine ear. Anyway, it worked. Its vibration made the room shake as though an articulated truck had thundered down the narrow street outside, sent that way by a Satnav device possessed by a trickster deity suffering from ennui.

The Air-Mage began to shrink, spinning like a whirlwind made from coal dust.

Vi's feet came to rest on the floor, the scuffed soles of his worn leather sandals meeting the violently tasteless carpet and doubtless wanting to recoil in horror. He raised both arms, his right hand holding his staff aloft and the left empty, with fingers splayed. As his adversary shrank further, he kept the right arm high and lowered the left so that his hand was held out before him at waist height, palm up.

The Air-Mage, now reduced to about the size of a football, came to float a few inches above Vi's open palm.

Vi moved his staff into a horizontal position above the shrinking ball of charcoal-coloured vapour, all the while whispering a spell to compact his vanquished opponent further. After the final word was uttered, he directed a breath into the space between his hands.

They're really quite special, Air-Mages. Their primary element is Air, hence the name, but they also tend, in many cases, to be adept at calling Water and just enough Fire to reduce anything to ashes. Huge potential for mess and, in the more powerful cases, costly property damage, especially when they're training, though you could say that for most of us. The payoff is great for these guys, though; I mean, the lucky fuckers can *fly*, for a start and, as if that weren't enough, imagine being able to turn yourself into a *thunderstorm*. I had to confess I'd always envied their flamboyance.

He tried a few last lightning bolts as a parting shot, but didn't have the strength in him, and only fizzed and sparked like a toaster on the blink. It was rather a damp squib, as Mage defeats go, to be honest. He crumpled weakly and was banished to a dimension of Vi's choosing — hopefully a nasty one. This was no mean feat. Vi had grown strong.

As the victorious Vi stood panting in the centre of the room, the Shroud dissipated into the dark corner behind the fruit machine whose lights flashed in a way that made it look as though it was having a seizure. A faint hint of burning lingered in the air, which was then absorbed into the curtain fabric to join the remnants of cigarettes smoked decades, possibly even centuries, earlier.

I gave a yell of triumph and leapt off my chair, the most exercise I'd done in ages. I went to Vi, who was still getting his breath back. "Nice one, mate," I gushed, clapping him on the back so hard I almost knocked him over. Then, calmer, gripping his shoulder, "you've learned a bit since last time we met, eh? Wow." I released my grip and gave him a round of applause.

The old bloke eyed us with suspicion from his corner, his bloodshot eyes burning in the gap between the peak of his flat cap and the top of his newspaper. He looked from one to the other of us, cogitating, gave an unpleasantly textured cough in lieu of any verbal offering, then went back to his tabloid.

Vi glared at me. His eyes burned with a fierceness that was new to me and spoke of real authority. He held my gaze while the blue light in his irises faded until they were their usual deep brown under the rim of his crumpled, and now lightly toasted, hat.

We returned to our places at the bar. The room was back to its ordinary, pubby self, and he was once more canine.

He jumped up onto his chair and licked at the singed patches on his coat. "It'll heal," he said.

I topped up his bowl, and, glowing with admiration, watched him lap greedily at his beer. He made a right bloody mess; foam went everywhere and my right hand and forearm were treated to a liberal shower of crap lager. I downed the rest of my drink so as to avoid contamination.

Reg was in front of me on the other side of the bar before my empty glass had made landfall on its frayed beermat. He has enough psychic power to make me suspect that he is, in fact, a Yoga Master. I nodded assent to a new pint being poured, and gave him a knowing smile. He ignored it. Perfect equanimity, just as I'd thought. The full glass un-levitated down a minute later, and I picked it up and sipped the divine in ale form, thanking the Makers once again as I did so.

Vi regarded me flatly and raised an eyebrow. "Another pint, Ernie, really? We need to leave."

"Mm? I'm not going anywhere." I tried my innocent voice again.

The room was empty now, but for us and the old bloke, who was still buried in his paper, and a barely visible new stain on the carpet.

"Alright," I sighed after I'd kept Vi waiting another minute, "I'll indulge you for a bit. You'd best be warned though, I'm keeping a tab. And," I wagged a fingertip at him to show I meant it , "I'm charging interest this time."

"Naturally," he said.

I scoffed and turned my head away from him so he couldn't see my expression. I caught it myself, reflected unflatteringly in one of the mirrored panes above the back bar. My face floated over the canopy of the tubular metal forest made from the free-pour spouts of rarely touched liqueurs in varying hints of aggressive and saccharine. It was wearing a most disapproving expression. I averted my gaze. I'd stared myself out in under five seconds.

"Sure," I said. "Of course."

Vi patted my arm. "Come on, Ern. Leave your pint and let's make tracks, eh?"

I dismissed him with a tut, and shook my head. I took a few sips with my eyes closed, and tried to pick out the most boring sounds around me, as if I could dispel this unexpected turn of events with stubbornness alone. It wouldn't have been the first time.

I opened my eyes, and looked into the mirrored glass on the back bar again, behind the free-pour forest. My face looked washed-out even in the tinted glass, my skin not its usual golden hue but the colour of piss-stained sand, with distinctly waxy overtones. Or would it be undertones? I looked like I'd borrowed a face, picked a discarded mask out of a bin and slipped it on.

As my mind shuffled toward the inevitable decision, weighing the good against the bad, I prayed for some of the former and as little as possible of the latter, which is all one can ask for in life, is it not?

"Alright," I said. "I'll come with. Hang on a minute, though. Just gotta go for a wee." With that, I alit from my chair and made for the Ladies.

Two

As I washed my hands, I leaned forward to scrutinise my face in the scratched mirror under the lav's fluorescent light. The mirror clung to the wall above the chipped porcelain sinks and perpetually empty soap dispenser. I regretted my decision already. It showed in my eyes: I saw a hint of doubt flash in my sage green irises, spied the pinch in the skin above my cheekbones, and that was ample evidence to convince me. I hadn't thought this through at all, had got carried away in all the excitement. Violet, cunning hound that he was, had taken advantage of my good nature and my beer-lowered defences. What an idiot I'd been to fall into that trap again.

"By the Makers, Earthfield Rockwood, you're a damned fool," I said to myself, my voice as cracked as the veneer on the porcelain sink. Yep, that's my full name, but I prefer the abbreviated version, although, as a friend pointed out to me a while back, it does somewhat lack gravitas; it's like Gandalf saying: "y'alreet pal, just call us Gaz." Nevertheless, I've always preferred "Ernie."

This was pretty much what happened the last time, as far as I remembered: I agreed to something without properly assessing the consequences, involved myself in a brawl that got extremely out of hand, and ended up in this state. Drinking alone, wearing not the flowing attire one might expect from a powerful senior Mage but a holey purple jumper and my black tracksuit bottoms with the fluffy insides and deep pockets you could — and I frequently did — lose stuff in. Fivers, mostly. Keys, sometimes. Drugs, far less often; I'm pretty vigilant where those are concerned.

But, looking around, I didn't see a way out of it. There was no way I could escape from the toilet window: it was barred and, in any case, far too small. I'm not as nifty as I was back in the day.

I wiped away fresh tears, then dragged myself back into the lounge bar to find Vi and meet my destiny.

We walked back to my place without speaking. The afternoon was as drear as my spirits. The fine mizzle that hung in the air had quickly soaked through my clothing and was working on the barrier of my skin, though the cold and the damp had taken up residence in my bones quite some time ago.

Vi cleared his throat. The sound came out as a gruff not-quite-cough, not-quite-bark. It was enough to snap me out of it, though; untwist my mental helter-skelter. I looked down at him.

He was padding along cheerily beside me, eyes bright and ears alert. I should probably have put him on a lead so as not to arouse suspicion, but nobody we passed seemed to notice. It was fortunate that Vi's Change-Form had settled into such an innocuous one. Quite a masterful ruse on the part of his predominant Elements, actually, since anyone would immediately judge him to be a thoroughly good boy and never suspect him of being able to, say, banish would-be assassins to another dimension. I imagined the reactions we'd be getting if people were seeing a Pit Bull rather than a golden Lab trotting along, leadless, beside me. In any case, he was a peaceful sort. Most of the time.

"I am truly sorry, you know, about Elias and everything," he said, making no effort to conceal the fact that he was speaking to me in English, plain as owt.

I glanced around nervously, but we were still ignored. I couldn't think of anything to say, so I didn't.

We got to my place. I let us in, and led the way down the dark central corridor of the house, past groaning bookshelves and over my boots that were scattered across the floor, and the litter tray I kept there for the cat who visited from time to time.

I shivered. "Boiler's on t' blink again," I said over my shoulder. "Sorry about the cold." The house was like a bloody tomb. I showed Vi to the living room, and lit the fire. "Should warm up soon," I lied, rubbing my palms together briskly.

"We don't have long," Vi said. "We need to set off as soon as is feasible."

"Huh?" I said, in a final attempt to feign ignorance, as I rubbed my cold, damp arms.

"You know, for the thing. The job you've agreed to help us with."

I stopped rubbing. "Oh."

"Might be one or two more of the Heartless Ones about," he added perfunctorily as he trotted to the sofa and jumped up onto it. "Where there's one, there are bound to be others." He pulled the blanket I kept rolled up along the back of the sofa's sagging cushions down onto the seat, tugged at it to unravel it sufficiently, and curled up, wrapping his tail about him.

"Make yourself at home," I said.

He just looked at me with those placid brown eyes. Was this a test? I wasn't fully convinced by his argument about more of the Heartless Ones lurking about, but he did have a point. Though we'd done away with most of them years before, and their leader had been under lock and key until very recently, we'd be foolish to assume they'd died out. It certainly didn't make sense to hang around and wait for them to show up. This was the closest brush I'd had with that lot in years, and I didn't like being caught on the back foot. Or, more accurately, caught sitting on my arse, getting pissed.

I stood in the centre of the room for a moment, hugging myself as I tried to will some heat into my limbs. It did no good, and I consigned myself, with a sigh, to being forever chilly. With that decision out of the way, I was unsure what to do next. Ah, that was it. I looked at the far side of the room, where sat a large armchair that wasn't pushed all the way back into the corner. I walked the four paces over to the chair and moved it aside by pivoting it on its rear left wheel. The other three left curved dents where they'd pressed into the floor, unmoved, for these past five years, and dark tracks behind them in the layer of dust on the carpet.

As soon as I caught sight of the old case I'd shoved into the corner behind the armchair, my soul sank into a dank hollow. The past had finally caught up with me, and it had been hiding in plain sight all this time. I broke down in tears. Seeing the prison I had packed my old gear into, and newly aware that the house was no more than a slightly larger one I had arranged for myself, I was now conscious of my loss as an unstoppable destructive force that could rip tree-roots from their darling earth.

I knelt in front of the case, reached to get the key from its place on top of a dusty tome I'd never read, at least, not that I recalled, and bent to undo the stiff lock. My hands tremored so violently that I couldn't connect the key with the keyhole at first. "I can't do this," I whimpered. I opened the case, and the smell of dust and love and pain rose up from my old stuff like bubbles of gas from rotting matter on a lakebed.

Vi jumped down off the sofa, padded to me, sat, and licked my hand. "You can. You're strong enough, Ernie," he said. "You are Earth. Use your roots." He nudged my arm with a wet doggy nose.

"You would bloody say that, wouldn't you?" I said between sniffs. "And I know very well who and what and how I am, thank you very much. But..." I flexed my fingers, feeling the tiny creaks and groans of joints that had borne too much weight, wielded too many heavy weapons, yet now were sorely, woefully out of practice.

Vi sat down. "We understand how hard this is going to be for you. Seeing him again."

"It's not *him* I've the problem with. I can't wait to split *his* head in two like I almost did the last time." I clenched my hands into fists. "It's what he reminds me of that's the problem. He killed my El..." I could barely speak his name aloud. It hurt so much, yet I wanted to cleave to the word as though to let it go from my mouth would be to lose him all over again.

The however-many ales I'd had suddenly sat wrong in my stomach. I pushed myself to standing, ran to the bathroom, and voided a couple of pints' worth of fetid yellow, dotted with the last remaining undigested chunks of the fried egg sarnie I'd had for breakfast. Some came out of my nose. It was disgusting. The interval between making and eating that sandwich, and bidding the last of it farewell, was quite a lot of beer ago. I coughed and spat, then went to the sink to rinse my mouth out with cold water. I splashed a little on my face, pointedly avoiding eye contact with the mirror. I'd had enough of the things. I sat down on the edge of the pink plastic bathtub stained with tide marks that long predated my residence in this hovel, and wept anew, which worsened my headache.

A cautious scratching at the door preceded a pleading canine whinge. "Come on, Ernie. You can do this. We all need you," said Vi, his voice coarser through the flimsy planks of the door.

"I don't want to know everything again if this is what remembering only part of it feels like," I said limply.

"You don't have to bring it back all at once. You can perform the Restoration in stages, and rest in between to give your mind time to catch up. That's the safest option, anyway, considering."

"I know." I sighed, swept my hair off my face, and stood. I realised then how hungry I was, and how faint I felt. I swooned, and had to place a hand on the wall to support myself for a moment while the black dots cleared from my vision.

"You okay in there?" Vi called.

"Hungry," I said. "Not feeling great, to be honest." I staggered to the door, and opened it. Two Brazil nut brown eyes looked at me from the Mage's face. He was in man-form again, wearing that cute robe and hat of his.

He beckoned for me to follow him, and we went into the kitchen. I sat down on a dining chair while Vi set about gathering the makings of something that could pass itself off as an edible meal; quite a challenge in this place. While he fussed over ingredients and pans, humming a tune to himself, I sank further into my seat. I closed my eyes. All I could see behind my eyelids was Elias, as vital and beautiful as he'd been the day he died. His face, his eyes, his arms opening out to embrace me. Would it always hurt so much? I couldn't bear the thought of it.

☙

I was startled by the sound of a cupboard door closing. My eyes fluttered open, and I wiped drool from the corner of my mouth while wriggling back to an upright position. Must have nodded off for a few minutes. I closed my eyes and took a few breaths, thinking I may have been seeing things; but when I opened them and turned to look again, there it still was, on one of the coat hooks on the back of the door, looking deceptively inconsequential.

"By the Makers, Vi, you utter bastard. I can't believe you've done this."

"Hm?"

"Don't 'hm' me, mate. That was a serious breach of boundaries."

The cheeky fucker had only rummaged through my gear and got my Skin out of the case. To the normal person it would look like nothing more than a satin dressing gown, but it was far more than that. Like Vi's get-up, this garment was a clue as to my appearance once I Changed, which I hadn't done for a very long time. I was surprised it looked in such decent nick: its green and brown satin, the colour of beech leaves and bark, was creased but not moth-bitten. It wouldn't have mattered either way if it had fallen to bits, since the garment itself was no more than a graduation certificate: it holds no actual power on its own; it's more what it symbolises that counts. The Change-Form itself is a co-creation between a Mage's combination of

Elements, and we just have to hope it's something we can work with.

I've always been embarrassed by mine. It's crap for sword fights, or anything fights for that matter, and not good for flying or leaping or running either. There have been very few Earth-Mages who Change into trees, and I'm one of 'em, since I also have a smattering of Wood energy, though I've no idea from where. Elements are hereditary, and we tend to have one that predominates, a decent amount of a second, and a little of a third. My family is Earth on one side and Mineral on the other, which is what makes my Change-form so powerful. I'm Earth first, Mineral second: a tree as solid as rock. Impervious to fire. Impossible to drown. Basically, I'm really bloody hard to kill.

Most Earth-Mages have the Change-Form of some creature that walks upon or inhabits the ground, which gives physical mobility and plenty of options for pretty fur and a nice tail of some sort. Vi, for example, is predominantly Earth, and his secondary element is Water. His Change-Form being canine is perfect, because what self-respecting hound doesn't love mud? As a golden Lab, he gets to roll around in it far more freely and more often than he would in human form. I've always rather envied him the ease with which he Changes; it makes it seem as though he's exercising a choice. The truth is that we don't get to select our Change-Form, though some manifest more commonly than others. Those of us who don't slip so smoothly into a comfortable relationship with our Form just have to find a way to live with it.

The tree thing got me horribly bullied for a while when I first discovered my own Form — my classmates were all Changing into deer and cats and ferrets and the like — but that soon stopped when I Changed in the playground. My roots broke its tarmac surface to pieces as if it were sugar glass, and the lead bully, who was standing close to me, was impaled very messily on a branch. I got into a right load of trouble for that; had to spend some time in the Correctional Centre for Wayward Magical Youths. It was worth it, though, for people to stop bothering me. Only problem was, the Centre is where my path first crossed with that of Richard Grey.

It sickens me to think of it now, but he and I were actually friends at first, bonding over a disdain for cliques and conformity. My fuck-up was that I mistook our shared outsider-ness for a shared worldview. Slowly, as I got to know him, I realised that what in me manifested as an embarrassed reluctance to join in and an awkwardness in groups, in him became a burning, vengeful resentment and an obsession with separation — one he would come to act upon. He slowly built a following (or a clique, one could say, and the irony of this should be lost on no-one) of other disaffected magicians, a group which to my credit I refused to join. There were only a dozen of them even at their height, and it seemed to the rest of us that they weren't a credible threat given our superior numbers. Nobody took them seriously until the Mage-killings started, a mistake that cost us all dearly, but some more dearly than others. I shook my head and exhaled, wondering, as I had many times, what I could have done differently.

Vi stopped chopping the garlic I hadn't realised I had in the fridge and turned to face me. He placed his hands on his hips, channelling some heavy maternal vibes. "The poor neglected thing needed airing," he said blithely, as though one of my most precious magical artefacts was just a bed sheet that had been folded up in a drawer for too long. Mind you, that was kind of how I'd been treating it.

"It's not right to keep it cooped up like that, even if you haven't worn it since Initiation," Vi continued. He shook his head and turned back to his chopping.

"You could've asked first," I muttered.

"You'd have refused, though, wouldn't you, eh? Stubborn goat," Vi projected over his shoulder. "And besides, you looked so innocent snoozing away there. I didn't want to wake you."

I could hear the smirk in his voice. "Whatever," I said, distinctly irked.

The last time I'd seen my Skin was when I'd shut it away along with everything else that reminded me of my Clan, my Element, my true identity. And Vi was right: it was criminal to have kept it locked in that case all this time. An act of self-harm, as was the magic I'd worked to dissociate myself from my Magehood. I'd wanted it to be the last magic I ever worked.

It was a spell not many have the grounding for. Flesh-magic with a ten-thousand-to-one chance of success; but I did it. I magic-ed my own brain into submission, suppressing even the most rudimentary magical skills and altering my physical appearance and my energy signature so I'd be spiritually invisible, or so I'd thought. It was nice while it lasted. Okay, not nice, just uneventful, which, after all the death and fighting, was exactly what I thought I needed. Nobody had the right to stop me, since it is enshrined in our Constitution that a Mage may work magics of any type, no matter how harmful, on themselves as long as they are of relatively sound mind — which I certainly wasn't, but I did it sneakily before anyone could stop me, then retreated here, to the nondescript small town I'd moved to as a kid and lived in during the years prior to my Initiation. I don't know why I came back here really. Habit, I suppose. But staying wasn't an option now, with the Mage-Killer back on the prowl.

THREE

Tomatoes from a newly opened tin sizzled in the pan, along with the garlic and half an onion that had seen far better days. Vi whistled to himself as he stirred. I usually can't tolerate whistling, but the irritating noise faded into the background when I stood up and walked to where the wire hanger on the back of the kitchen door held my long-neglected Skin.

Now, facing this ceremonial garment again after so long, every inch I moved carried me a little further back in time, a little further into the fog, and it thinned as I passed through it, thickening again, protectively, behind me. I felt uncomfortably close now to everything I'd turned my back on. I stood blankly, scalp tingling, skin cold, facing the back of the kitchen door, staring like a proper mad person instead of one who has, due to profound shock, taken only temporary leave of their senses.

The bang of a cupboard door startled me and dispersed the fog. My head whipped round and I glared at Vi. He stood, wooden spoon in one hand, his eyes rueful. His other hand rested on the handle of the cupboard I kept cups and glasses in. "Sorry," he said, "just looking for pasta."

"Oh, yeah, it's there somewhere," I said flatly, and turned away from him again. I pulled back from the sounds of good-natured muttering and rootling until they were just a numb vibration somewhere else.

I was close enough to smell the fabric now. Heavy with use, and not a little resentful at having been ignored for so long, it bore the lingering remnants of frankincense, patchouli, and other fragrances long forgotten. I shifted my weight from side to side, feeling the bandy floorboards under the kitchen's scuffed linoleum flex beneath my feet. Slowly, slowly, I reached up a trembling hand, and took heavy satin in my fingertips. I knew that Vi was watching me; I could feel those eyes of his boring gently into my back, if such a contradiction were possible, while he pretended to stir the sauce. The click of the kettle coming to a boil took his attention away from me, and I unfroze. I ran satin through my fingers, then took the weight of the fabric into my hands and examined it, rubbing it across the flat of my cheeks where it soaked up tears. *Be useful, these will*, a neglected part of my brain noted. I shushed it away: "Not now, please," I whispered. I let the Skin fall back down, and it swung from side to side on the hanger.

"Grub's up," said Vi from behind me.

I turned. He had laid the table with plates and cutlery and napkins and was dishing up steaming piles of food. He'd rolled up his sleeves to expose lean, muscular, heavily tattooed forearms. All evidence of the fight in the pub had already healed — a testament to his strength — and I saw that he had indeed acquired a lot of new ink. Lovely work, too. His display of manners was strangely formal, and I didn't know whether to laugh or cry. I was touched by the effort he'd put in, even if it had been nothing more than a transparent attempt to butter me up. We both knew I'd be leaving with him. There was no need for pretence, but I couldn't argue. A good meal would be the best way to start the journey. This was Vi's affable nature plus a wheelbarrow-full of classic Earth pragmatism, and I appreciated both.

"Pepper?" He stood, paused with the pepper mill over my plate.

I smiled feebly, and nodded. "Lots. Ta," and I watched as he ground a large amount of coarse black pepper over my food. No such thing as too much pepper or garlic.

We ate in silence. Vi had impeccable table manners for a man who spent much of his time as a dog. I refrained from commenting for fear of patronising or offending him, especially after all the trouble he'd gone to with the food, but I couldn't hold back from watching him as he ate. Put polite amount of food onto fork. Lift to mouth without incident. Open mouth just enough, insert food. Retract fork, retaining food in mouth. Chew, mouth politely closed. Swallow. Repeat until plate empty, and without scraping or clanking fork too much. It was beautiful.

After I'd swallowed my final mouthful, I ran my finger around the edge of the plate to mop up some sauce, then I lifted the plate and licked it clean, partly to signal to Vi that if he wanted to do the same, or even put his dish on the floor and take dog-form to relieve it of any remaining scraps, I'd be fine with that. He did neither, and simply leaned back in his chair, smiled, and patted his belly.

I pushed my plate away and burped loudly. I hadn't meant to, but it broke the silence, and both of us laughed. I couldn't remember the last time I'd laughed — well, I could, but not for real.

Vi picked up the dishes and took them to the sink, then got to washing. I normally would have offered to wash up since someone else had done the cooking, but he seemed happy enough, humming away to himself amid an excess of bubbles. I leaned onto the tattered upholstery of the backrest of my wobbly dining chair and retreated into the thoughts that were waiting for me.

I returned to myself when Vi touched me gently on the arm. Had I dozed off again? I sat up in my chair. My arse cheeks had gone numb. I stood up and, though the muscles were stiff, I was glad to notice that my legs felt a little stronger than before.

Vi went into the living room. I heard things being moved around, which meant the cheeky so-and-so was snuffling about in the case again. He emerged in dog form, with my wand held between his teeth. He flicked his head sharply, throwing the wand into the air for me to catch, which I did purely on reflex. Very crafty of him, that was; to hold a wand is to accept responsibility for one's Magehood. It's the final act in the Initiation. A binding contract which still stood, even though I'd deliberately forgotten all my magic. Looking very pleased with himself, he trotted to the back door and whined to be let out. Seriously? Could he not use the bloody bathroom like the rest of us? You can even train cats to crap indoors, for Earth's sake. I glanced at the litter tray — no, that would be too weird. "You'd better not be expecting me to pick up after you once you've been, mate," I said.

I unlocked the door and let him out into the garden. Truth be told, I was relieved to have a few moments to myself. I didn't know when my next chance of some peace and quiet would be. I went through into the living room to look at my old gear again and to pick further at the cracks forming in the protective wall I'd built, but I had to return to the kitchen to let Vi in when he scratched at the door a couple of minutes later. He came back inside, tail wagging, crossed the room, opened the cupboard under the sink with a honey-coloured paw, grabbed a bag from the pack I used for cat litter, and trotted back outside with it held in his teeth. A minute later he came back, and I opened the bin for him to drop the bag in. He did so, then sauntered into the lounge as if he owned the place.

I briefly worried that one of the neighbours might have witnessed a dog pick up its own business in my garden, a sight I had certainly never seen, but it was a rainy Saturday afternoon; they'd all be watching telly or down the pub. I locked the back door and followed Vi into the living room, shaking my head in near-disbelief at the bizarre turn my afternoon had taken. Only about an hour ago, I'd been enjoying a quiet pint. I wondered forlornly how long it'd be until I had another one.

"Right," Vi said from the blanket he'd reclaimed on the sofa. "We ought to go as soon as possible, really."

I knelt on the floor. "I know."

I picked up my laptop from where I'd shoved it halfway under the sofa before I'd left the house a few hours earlier and opened the lid. Once the geriatric machine had yawned itself conscious, I opened a new tab in the browser, found the booking web site, and plonked the laptop on the sofa next to Vi.

He tapped at the keys for a while, frowning. "Gosh," he said, "it's so pricey these days." He sighed, paused a moment, and a mischievous grin slowly bloomed on his face. "The Clan's covering it, anyway, so I suppose I'd better book us First Class."

"You sly old dog," I said, and I smiled at the thought of adequate legroom and free cups of tea, even though I knew it'd be served in one of those miserly thimbles you could eke about two sips from. I like my tea to come in a proper mug, you know, one the size of something between a cauldron and a skip.

Vi barked happily, pleased with his polite disobedience.

"Steady on, mate," I said, smirking. "You'll have to wear a lead or they'll not let you on. Pretend you're my obedient little pet."

He put his head on one side at a jolly angle. "I know," he said affably. "It's a modest price to pay for your assistance."

I could tell from the shock that erupted on his face that my expression had instantly darkened.

"That is *not* my price, mate," I glowered. The atmosphere grew charged, as though a fairly benign raincloud had decided that actually, no, it was in foul humour today and would now spread and boil an anvil head above us, and it was hovering as it did so, eyeing which bits of human, canine, or furniture to zap with lightning bolts.

"I wasn't suggesting—" Vi tried to backtrack, and I knew he hadn't meant to insinuate that I'd be helping for free when they still hadn't properly compensated me for last time, but I was in the mood to be a bit difficult. The least I could do at this point to feel any certainty was to uphold my reputation for being a git. I took a deep breath and slowly exhaled, counting to ten. "Sorry. There was no need for that."

We were on the same side, after all; what was the use of bickering? Why waste energy on being an arsehole when I'd need all the strength I could scrape from the bottom of the metaphysical barrel for whatever awaited? I hadn't raised my voice in such a long time, though. I felt awkward. I wasn't sure what to do next. I'd surprised myself.

I was roused by a polite canine cough. "You alright, Ernie? Want to talk about it? Quite understandable if you're having second thoughts."

I was, of course. Second, third, fourth, and fifth thoughts, actually, and I knew that none of them would change the fact that I couldn't avoid what I had to do. It was horrible, but so was my life here, the one I'd collapsed into, and that wasn't life at all, not really. I took a deep breath in, blew it out, and gave a half-arsed smile of acquiescence. "So, ah, what time's the train then?" I said, "and where is it we're going, exactly?"

Vi shook his head. "Never you mind. It's best you don't know at this stage. And we've got an hour yet before we need to be at the station."

I jumped to my feet. "What! Only an hour? Best get moving, mate; the buses round here are really unreliable. I've cut it fine way too many times." My head blared a warning that I was careening towards overwhelm, but I ignored it. "Come on, then, let's get cracking," I said, before swooning again and losing my balance. I arrested my fall — in the clumsiest manner possible — by flinging my upper limbs around the arm of the chair I'd pulled out from the corner. I clung on as though it were a life raft made from brittle wood and musty velour and turned my head to take a look around the living room that already felt as though it belonged to someone else. A mood hung in the air, as though the room itself was informing me that I had now completed my term as custodian and it was chucking me out. Maybe I should have looked more closely at the rental contract:

inspected it for clauses about the gaff evicting me when it'd had enough. It was unceremonious, to say the least.

FOUR

e waited at the bus stop in the rain. It was one of those that's just a pole with a sign on it, rather than having anything as helpful as a shelter to keep the weather off, or even an up-to-date timetable — not that it would have had any bearing on what times the buses would actually arrive, if they could be bothered.

I had a battered holdall with my essentials inside it slung over my shoulder, and Vi was in dog form. We needed to pass for normal, or as close to it as a pair like us could manage, the idea of which is, frankly, hilarious. I'd done the best I could to find Vi a collar, which meant kitting him out in a Day-Glo pink studded belt I used to wear to raves, plus a lead I'd dug out of my bedside cabinet's deepest drawer. This had studs on it, too, though it was of a somewhat different stylistic bent. I'd trimmed a few inches off the belt so it was the right length for his neck.

"Really suits you, mate," I'd said as I stood back, kitchen scissors still in hand, to admire my handiwork, but he didn't seem convinced. He was too polite to say anything at the time, but he had the look of a tolerant family pet the kids have dressed up in a frilly pinafore and bonnet. "Ah, come on, it's a perfect disguise for a warrior of your calibre." He chuntered under his breath at this, so I didn't push things further. He did look fabulous though.

The rain persisted. Luckily, I was still damp from before, though I worried about my stuff getting wet in the holdall; its waterproof days were far behind it. I peered along the road, craning my neck. No sign of the bloody bus yet. Typical. It's remarkable the difference a few minutes can make to a journey, how that distance between having plenty of time to not quite enough can be a splitting of seconds. I looked up and down the street. There was very little traffic. Suspiciously little, in fact, for the time of day.

I shivered. I was cold from the rain, but this was something else; a sensation of something closing in around me, and icy fingers stroking the length of my spine.

A movement across the road caught my eye — was that a wisp of smoke I'd just seen in the doorway of the café on the corner opposite? I tightened my grip on the lead and gave it a quick tug to get Vi's attention.

"D'you smell anything sketchy over there, mate?" I whispered.

Vi sniffed at the air. The fur along his spine bristled. He leaned forward, pulling at the lead, frowning, nose lifted, but said nothing.

"It might just be nerves, but I really don't like the feel of this," I said, trying to keep my hands from shaking. I looked right, then left, then right, willing the bus to come and rescue us.

When the headlights of the 42 swung into view from round the bend in the road, I stuck out my arm and waved it frantically. I made eye contact with the driver, who I could tell even from fifty feet away was having serious reservations about stopping. And who in their right mind would stop for us, the crazy old bird in the purple jumper with her probably incontinent dog that looked like a relic from the 1990s with that reflective fluorescent collar on, which, though ridiculous in one way, was actually sensible attire considering how dark the sky had grown.

I toned down the arm-waving, and the driver's expression softened. The bus pulled up with a hiss of hydraulic brakes, and the door swung open. I stepped in, glad to be out of the rain, and Vi jumped in after me and shook the water off his coat, drenching me anew. He looked up at me, chuffed with himself, and I pressed my lips together and exhaled through my nose. "*Mate*," my expression said. "*Seriously.*"

The bus driver side-eyed me, then peered down at Vi.

"He's my support animal," I said. "I have terrible anxiety."

The driver narrowed his eyes. He didn't seem convinced.

I tried, and doubtless failed, to conjure up my least anxious-looking smile and proffered a crisp fiver.

"Single to Central, for me and the little 'un," I said, my pitiable attempt at humour failing to inspire either laughter or sympathy.

The driver growled, probably in disapproval at being handed a note rather than as a value judgement on my appearance, but nevertheless I still felt personally offended. He threw me another hefty dose of shade and peered at Vi again, then flung the change at me before crunching the gear stick and flooring the accelerator pedal.

The vehicle's heavy lurch almost launched me off my feet. On the bright side, we'd set off at a good pace, which would mean we'd be less likely to miss our train, even if we did end up dashed to smithereens across the newly-paved bit outside the station, in full view of its row of new bus stops. Pride of the local council, they were, with their anti-homeless hostile architecture and their eternally-revolving display of pointless advertisements.

I cast a final glance at the corner café as we pulled away but saw nothing lurking in the shadowed doorway. I must have imagined that, too. Travelling was fraying my nerves already and we'd barely made a start. Goodness knew how I'd cope with the rest of the journey, not to mention all else that awaited. I cursed myself for an idiot, sent a quick appeal to the Makers for their protection, and felt hopelessly doomed.

"Come on then, mate," I said to Vi. "Upstairs or down?" We moved to the bottom of the narrow, twisted staircase that led to the upper seating area.

Just then, there was a *whump* as something hit the side of the bus. It felt like a micro-focused gust of wind, or a kick from a giant, invisible boot. I looked down at Vi. His ears were pricked up and his eyes wide. The impact again: *whhhhump*. It was forceful enough to almost pitch the bus sideways, and the wheels all along its right-hand side got a second of air time.

The driver swore floridly in a thick local accent and wasted no time in stepping on it. I leaned back, keeping hold of the handrail, and peered at his face in the rear-view mirror. He was looking around, boggle-eyed, with panic mashing his features into a confused amalgam of scarlet skin and bristly facial hair. It was quite something to behold. He wrenched the huge steering wheel hard right to pull out and overtake another bus that was stopped in front of us with its left indicator blinking.

"We must be making decent time if we're passing the bus before ours," I mumbled, and internally hailed the Fates responsible for the mysterious zone where timetabling meets traffic. "Let's stay down here, eh," I said more loudly, and me and Vi swayed our way to the nearest seats as the driver pulled the wheel back left to guide the bus into its correct lane.

Once seated, I turned and looked out of the window. Nothing there. No sign of anything untoward. Had I imagined the sound? The impact? It must have been something, to make a double-decker bus shudder like that. Vi jumped onto the seat beside me and rested his forepaws over my legs, transferring some mud and pavement grime onto my trousers. Given the circumstances, I didn't mind.

The bus cracked on at a great pace down the high street, its driver now in the grip of mania. He'd rolled the window down and was treating the outside world to a range of obscenities, so that the humble 42 now had an audience all the way to the station. We swooped past slow-moving cars and deftly, if narrowly, avoided the ones coming the other way. This driver was a legend and had evidently missed his calling as a stuntman. I wondered whether this experience had opened a door in him and led him to a style of driving he'd always wanted to try but which didn't tend to be asked of him in his day-to-day duties.

I had one arm over Vi and the other over my holdall on the seat between me and the window. And I was absolutely bloody terrified. My knuckles made bony peaks above the slopes of my hands. I leaned left to make regular glances out of the windscreen to assess the traffic and recalculate the probability of missing the train — but while that eventuality grew less likely, the chance of being plastered all over the windows and floors increased exponentially.

Only when the bus pulled in with a screech of brakes at the stop outside Central Station and I had thanked the Fates for our survival, did I notice the huge scratch-mark on the window beside our seats. It hadn't been there when we sat down; I was sure of it. I'd have chosen another seat as soon as I'd noticed something so wound-like. It had the look of skin raked raw by long fingernails or claws. The safety glass window was bent inward at the place exactly level with where the side of my head had been, and a fluvial plain of crisscrossing cracks haloed out around it. Why hadn't I noticed it before?

Vi *rrrrffed* softly, leapt off the seat, and pulled me along behind him to the door. We alit onto a damp, slate grey pavement covered in flattened spat-out wads of chewing gum like the blooms of a vile fungus, and he dragged me into the cool blandness of the station concourse.

Having already sent our tickets straight to my email, Vi marched me to the departures board. His eyes scanned the electronic brimstone numbers and letters, and found their target. "Platform Four," he said. "Other side, over the bridge. C'mon."

I didn't have time to work out which train he was looking at, and when he set off I trotted dutifully beside him. He still looked, to all intents and purposes, like a well-behaved golden

Lab and not one of the most powerful Earth-Mages who's ever lived.

He muttered under his breath, weaving a spell for protection and swift travel, I assumed, though I didn't understand the words. Passing hassled parents and their mewling charges, stressed public transport employees shouting into walkie-talkies, and gaggles of angular, loping, eye-lined teens, we took the steps two at a time.

"Come on, come on," Vi urged.

I almost chastised him for speaking in public whilst in dog form, but when I glanced around and saw that nobody was looking at us at all, I calmed down.

"Slight overkill this, though, mate, working proper magic in the station?" I said to him, almost laughing. His growth in the years we'd not seen each other had obviously made him as paranoid as he was powerful. He ignored my chiding and strained at the lead, pulling me across the high bridge towards the steps down to the furthest platforms.

When we turned the corner and started down the steps, I saw why Vi had taken his precaution: one of the Grey's soldiers stood at the bottom of the stairs. Well, "hovered" would be more accurate. She was floating about six feet off the ground. To be fair to myself, she was hard to spot: a Spirit-Mage by the looks of it. In my dulled state, she was barely visible as a shimmery patch like a heat-haze, which the other passengers would be mistaking her for if they could perceive her at all. As I stood on the third stair from the top, holding my breath, I could just make out the void in her centre, where her heart would have been, if she'd had one. My companion's superior skill had detected the coldness of the Grey while I'd blundered obliviously nearer. My own heart, which I was only marginally pleased to have still in my chest, sank. How unaware and ill-equipped I was. How awfully needy and dependent. And I'd done this to myself. What a bloody wanker.

Vi tugged me onward. "No, Ernie, you grumpy so-and-so, don't you dare stop now," he growled. "We're alright, but I can't keep this up for long."

My arms and legs began to tremble. A cold flood had spread through my intestinal organs and was trickling downward. Walking down stairs had become very difficult and, as I stared at the hazy patch that grew closer with every step we took, I clenched my teeth, making my jaw ache.

The Heartless Spirit-Mage floated above the foot of the staircase, casting this way and that to detect our presence. She was Veiled. This is a sort of close-range Shroud that shields an individual practitioner — as opposed to expanding over more than one or through a room — but she was clear as day to Vi and dim as dusk to me. I could feel the magnetic pull of her mind coming at us as she spread her net, drew it in, and spread it again and again, as patient and calm as the sort of fisher you'd never want to place your tackle-box next to. Our fellow passengers barely flinched as they walked below her, not realising what was hovering mere fractions of inches above their heads. I felt queasy as I saw a guy who must've been six-three, six-four, pass beneath her. The top several inches of his head went into the haze and he spasmed as though he'd been bitten by something, though he didn't look up. For a split second, a look of sheer despair came over his face, and then faded away once he was free of the shimmer.

Vi and I made our way past the Spirit-Mage without attracting her attention, though Vi was panting with exhaustion from keeping our defence up, and his paw-pads left sweaty prints on the ground. By the Makers, I hope she doesn't see the trail and smell an Earth-Mage in them, I thought. *Vi can't take two fights in one afternoon, and I'm no good for anything.*

A train, which I presumed to be ours, winced to a halt at the platform. The Spirit-Mage's attention was drawn. I felt her gaze as a tug of energy that made me nauseous. I hoped that it was the sound of the squealing brakes and not the Shroud that Vi had cast beginning to ebb away, that had piqued her interest but, regardless, it wouldn't be long before she detected us, maybe even the next time her attention scan moved our way. We were protected, but not for long. Maybe only seconds.

I accelerated and overtook Vi to cut scalpel-like through the clots of people milling on the platform with their cases at their feet, and Vi quickened his pace behind me. We got to the edge of the platform at the perfect spot for a set of doors to open right in front of us, thank the Makers, and jumped with unlikely nimbleness up the step and onto the train. Luckily, only a few more people seemed to be getting on; the rest of the crowd continued to stand with their luggage, staring blankly at the black and yellow departure screens and glancing down at their phones every few seconds, blue-white glare reflecting on their faces.

The train doors closed, and the machine juddered into movement, coughing smoke upwards from its filthy diesel exhaust. I imagined birds flying overhead, wearing those pollution masks cyclists use. Inside, the train was one of those relics that felt more like an old school bus, complete with grubby windowpanes and upholstery that emitted puffs of dust — and no doubt also mould spores — whenever you ventured to move on your seat in search of elusive comfort, since any padding in the cushion had long since either disintegrated or been sequestered by nesting rodents. The stench of over-pressed brake pads and strained cables hung heavy in the air, making it smell of headache.

I hunkered down into my supposedly First-Class seat and, as the train began to inch forward, I risked a glance back at the bottom of the stairs that led down onto the platform.

The Spirit-Mage had moved: she was now directly outside our window and scanning left and right along the platform.

I yelped, and leaned away from the window, my mouth hanging open. Vi lolled beside me, unable to sit upright. His weight rested against my ribs; he was worn out from keeping a Shroud around both of us that was strong enough to fool another Mage. I couldn't ask any more of him now. I resigned myself to my fate, and slid down in my seat, dragging Vi with me. He was limp; exhausted. If this was our end, what a place this was to go. I prayed for a swift and merciful death.

The train coughed as it picked up speed with torturous leisure and, after a moment, I risked a look back.

The hazy Spirit-Mage still hovered on the platform. We'd evaded detection, for now, but the real question was: how did the Grey know our movements? Either someone had tipped them off, or — and I wasn't sure which option I preferred — they'd been watching me the whole time, waiting for the day I decided to reprise my old role, dust off my gear, and consign my feigned oblivion to true oblivion. I felt sick. I turned away and set my intention to the journey ahead, away from what I'd left behind, which, come to think of it, wasn't much barring a massive book collection, four and a half pairs of sturdy boots and a cupboard inadequately stocked with food — and not even interesting food at that. I hoped the neighbours' cat would be alright, the one I'd been feeding for a while. He was a good cat. Huge and black and fluffy. I'd left the cat flap unlocked, so there'd be space for him to sleep at least, get away from the noisy house he lived in with the kids who ran riot at all hours. Them I wouldn't miss, screeching through the thin walls.

A fuzzy voice announced the train's destination and began to reel off a long list of stops.

"Well?" I said to Vi. "Where're we off to on this jaunt?"

"End of the line," he replied. "A place you know intimately."

"Fuck."

The end of the line was Clifford's Bay, the town I happen to have been born in. It's a quaint(ish) settlement, unfairly renowned for its huge population of octogenarians when it also boasts a statistics-distorting violent crime rate. I can claim a proud part in the town's history, since I was partly responsible for said statistics in my youth — but those are fire pit stories that aren't for telling now.

The man after whom the settlement was named, old Cliff himself, was a fascinating chap. A gentleman of copious wealth (isn't that the way with fascinating chaps?), he'd moved to the coast several centuries ago and set up a spiritual retreat centre to provide healing and various other services including divination, curse-breaking, curse-making, and fine dining to the local populace. Being, as he was, extremely talented, his reputation soon spread, and the business became lucrative, drawing custom from across the realm and beyond. With the proceeds, Clifford built an opulent house and a series of outbuildings overlooking the bay with easy access to the beach. And, over time, between the various esoteric and culinary services he offered and his side gig — rum smuggling — he became a lynchpin in the local community.

Unbeknown to the townsfolk, however, our Cliff was also a powerful Earth-Mage, and it just so happened that his land covered a highly auspicious area where deep telluric forces are conjunct. So, parallel to his indisputable good works in the town, for many years he also headed the Clan into which, generations later, a young, wet-behind-the-ears and vandalism-inclined Earthfield Rockwood would be Initiated. The man was a great magician, and my great-great-great-great-great-great-great uncle. Returning to the town was going back in history, delving not just into my own past but the life of my distant ancestor. I wished I'd been going back under brighter circumstances.

Ten minutes into the journey, I dozed off. When I woke up, we were two stops from the end, and Vi was in human form. I wasn't sure that a jauntily-attired Mage would attract less atten-

tion than a dog who occasionally spoke in beautifully-enunci-
ated words, but there we had it. Wordlessly, he unzipped my
holdall, placed inside it the collar and lead he'd relieved himself
of, and zipped the bag closed in a way that made me refrain
from even whispering anything affectionately sarcastic.

Five

We made our way along the baked concrete platform towards the shambles of construction materials that passed for a station building. It squatted before us beneath a warped roof that looked suspiciously asbestos-y and was likely in contravention of a number of other regulations too, since it appeared to have been attached not with nails or studs but dried spit. My eyes tracked downward to the beige walls whose paint peeled like picked skin, revealing a sickly dermis of sun-bleached wooden slats.

"Bloody 'ell, this place has really tanked since last time I was here," I said under my breath.

An intense heat rose from the paving, slamming upward with such force that I swayed with every step. Sweat slicked my forehead and made my scalp itch. I took a hairband from my pocket, and tied my hair back. It was good to get it off my neck, though it left me vulnerable to sunburn.

A train was due to depart from the opposite platform, and the temptation to jump down onto the tracks, get over there and climb on board was almost irresistible. I would have done it in a flash had I not suspected that my bid for escape would be thwarted by some white-shirted avatar of bureaucracy in a high-viz jacket and some kind of horribly wacky tie, citing health and safety legislation beneath a shapeless flannel of greasy hair. Not to mention the Spirit-Mage who'd be waiting for me at the other end of the line.

Everything I could see as I looked around the bottleneck squeezed closer to the building was clad in a shell of pebbledash that coated every surface as though it had been airbrushed on. It lent that particularly depressing ambiance that seaside towns not blessed with at least a ribbon of tourist-trapping quaint old buildings along the seafront often have. Clifford's Bay has a decent esplanade, but the town itself consists largely of bungalow-pocked estates where the husks of burned-out vehicles give a profane nod to the stone gateposts of old.

"Nearly through," I said to Vi, who looked distinctly overheated in his hat and robe. Not much further now. I urged the shuffling horde onward.

Finally, after dealing with a particularly officious ticket inspector, we were through. We stumbled into the living room sized ticket hall and almost tripped over our own feet about three paces later as we were puked out of its lone exit.

Vi took off his hat and used it to wipe the sweat from his forehead. I tilted my head back to open my chest as if I had never before tasted air, and we took a few lung-filling breaths after our respective fashions.

A minute later, my core temperature was less alarming, and I felt ready to carry on.

"This way," Vi said, inclining his head to indicate I should follow him along the side road that led to the right, away from the main strip and its relatively large crowds.

We walked a few paces, then I stopped to look behind us and Vi stopped too, ever the patient friend. There was nobody about.

"My senses will be somewhat finer if I Change," he said.

I nodded to signal that he should go for it, and turned to face the other way for a moment. When I turned back, he was his doggy self again, and I had to restrain an almighty urge to get the collar and lead out of my bag and subject him once more to the accoutrements of canine raver submission.

His dark brown eyes met mine and looked deeply for the first time since we'd left my old place, which felt like a century ago even though it was only about two and a half hours. I was glad I hadn't taken the lead out again.

Vi gave a little snuffle and started back up the lane. "We're going to see old Wilbur," he said over his shoulder. "Did you ever meet? Funny sort. Water-Mage who goes for dips in the sea to Change into a jellyfish. A really sting-y one, too; it's got them in serious trouble more than once."

Wilbur and I were acquainted, as it happened, having chatted and drunk a lot between bands back when Vi was gigging, but I was too knackered to indulge in nostalgic stories now.

"It's only a couple of minutes this way," he said, "just a street away from the seafront, but hardly anyone takes this shortcut."

The breeze blew a faint whiff of urine to my nostrils. Vi dragged us on, back out into the searing sunlight that bleached out the colours of the quiet residential street. Parched roses browned in front gardens and windows on the sunny side of the road had their curtains drawn against the glare. It was afternoon going on early evening, but the heat of late summer blazed unrelenting, even as the humidity grew with the clouds brewing above.

We were almost at the end of the street now, and the breeze carried the aroma of the sea. It tugged at my heart, making me wish I could just run to the beach and throw off my clothes and sink into the water, but I beat back the urge, took a right turn and followed Vi along the pavement that was featureless but for stubborn bursts of desiccated grass that thrust their brittle blades between the paving stones.

My gut told me something was up just as the angled roof of the Golden Sands Retirement Complex came into view beyond the lower buildings in the foreground. I imagined I'd smelt blood, then noticed the gooey droplets on the pavement. They were blue-green rather than red-brown. Not blood. Unless, the thought dawned horribly, it's Water-Mage blood? Vi gave a desperate whimper and sped up, and I kept pace with him, my heart rate ratcheting up in shambolic lurches.

We turned right, coming off the level pavement and up onto the wheelchair ramp that was the closest way to get to the main entrance, although not the quickest; it snaked back and forth at its gentle incline and we followed it. I considered jumping the wall but that could have been noticed; it wouldn't do to be fooled by the quiet for the second time in one day, and the quiet felt so intimidating that I thought it best to go along with it.

A majestic long-haired tabby cat lounged on the low wall outside the reception area and a nasty little nagging feeling sparked into life in my mind: a feeling that this cat was familiar to me, somehow, and I suspected the truth was lurking beneath a layer of deliberate forgetting. Something internal began to feel less stable than it should have.

"I wouldn't go in there, if I were you," the cat said languorously, stopping me and Vi in our tracks.

Vi gave a short yap.

"Hush!" I commanded, my voice coming out too loud.

Vi gave a defiant woof and ran in through the open double doors. I almost shouted after him, but thought better of it. I stood on the path, my eyes darting from the cat to the clusters of bright flowers in the window boxes, to the drops of blood on the grey paving slabs. They were bigger here. I looked down at my feet and saw that I was standing on one that was more like a smear, a mark left by the sole of a boot worn by someone fleeing a horrible scene. My stomach lurched, and I leapt aside. This brought me closer to the cat, who simply observed me with that sardonic grace that most cats have. She seemed almost to smile at me, then sighed tolerantly and spoke again.

"I did say just a moment ago, if you'd been listening, that I wouldn't go in there if I were you. It's not a pretty sight, I'm afraid. Your friend will find out soon enough, though. Foolish hound." Her voice was clear and calm, the voice of someone accustomed to Being In Charge, and who likely also excelled at it.

"That daft pooch is braver than I've ever been," I said, meaning to defend Vi's character but instead besmirching my own.

The cat looked me up and down, taking her time. Her eyes lingered on my scruffy clothing, my unkempt hair, my sweaty face, apparently disapproving of the whole picture. "Mm-hmm," she said, and began to wash herself. If licks to one's own arsehole could ever be sarcastic, these ones certainly were.

I found myself getting irked. She must be with the Council; nothing else could explain that level of pomposity. I usually find cats very down-to-earth, but this one was a pain in the back-side.

She finished licking. "You won't remember me yet, Mage Rockwood, due to my association with magic you took great pains to erase, but I'm with the Coun—" she began to say, but I cut her off with a dismissive flick of my hand.

"It's too hot to dickhead about with formal introductions," I snapped. "You know who I am, so why don't we just dispense with the spreadsheet tick-boxes and you tell me what the bloody hell happened here?"

"Very well." She folded her front paws, then got distracted and took to grooming one of them, running the underside of her claws through her teeth and teasing between the paw-pads. I am greatly fond of an impromptu groom myself, but this was hardly the moment. I cleared my throat.

"Oh! Yes. Alright." She lowered her paw, licked her lips, and cleared her throat. "If you hadn't guessed as much, there's been, ah, a bit of a murder."

At that moment, a howl stabbed the space between the open first floor window and my ears.

"I did say it wouldn't be p—"

"Shut up," I said. "I heard you the first time." I walked to the wall beside where the cat still lay in elegant repose and sat down. I bent forward, taking my face to within three inches of hers. Her pupils dilated.

I bent my face even closer. "*What. The fuck. Happened?* If you please."

Vi walked back out of the open doors, still in dog form. He slumped down at my feet, whining. I reached down and placed my hand on the side of his neck and stroked his golden fur. He turned his head and nuzzled my hand, a gesture so small and so great I couldn't help but cry.

The cat sat up, sniffed the air, and looked around. Her pupils became slits. "We don't have long," she said.

"Tell me something I don't bloody know."

"There's no need to be rude. I'm on your side."

"Fine."

"All I know is," the cat said in a hushed tone, "I arrived for a scheduled appointment we kept regularly, every week, and something felt — different. So instead of going straight up, as I usually do, through the main doors and up in the lift—"

"What? How do *you* go up in a lift?" I stifled a discourteous laugh at the mental image of a cat sauntering into a building and calmly pressing the "call elevator" button. Would she give a well-practised leap to hit it? Was there a low table or something she could stand on? I felt an impatient paw tap my leg. "Sorry," I said. "Got distracted."

"It's easy," she said, "the Reception staff think nothing of it, and the old dears love that a cat can just wander in and out. Lends the place a homely air, which is great for business. It's a saturated market round here, but it still behoves one to maintain a competitive edge. Anyway, there's always someone going into or out of the lift, so all I do is get in and wait and they know where I'm going. However, this time, for some reason, I did not. Instead, I walked along the corridor to the left there and went up the stairs. They come out just a couple of doors along from Wilbur's flat, and the door's often open for ventilation at this time of year. Even though it's a fire door and should always be kept shut—"

"No more tangents! Sorry, but, you know, time and all that."

"Yes. Alright. Well, as soon as I stuck my head round the corner at the top of the stairs, I smelled the blood, and had a feeling how much of it had been spilled, and I knew it was Wilbur's blood. It smelled so, well, sea-ish. I could see that the door was open, so I crept along, and," she looked away for a moment, then looked down at Vi, into his eyes, then up at me. "There was nothing I could have done. I'm so sorry. It was recent. But there was no sign of whoever'd done it."

A ripple of something worked its way up from the pit of my belly. I had no idea what it was or why it wanted to know this, but I said: "What condition was the body in?"

Vi looked up at me, horrified.

"Don't start, mate," I said, shaking my head as though the words had simply been put into my mouth by an unseen force. Which they kind of had. "I'm really sorry, but, I mean, how did the scene look? Was the corpse—" I leaned forward, "*intact?*" By the Makers, I felt awful for asking this and I still had no fraction of a clue why I'd done so. I awarded myself a hundred million wanker points and braced myself for the offended reactions.

The cat's brown tabby fur seemed to grow a shade lighter, and she shivered despite the heat of the afternoon, but she didn't have a go at me, for some reason I couldn't fathom. "I'm surprised you'd ask that before being Restored, and I don't want to unsettle you further, but Wilbur's eyes were, uh, gone," she said, almost under her breath.

"Oh," I said, screwing up my face. "Also, eww. Urrrrgh. Not good."

I looked up at the open first floor window and flinched at the lurid image in my mind's eye. I saw a body sprawled on the mustard yellow living room carpet. I had no idea whether I was seeing this right, since my extra senses were so dulled, but the image was strong. There was a shocking amount of spilled blood on the floor, deep, deep oceanic greenish blue, fresh but cooling, and the first flies were coming to lay their eggs in the plucked eye sockets. They crawled along the rivulets of blood and the threads of exposed optic nerve drying out and curling like blades of grass in the summer heat. I snapped my mind's eye shut. That was more than enough of that.

"Right," I said, looking at the cat then at Vi. "What next?"

"Well, first off," the cat said, "we could do with not sticking around here, really. We only just missed whoever did this, and we don't know whether the assassin was acting alone." Her ears went back and she looked nervously up and down the street. "It's too quiet," she whispered, leaning close to me. She smelled of perfume, which was a bit out of the ordinary for a cat, to be honest.

The sound of the approaching car was a faint shushing drag I heard in the distance before it came into view from the direction of the seafront. We held our breath.

The car trundled laboriously along the road at a speed well below the regulation for traffic in a residential zone. It took forever to pass us and we followed it with our eyes, still holding our breath. It was a rusty little VW, so ancient I wouldn't have been surprised to see it in an archaeological museum. It puttered along the street, wheezing from an exhaust pipe that looked as though if the car went over any bumps, it'd clatter down onto the asphalt and remain there to weather like bones exposed by a rock slide from a cliff full of twentieth century fossils.

The driver was an old geezer wearing a brown tweed jacket, a flat cap and leather driving gloves. He had the windows shut, I noticed, and there was no way that relic of a vehicle had air conditioning, but he didn't so much as look at us. He was hunched over the steering wheel, deep in concentration. The car continued on its glacial way and passed out of view, the sound of its engine fading like the last notes of a heavily pollutant song.

I wasn't sure exactly what kind of drama I'd been expecting, but I realised then how tense I'd been as I'd waited for some esoteric meanie to open a portal and burst flailing through it, or for the driver of the car to shapeshift into something supernatural and very angry. I exhaled with relief and, at the sound, Vi and the cat snapped their heads round to glare at me. They'd clearly been as tense as I was. My fingertips were tingling. I needed something to eat and drink and a nice sit down somewhere cool where I could regroup. The day had rather rapidly gone to the dogs, so to speak.

The cat read my mind. "The Clan House of Earth is accessible through a doorway nearby. I wonder how many people are aware that the Old Path is slap-bang in the middle of their town," she said, and made a little clucking sound. "It's usually not preferred to go that way, but these are special circumstances. I'm sure we won't be reprimanded. We'll head there as a first move and then float some ideas for next steps, in consultation with the Council, of course. It'll all have to be fully risk assessed and the proper forms signed."

"Of course," I said, surprised at the cat's willingness to break a rule. I let her corporate speak slide, but it made me hazily remember a bit about the Council and how I'd never been able to stand how bloody bureaucratic they are and how I'd always done my best to avoid having to deal with them and their tedious forms and data. However, griping about it now when we were being offered their help would have been bang out of order. A dwindling cohort of Elemental Mages can't be choosers, as the old adage goes.

"What's got into you, mate?" I asked Vi, who looked unduly gleeful.

"Oh, it's just ah," he said, embarrassed that I'd noticed him perk up. "I've never been to the House via the Old Path. I've always wanted to, since reading about it during my training. S-sorry, Ern, didn't mean to be inappropriate. It'll just make a change from normal, you know? The usual route gets boring after the first few hundred times."

"Mm," I said.

Everything felt too hushed, too dead. Why hadn't an ambulance come, or a coroner's van? Maybe the Retirement Complex people hadn't found the body yet.

I stood up and walked across the pavement to the Reception window. I bent to peer between the slatted blinds that were pulled almost closed against the afternoon sun, and squinted. The office was empty, just a couple of computers at desks where the chairs were pushed away as if someone had got up and left the room in a hurry. I straightened up and winced, flexing the shoulder carrying the holdall.

A scream pierced the muggy afternoon air from the open window of poor Wilbur's flat. That was our signal to get away, and sharpish. Though I had one or two questions for our feline guide, I piled them up in my mind and tucked them into a pocket for now; my self-preservation instinct was still strong enough to recognise where the most immediate danger lay, even though I also knew that an apparent friend was sometimes more of a threat than a blood-soaked room, a defiled cadaver, and a terrible scream.

The cat stood, stretched and jumped off the wall. "That's our cue to leave," she said.

Vi leapt over the wall to follow her and I swung my legs over and let myself down slowly, not enjoying the feeling of the top layer of sun-heated red bricks digging into my palms. Luckily, the wall wasn't high; I'd sprained my ankle once doing something similar in greater haste, and it wouldn't do to get myself hurt like that now. The three of us crossed the recently-mown lawn and the well-tended flowerbed full of obscenely bright and smiling pansies, and stepped or leapt in unison, according to leg length and number, over the low box hedge.

The cat trotted off in the direction of the seafront, and Vi and I followed. We had to go at a brisk pace so as not to lose her. I shifted the cumbersome holdall from shoulder to shoulder and was soon sweating liberally. I probably should have taken my jumper off. It would have been awkward with my bag, though, and the network of scars all the way up and down both my arms would have attracted too much attention. So I endured the itchy jumper for the time being and was grateful when we came into the shade of a church tower. I felt as though the breeze was coming off the ocean specifically to make its kindly way between the garment's loose-knitted fibres to my clammy skin.

Vi lay on his side on the grass at the edge of the church yard, panting. I put all my effort into staying upright, but enjoyed the soft green surface and the feel of the earth beneath it. Noticing the Element, its depth and strength, I felt supported. We rested for a few moments, but the cat quickly pressed us on. Fluffier and calmer than both of us put together, she crossed the road, looking carefully in both directions even though there was no traffic. She ducked onto an overgrown path that went along the side of the church graveyard and slunk along it with her ears pricked up and her tail sweeping low from side to side. I crouched instinctively so that no branches would hit my face.

My holdall kept swinging down off my shoulder and I shoved it back into place with my elbow, annoyed, every fifteen seconds or so. I could hear the sea, but it felt like it could be in any direction now, or all of them. I'd lost my orientation here, of all places, somewhere it should be easiest to keep it with that big blue salty bastard so close by. Not like you can mistake the ocean for anything else: it is a bit of a feature.

The cat stepped into the long grass beside the path. "Come on," she said. "We're very nearly there." She turned off the path and trotted into the undergrowth.

Vi went ahead of me, jumping over the long grass beside the outstretched branches of some thorny fruit-bearing shrub. I'd never seen one like it, and I of all Mages should have known what it was. Mind you, I'd not done the Restoration yet, had I? If this was a magically potent plant, I wouldn't know until later.

Its thorns were formidable and I instinctively pulled my arms away as I passed.

We reached a broad clearing. The ground was flat and the grass short and tidy, as though it had been mown. But, I thought, why would anyone mow the grass in the middle of the woods? Yellow-green light filtered through the leaves of tall ash, birch, and sweet chestnut trees, and we stopped walking to look up into the canopy and bathe in it. Even though we were not far from the path beside the church yard, if distance were to be measured in the number of steps we'd taken, I suspected we had in reality travelled a lot further.

I expected the cat to perform some kind of magic and open a portal or something, but she chirruped for us to follow her and led us straight through the clearing. She plunged into the green woods on the far side, and we walked along a narrow, winding trail for a while. I wondered what energy I might have detected in the air if my senses had been sharper. The path twisted and turned so much that I felt as though we were going around in circles, doubling back on ourselves. I stopped, once, and looked back. There was no path behind me. The undergrowth had closed it off completely. I turned, afraid, and caught up with Vi and the cat.

"Keep up!" she said in the breezy manner of a school sports teacher, "Don't want you getting lost."

I didn't need telling twice, and kept up, the Old Path drawing closed like heavy green curtains at my back.

We came eventually to a wooden gate caked in peeling brown paint. It looked at first like it was there by accident or fly-tipped in the woods, though I could see no evidence of retired electrical appliances or shopping trolleys nearby, and the ground was mercifully free of stained underwear and used condoms. I concluded from this that the gate had not been abandoned but was here by its own choosing. But it was weird. The wood beneath the peeling ribbons of paint was dry and splintered. One might only have to exhale onto it and the doomed thing would give way. It didn't look like it led anywhere or guarded anything.

The cat scratched at the gate and meowed loudly. Definitely an attention-seeking meow, that one. Vi and I exchanged a questioning glance.

The gate swung open silently to reveal an attractive garden with a modest number of pub tables overhung by thick leafy boughs that reached towards one another. Birdsong floated out on air that was cooler than the air on this side of the gate, though still warm with summer's gold. I peeked in. Large terra-cotta pots stood at intervals along the wide garden path, boasting a number of strong, healthy cannabis plants. The breeze carried their aroma intermingled with the delightful scent of the garden's flowering plants, including the wisteria vines that thickly coated the wall, throwing out an abundance of grape-like clusters of pale purple flowers from their twisting, spiral-ended stems. I also smelled creosote drifting from the recently treated and reassuringly high wooden fence that had appeared when the gate opened: a smell I've always liked despite its air of being manufactured. It has a robust, earthy quality. Standing on the threshold, something within me tentatively began to open.

"Go in, then," the cat said. "She's waiting."

I took a couple of steps forward and passed through the gateway with Vi at my side. I felt like a shy child on the first day of school.

The gate slammed closed with such emphasis as to make the ring-shaped handle attached to its latch fly outward and bounce a couple of times when it landed back down on its mount. All of this was soundless; I could almost sense the burrowing of the worms in the fertile ground below it.

I noticed that the back of the gate was quite different from the front. It was sturdy and reinforced with studs and braces.

As soon as the bolt slid home — which it did quite by itself — strong vines reached out from either side of it, moving towards each other like lovers' hands. They connected, and knotted deeply together, as tight as the most earnest of promises, though far longer lasting.

"Ohhh," Vi said. "So *that's* where that gate leads to."

I became aware of someone behind me. A shiver went down my back.

"Hullo, darling," a lilting voice said.

I turned, even though I already knew exactly who it was. "By the bloody Makers, it's you," I said.

SIX

Serenity de la Guerre – Rennie for short – stood before me with her arms outstretched, apparently expecting a hug or something. I noticed that around her neck she wore the flame-form pendant that signalled her status as Chief Mage of the Clan of Fire.

"My dear old friend," Rennie spoke-sang in a tone that shifted like the colours of her Element. "Darling! It's just *so* good to see you after all these years."

I made no move to walk towards her, and she lowered her arms.

The cat gave a bright chirrup and padded to Rennie with her tail held upright in a gesture of trustful greeting. Rennie bent down to stroke between her tufted tabby ears.

I watched, transfixed. I needed a second to take in the scene, really make sure I was seeing what and who I thought I was seeing. Yes, I was. And very much there, too, was she: Rennie the Ruthless as she'd once been known — Rennie the Useless as I'd come to bravely call her behind her back. Long story short, she'd got promoted, very quickly got comfy in her plush new House, then neglected to join me in the mission that lost me my partner, my hard-earned status, and plenty more besides.

She tilted her head to one side. The Firestar dangling over her solar plexus flashed and flexed as it caught the light. "Oh, come now, Ernie, you're not still upset about *that*, are you?" she said, astutely aiming a flame-tipped arrow straight at the heart of my resentment. She smiled at me through the weight of the question with disturbing innocence; all heart and no conscience. She was the epitome of Fire, after all; one was bound to get fried if one got too near. It was in her soul and in her fidelity to her mutable nature, and I knew this as well as anyone. It would be wrong of me to hope for her to change the way she was. I also knew that she had the most wonderful, warm, blazing-orange spirit, for all her inconstancy, though I wasn't prepared to admit it there and then when I was reeling from the shock of seeing her for the first time in years. "I had new responsibilities to tend to, you know that, darling, and Earth-slinging wasn't that high on my list at the time."

"Didn't want to get your hands dirty, you mean," I said in a low voice.

She nodded sadly at me, all the playfulness spent like exhausted fuel and just the real emotion there burning the air between us.

"You are right, old friend," she said. "I am sorry, you know, about the way things — blew up."

Lovely turn of phrase, that, considering that things had blown up, in the most literal sense. I might have laughed, but I wanted to give no ground, and pulled my best stoic face.

"Wasn't expecting to see you in person," I said, as levelly as I could manage. I felt like the air temperature had shot up by a good ten degrees since the gate had shut, and I suddenly felt absurd standing there with my scruffy holdall still slung over my shoulder and wearing a seasonally inappropriate woollen jumper. I had no need of it now I was on safe ground, so I threw my bag down, peeled off the offending garment, and dropped it onto the lush grass at my feet.

Rennie recoiled at the sight of my scars, though her irises flashed scarlet, thrilling just a little to the ire and power that had caused them.

"Oh, of course, sorry, Rens, mate," I said with as much incredulity as I could muster. "Forgot you've not seen this lot in the flesh." I smiled, and held my arms out before me so she could get a good look. I wondered whether it would honour my beloved's memory more if I were to scream at her, to challenge her to a fight, or simply keen and wail and beat at my chest. I felt awful for this, but the truth was that I was simply too exhausted to open that wound any further. I'd been through too much. She'd done wrong, yes. But I didn't see any benefit in arguing with her when I had a far bigger problem on my hands, which was, after all, the reason I was here. I inhaled a lungful of air, letting it fill my chest completely, then exhaled with a deep sigh.

Rennie watched me with a serene expression on her face. She stood bolt upright, but in the style of a warrior monk rather than a blustery military officer, looking unnervingly calm. She smiled, showing her irregular teeth. "I really mean it, you know; it is good to see you. And I really mean it when I say I'm sorry. I've come to make amends. I should have supported you back then, and I didn't, and, well, here I am now."

I'd cooled down enough by now to have a respectful exchange of words. Well, kind of. I wanted another dig first.

"So," I said after a tiny nod of my head to acknowledge, if not accept, her apology, "I'm given to understand from our Vi here," and I glanced down at Vi, who was rolling about in the grass underneath one of the pub tables. Hopefully, he wasn't coating himself with fox turd, but he could wash that off easily enough himself. He'd been very polite with his garden visit at my place, after all.

Rennie coughed to get my attention and I picked up the thread of my accusation again.

"Ah," I continued, "I understand from our Vi that my superiors have need of my skills, since they've been negligent enough to let the infamous Mage-Killer slip from their oh-so-watchful sight," I purred, smiling coldly.

Rennie bowed her head. "Yes," she said carefully. She was struggling not to lash out at me; I could feel it. "Yes," she repeated. "It was unforgivably careless of all of us to lose him," she visibly quailed at this, her flame of pride momentarily dimmed, "but you are the only one who knows how to do the Grounding and Keeping rituals properly and safely. We need a

Mage whose energy is totally solid. And you always were the most solid of us all, darling."

"It didn't exactly take the greatest mental leap to deduce that this was what you were after," I said. "My question is: after suffering so much loss and death, could we not have avoided a situation where I would be the only Mage left with this knowledge in its useable form?"

I looked at the cat, who stood quietly at Rennie's side. "Actually, it's you I should be really laying into about this, since the Seven Clans don't even have a leader at the moment. Aren't you Council dickheads training people anymore?" I stared at her, and felt stronger than I had in a long time. Her ears dipped slightly. "And," I added, "I don't even *have* this knowledge yet, because the Restoration isn't done. It's not even *begun*. Some things have been popping back since Vi came barking, but I've not let the rest of it in yet. Brought my stuff, though. Well, the important stuff."

My holdall lay on the grass like a deflated bagpipe, with just a few tell-tale lumps in its skin to signify the presence of its contents.

Rennie began to cry. Two tears of equal size flowed down to evaporate in steam on her cheekbones like seawater wave-thrown onto a fresh lava flow. Her shoulders slumped forward, and she raised her hands to her eyes and covered them with the flats of her palms.

The cat hung her head, and spoke almost too softly for me to hear. "Yes," she said in a small, delicate voice. "In hindsight, we should have managed the situation more effectively."

I stayed quiet. I was dying to find out what she'd say next. Even the bees buzzed more softly, listening in, or perhaps I was focusing my attention on a single point in a way I hadn't done for a long, long time and letting everything else fall away. But neither the cat nor Rennie offered further words.

I looked to the side of me and saw that Vi was standing there, just to my right, man-formed. Huh. I'd felt all the Changes he'd undergone since we'd met, barring the one that happened during my nap on the train, sensed them beginning and then noticed a sort of tearing away as he completed the process. It's an energy in him that rises gently, rippling from his feet; very different from how I remember my own Change feeling. From what I've read and the conversations I've had over the years, I understand that each Mage experiences their Change uniquely, depending on their predominant Elements and their Change-Form, but I didn't want to ask him directly; this information is best volunteered. I'd have giggled at the sight of his robe and hat Skin again, but I wanted to enjoy the impact I hoped my sternness was having on the cat and Rennie.

Unexpectedly, Vi put his arm around my shoulders and pulled me gently sideways so that I was leaning against him. His fingertips stroked the top of the long scar that was a trough gouged into my flesh from clavicle to wrist.

I let him support me, and was grateful for how trustworthy and strong he felt, but did not break my attention away from Rennie and the cat. Rennie's apparent contrition was charming, and I knew that, as a Fire-Mage, she was not and could never be one to ruminate in the way I do. A couple of sentences didn't feel like enough, but I knew that they would have to suffice.

The cat looked up at me with sorrow in her eyes. "The Council deeply regrets your loss, and the circumstances under which we are now asking for your help. But the fact remains that we need your help. Urgently. Please."

I nodded grimly. "I don't see that I have a choice. Mark my words, you'll be getting an invoice as soon as this is over, I need a bunch of new gear."

"Of course," she said. "I've already spoken with the Accounts and Supplies departments."

I narrowed my eyes but, suspecting that I was about to press the matter further, Rennie nodded briskly and gave a single, loud clap. "Right. Now that's settled, we must perform the Restoration at once. Undo all that self-destructive jiggery-pokery of yours, eh, Ernie? Let's go indoors and get down to business." Her voice shone as it ever had, keen as a sunbeam in a grey valley. Thinking about what was to come, I felt decidedly less bright.

Seven

The "jiggery-pokery" to which Rennie had so casually referred was quite an achievement in magical terms. In fact, I was proud of it. It was also a highly irresponsible and dangerous act.

The Dissembling and Reconfiguration, to give the working its correct title, has only been done successfully a dozen or so times over the past millennium and attempted on far more occasions. What you do is systematically go through your memories looking for specific things and remove them in the sort of way you might employ dynamite to remove an unsightly blemish. In my case, it was knowledge of magic I wanted to remove, so I couldn't make any more mistakes serious enough to cost someone their life. But it's not just about going through the filing cabinets and taking out a folder here, a pen drive there; it's all interlinked, and extremely hard to disentangle, hence the likelihood of getting it hideously wrong. Results in unsuccessful cases have ranged from mild amnesia to head explosion.

Consequently, the "DNR," as it's come to be known, is regarded by many as nothing more than a procrastinatory form of suicide: Russian Roulette with flesh-magic rather than a gun and a single bullet. One has to be in a certain frame of mind to consider performing a working so aggressive and, if there were such things as statistics, they'd reveal that Mages who opted to do so could be described, in all cases, as downright bonkers. Actually, what the bloody hell was I thinking? *Of course, there'll be bloody statistics! The Council will have a tonne of files on the subject!* I thought. I made a mental note to ask the cat once I'd come round — if I remembered.

"So, time for a bit o' the old Restoration then, hm?" I said awkwardly, my throat tight with anxiety. I gulped. "Oh, heck."

"Come on, Ernie, you'll be fine," Vi said, and placed a hand on my back. He didn't force me in the direction of the doorway, as such, but there was definitely pushing. I had no choice whatsoever in what was about to happen to me.

Hey, at least you won't be roped into cleaning-up duty if your head explodes, mate, the more morbid part of my brain helpfully pointed out to the rest of it. This was not reassuring in the slightest. I'm usually quite sanguine, but that bit of my personality had evidently taken its leave.

Rennie winked at me, linked her right arm through my left (which surprised me, because of the scars) and walked me too briskly for comfort along the path through the garden. The cat trotted ahead of us, nose and tail held high. We strode past the fragrant plants and bypassed the low, bulky pub tables you could while away so many afternoons at. I looked at it all with a great yearning in my heart, imagining that they were not empty but filled with Mages of all persuasions, talking and laughing and sharing time, as they would have been before all this mess and hopefully would be again one day. Vi quietly observed me as he kept pace, padding along a few feet behind.

As we crossed the threshold, my eyes widened and my heart soared. I felt assaulted by the beauty of the room. The walls on one side were lined with bookshelves and on the other were tall dressers and cabinets I couldn't wait to poke about in. At intervals along the walls were stout struts made from living tree trunks. I traced their natural curves upward to clumps of leaves and the ceiling made from boughs between which was a sky hung with lights like dancing fireflies. Large rugs mostly covered the floorboards, and cushions and bolsters for lounging on were dotted about the place. And it was warm. I envied those who lived here in such homely comfort.

Rennie led me into the room. She released my arm, turned to face me, and placed her hands on my waist.

"It's yours," she said. "Welcome home."

"What d'you mean, *mine*?"

She smiled, laughed, and moved her hands to my upper arms, shaking me gently. I felt like an idiot, but one who, at least for now, awoke some affectionate instincts in others, though only the Makers knew how I was managing it or for how long it might continue.

"You heard me, Earthfield Rockwood, you great oaf. This is yours, along with the Chiefship of the Earth Element, if you'll have it, once the Restoration is complete."

"Eh?"

"This is the House of Earth," Rennie continued with uncharacteristic patience, "and you're the boss. Well, you will be once we've sorted your brain out and caught you up on one or two things." I got the feeling that "one or two things" was an understatement, but kept that to myself for now.

"So," Rennie continued, "this is basically your manor house, if you like to think of it that way. It's the one we built after the last one was destroyed. It's been home and HQ to your Clan for almost five years now. Welcome."

I looked around the room, studying the details of the beautifully carved wooden furniture, the woven rugs and drapes in my favourite hues of green and purple, and the huge fire pit in its centre, around whose hearthstones one could entertain friends, acquaintances, and strangers for endless, joyful nights. All the life I had denied myself was laid out before me, and it was overwhelming. A cold flush spread up my arms and legs, and I swooned.

"Feel sick," I managed to say, my words slurring together. Vi caught me as I collapsed sideways. He carried me across the room to a low couch, where he deposited my limp body among an assortment of plush velvet cushions. As I sank into them, scents of incense and flowers were released from the fabric.

Rennie sidled over and knelt on the floor beside the couch. She felt my forehead with the backs of her fingers, peered into my eyes, then took my hands in hers. "You're a bit too chilly, darling," she said. "I'll make you one of my specialities to perk you up a bit, then let's get going. We've no time to lose." She swooshed across the room to one of the cabinets. I heard doors creak open, and a clink of glass.

Vi grabbed a cushion, dropped it onto the floor where Rennie had knelt, and sat down, cross-legged. His hat had slid down his forehead and covered one eye. "Really must adjust this thing; stitching came loose in the fight," he said to himself. Then, to me: "When we finish this business, Ernie, you can stay here, reclaim your place, eh? There'll be no challenger. We want you back, unanimously. We voted on it last week."

I was overcome. "I don't know what to say."

"You don't have to say anything now," Vi said. "One step at a time. We need to Restore you first. Speaking of which, might as well start getting stuff ready then, eh?" He got up and went to one of the bookshelves.

Rennie swooshed back across the room holding a generously proportioned tumbler. It was two thirds full, its single ice cube looking lonely as it floated there in its highly flammable amber sea. Orange vapour rose from the glass. "This'll put hairs on your chest," she said, grinning. "Come on, sit up, and get this down you."

I pushed myself upright, and Rennie moved the cushions into position at my back. I felt like an invalid but had to admit to myself I was loving the attention.

"This," she said, handing me the glass as if it were a ceremonial chalice, "is 'Flame of Health.' Its recipe is a closely guarded secret. All we Fire-Mages carry a good-sized flask of this stuff on long journeys. Many's the time it's kept one of my Clan alive against the bitter cold of night on the road. I keep a flagon of it in your booze cabinet with the rest of the fortifiers and medicinals. Now, darling. Drink."

The ice cube had already melted. I lifted the glass to my nostrils. The fumes were so powerful I felt tipsy already, and my cheeks flushed. "Dare I ask for any clues as to what's in this stuff?"

"Absolutely not," Rennie said. "If I told you, I'd have to kill you." She smiled like a Great White that's just got a whiff of fresh blood in the water. "All you need to know is it's a tonic for warming the body and the soul."

I tipped the glass with great care, wet my lips, and licked the fiery liquid off them. "Oof. Bloody hell." I waited for my tongue to cool down, took a sip, nodded. "Not bad, this stuff." I took another, larger sip. As I swallowed, I felt a glow of vitality working its way down my throat and into my belly. Rennie watched proudly as I sipped the Flame of Health and, before long, the glass was empty. I sighed and leaned back on the cushions, feeling more composed than I had in some time. "Great stuff," I said. "Really great."

"It is," she agreed. "And no, I'm afraid not."

"Afraid not what?"

"You can't have any more," she said as she prised the tumbler from my grip.

"Bollocks."

"It's for emergencies only," said the cat, who had just trotted through the cat flap in a wide, heavy wooden door on the far side of the room. "Glad to see you're looking better, Ernie. Vi, have you found the necessary volume yet?"

"Getting there, cat," he said. He'd pulled a couple of weighty tomes off the shelf nearest to him and was leafing through them in the manner of one who is looking for Something Deeply Important.

I allowed the Flame of Health to seep into all my corners and soothe my achy bits. My body hadn't felt this good in years. My spirits buoyed by this sensation, I let a new thought in. Yes, the thought whispered to me. Then, *yes!* I could reclaim my rightful position as Chief of the Clan of Earth. No bother. I'd have plenty of folk buying me pints then, that was for sure, and I chuckled weakly to myself as I let my head tilt back and my gaze roam the pretty lights on the ceiling. A part of me wondered whether I'd regret this once I remembered all my magic and therefore also the responsibility that comes along with it, but, for now, I was enjoying myself in an uncharacteristically carefree manner.

"Goodness, she's delirious again already," Rennie said to Vi, frowning, her voice concerned. "She must be very sick."

Vi looked up from his research, leaving his index finger resting on the page to mark his place. "No, she's not," he said, shaking his head. "I've seen that look before. Probably just thinking about beer."

I giggled to myself. Gosh, but the ceiling really was pretty.

"I see," said Rennie. "Well, we can all have one after we're done. We'll have earned it." She thought for a moment. "Or maybe I'll have a bourbon. Yes, that'd be better."

Since nobody had asked me to move yet, I stayed put, allowing the well-stuffed cushions to support my back.

"Where's your Skin, Ernie?" asked the cat. She was sitting on the dining table, tapping at something. She peered at me over the rim of her wire-framed glasses.

"My bag," I said, reaching out a scar-lined arm and waving the hand about feebly as if the holdall would magically float to me from where I'd left it in the garden. Oops. Forgot about it completely. I hoped no Faeries had carried it off, thinking it needed a new home. I was in no state for negotiations. I had no intention of getting up, though, and I waved my arm more emphatically on the off chance it might make something happen. It didn't, and even if I'd had a sniff of the Air- and Spirit-Mages' gift for Close-Range Drawing, another skill I'd always admired, the bag was just out of range.

"Ah, of course," said the cat. She chirruped, and a freckly young wizard clad in a hooded brown robe appeared through the doorway beside us, drying his hands on a dishcloth.

"You rang?" he said with a sardonic drawl, and regarded the cat from beneath a tousled mop of black hair and some of the shapeliest eyebrows I'd ever seen. I liked him already.

"Eric, darling! Lovely to see you," said Rennie. "Would you be so kind as to fetch the almost Chief Mage of your Clan's terribly unassuming and not-very-heavy luggage from the garden, please?"

Eric nodded. "I'd be delighted," he said with a warm smile. He chucked the dishcloth into the kitchen and strode through the chamber, his robes swishing around him. He disappeared into the garden, then reappeared a few moments later with my holdall clutched to his chest like something precious. He placed it carefully on the floor beside the couch, then strode back towards the kitchen. "Stew's nearly ready, by the way," he said from the doorway.

"Thank you," I said. My stomach growled in anticipation of food. "Shall I help set the table?"

"Hold your horses, you," the cat said. "We'll eat when we're done."

The way the vibe changed told me I wasn't the only one disappointed by this news.

"Violet, Serenity?" the cat trilled. "Move the rugs, get everything and everyone into place, and let's do this."

Eight

Vi and Rennie did as they'd been instructed. Rugs were folded back to expose a large area of the floor, which was swept by Eric who'd swooped into the kitchen and returned with a broom and dustpan.

The cat surveyed the floor, giving it a sniff here and a tentative lick there until she was satisfied.

"This will do," she said. "Next, we need candles, chalk, incense, et cetera. And the book, of course. Violet, did you locate the relevant passages?"

"I did," he said. The volume he'd been inspecting was on the dining table. He picked it up and found the page he'd marked with a slip of paper.

"Right, everyone, let's take our places," he said.

I stood up and was pleased to note the strength that had found its way into my legs. That Flame of Health really was fantastic stuff. I understood why the Fire-Mages weren't fond of sharing it.

"Here, if you please, Ernie," said the cat, gesturing to a spot on the freshly swept floor. "Need a cushion?"

I shook my head. "I'll be fine," I said.

The cat narrowed her eyes. "Good."

Vi and Rennie sat down across from me, Vi cross-legged on the bare floor and Rennie on a large square cushion with her legs tucked to the side. Eric picked up the cat's tablet from the table, folded back its cover to make a stand, sat down on a zafu, and propped the tablet up on the floor a few feet away from him, its screen facing into the centre of the circle.

The cat trotted over and tapped at the screen. "Angeline?"

The screen showed an ordinary-looking office from the point of view of its desktop. An empty chair occupied the foreground. In the background, the door was closed. It was all very magic-meets-bureaucracy: metal, bracketed shelves stage right, groaning with ancient leather-bound books and a row of waist-high metal filing cabinets with assorted in-trays and magazine racks lined up atop them. Plastic pen pots barely contained an assortment of wands. The planner hanging on the back of the door was a chaos of scribbles and different coloured sticky notes, and doubtless also at least one inter-dimensional portal.

The cat sighed. "Angeline, are you there?"

Nothing.

"Angeline, by the Makers, we're ready! Where in blazes are you?"

The door was flung open and a woman burst in. An Air-Mage: wispy, cloud-white hair, a floaty azure gown with golden butterflies embroidered on it, and a faraway look in her pale grey eyes. I found it hard to imagine her firing lightning bolts from her fingertips. She was definitely on the floatier side of the Element — think of the hippie who teaches Textiles instead of the scary headmaster who floats along the school corridors like a thundercloud.

Angeline placed the porcelain teacup she was holding on a coaster on the desk and sat. She was wearing glasses with transparent pink plastic frames. They slipped down her nose. She pushed them up. They slipped again. "Sorry, boss," she giggled, tucking flyaway hair behind her ears, from where it immediately sprang free, releasing a cluster of dandelion seeds. "Won't happen again." She smiled sweetly. "I was on another planet. Time sort of got away from me."

"I can well believe it," the cat said tersely. "No matter, we're still waiting for Gary, anyway."

"Gary?" I mouthed at Rennie.

"You'll see," she mouthed back at me, and grinned.

I heard the cat flap in the kitchen door go and, seconds later, a huge, fluffy, black cat walked in. He looked very much like my erstwhile neighbour's cat. Exactly like him, in fact. The neighbour's cat, too, was pure black except for a few white hairs on his chest, and he, too, had a bit missing from the tip of his left ear, which made its tuft of fur slightly less tufty. His eyes were the same unmistakeable sulphur yellow.

"Hiya," he said, "nice to see you again. Thanks so much for all the kibble, and I do love that wood pellet litter; the other stuff really makes me sneeze."

"What the fuck?" I was very glad to be sitting down. I stared at him, unable to believe it was really him I was seeing. "Is it really?"

"Yep," he said, "it's really me."

"Oh. Well, uh, hi." I could think of nothing else to say.

Gary tilted his head to one side, thinking. "Mm," he said. "A radiator bed might've been nice, though; that poky little house is freezing."

"I'll bear that in mind," I said. "Does this mean—"

"What?" Rennie said.

"It means—"

Rennie grinned. "Don't be angry, darling," she said.

"You were—"

"Spying on you for the Council and the Clan, yes," Gary said.

"Fuck's sake!"

Vi observed me with interest. "You see, Ernie?" he said. "We didn't forget about you. We knew you were safe, because Gary was keeping tabs all along. We didn't want to worry you and thought it was best you just sort of quietly got on with stuff out of harm's way. We also knew you didn't want to work any magic; we thought just showing up might jeopardise your stability."

Well, that was one way to bloody put it. "You sneaky bastards." I blushed. I'd shared a lot of my darkest thoughts with Gary. I hoped he wasn't the type to betray confidences.

Eric was busying himself with candles and incense. He was also eavesdropping but had the good manners to stay out of the conversation.

Gary padded over and sat beside me. "I'll stand for the Wood element," he said.

Eric placed a wooden statue at Gary's feet. It was a lovely, curvy representation of the Lady of the Willows, wearing a magnificent crown and sitting on a throne of delicately inter-woven branches. Gary rubbed his face on one of them, giving his chops a good scratch and emitting open-mouthed, rattly purrs. The Lady seemed fine with it; I heard laughter in the back of my mind like the rustle of leaves beside a summer ri-verbank.

"Thank you, Gary," the cat said. "Ernie, you'll be Earth, obvi-ously, and Rennie, Fire. Violet, are you comfortable with Water, since it's your secondary Element, and with reading the words? You have such a steady voice."

"Of course," he said.

Eric placed a wide, shallow brass bowl in front of Vi, and a bottle of water, then picked up the stick of chalk and drew a circle on the floor around us all. He sat down and wiped the chalk dust from his fingers onto his robe. He picked up the lump of clear quartz from the floor in front of him and held it in his cupped palms.

"Eric, I see you've claimed Mineral. Good, that'll really help with your training; you need to get a good feel for all the Ele-ments. Angeline will be Air, and that just leaves Spirit. That's me."

Vi filled the bowl with water.

Rennie clicked her fingers, and the seven candles lit.

The quartz crystal Eric held began to glow white.

On the tablet's screen, Angeline went all glittery and started singing a high, lilting song.

Gary chewed at a point on the Lady of the Willows's crown.

I suddenly felt very Earth-y indeed; more Earth-y than I had in years. I felt a root grow down from the base of my spine, anchoring me in place, while all my bones filled with strength. I'd missed this feeling.

The cat began to chant. The light in the room dimmed, except for the candles. I closed my eyes and watched the patterns on the inside of my eyelids. Sometime later, the cat finished chanting, and the echo of her voice faded away. Sometime later still, I was shocked back into my body and my eyes pinged open. I had no idea how much time had passed. The cat nodded to indicate that Vi should begin reading. By the Makers, I thought, we haven't even started yet?

Vi picked up the book, found his place, cleared his throat and began to read. "Magics and Metaphysics, Volume Twenty-Three, Flesh-Magic. Chapter Eleven. Spells of Undoing, open brackets, Potentially Lethal, close brackets." He winced. "Sorry, Ernie, I shouldn't have read that bit out." He cleared his throat again. "Okay. Now. Everybody, close your eyes."

I reluctantly closed my eyes, and what followed is nothingness. Well, not quite nothingness. In fact, I freaked out completely. I came to on my back on the floor, with no idea of who or where I was, or how I'd got there. I panicked, started screaming. Fragranced smoke wafted into my face; no more desire to scream, and instead a pleasant numbness. I closed my eyes again, hoping things would be less confusing later, but for now I wasn't worried, for some reason. I was lifted up, carried, laid down on something soft. It smelled nice. There were voices. Unfamiliar voices. I didn't mind; they sounded lovely. They grew quieter as I sank down into the softness.

❧

When I opened my eyes again, I felt hollow, sort of scoured out. And I was so thirsty I thought I'd go mad from it.

A stranger knelt down in front of me. Tall blond guy in a robe and pointy hat. Good looking. Nice tattoos on his forearms, which meant he probably had them elsewhere, too. This made me smile and go all tingly. His robe had little white bones stitched all over it in a loose herringbone pattern. Very, um, unique.

"Is it just the drugs, or was this supposed to be the way it happens?" he said. His voice was soft and kind.

I peered at this eccentric, charming person. I had a weird feeling I should know him from somewhere. I hate déjà-vu: always feels like my memory is laying a guilt trip on me for not remembering something I should. I looked around the room. A large black cat was in the process of disappearing through a cat flap in a beautifully carved wooden door across the room, and a floofy brown tabby was sniffing about the place, but there were no other humans there but me and the blond guy. We weren't completely alone, though; I could hear sounds coming through the door to the kitchen, which I judged to be so because of the clink and clank of dishes and cutlery. Someone in there was humming tunelessly, and someone else sounded as though they were having a phone conversation. I smelled food. My stomach growled.

"Who are you talking to?" I said. The words came out funny. Was that what my voice sounded like? Come to think of it, what *was* my voice? Who or what was I?

I gave a start when the brown tabby cat jumped onto my lap. Then, since I was looking in that direction, I couldn't help but notice that my arms, which rested on top of the green and brown satin robe that had been laid over me, were covered in scars. Long, deep ones. I waited a few seconds for myself to feel shocked or repulsed by them, but the feeling didn't come. I held up my arms and looked at them and had a knowing that these scars were made in a time when the arms were lithe and muscular rather than soft and weakened. I decided to risk touching one and brought the tip of my right index finger to the bottom of the long fault line that ran from my left wrist all the way up. I shivered at the touch, at the difference in the textures of the scarred and unscarred skin, the weird smoothness of the scar like a valley scraped by glaciers over millennia. But I knew it had happened in an instant, and that I had escaped with my life by the narrowest margin.

"It's never that predictable what the short-term side effects will be. Or the medium- or long-term ones, actually, for that matter," said the cat. The cat. The cat had spoken. In an authoritative and elegant female voice. I must be imagining things. My day was getting very confusing all of a sudden. Come to think of it, I thought then, what was I even doing here, anyway? Then, as if to confirm my descent into rampant insanity, the cat spoke again.

"In fact," she said breathily, "it's quite exciting. This is actually the first time I've taken part in a Restoration of this magnitude since I took over at the Council's helm. So I suppose we'd better prepare ourselves for anything. She was unconscious for a full three days, after all, and absolutely would not be moved from this spot. Fascinating!" She looked at me as a vivisectionist would peer through cage bars at her next poor subject.

Oh, this was bloody great. Three days totally out of it, and no idea what had happened. At least this couch was comfy. My mind began to pick at the knot it had tied itself in, in a vain attempt to work out what was going on. As you would expect, with my world reduced to such a degree that the only thing I really knew for certain was that I was lying on cushions on a couch and was in a gorgeous but unfamiliar chamber filled with beautiful things, but with absolutely no memory of how I'd got there, I began to feel more than a little anxious.

The cat stood, trod a couple of tight circles on my lap, then arranged herself neatly, rested her head on her forepaws and closed her eyes. I could feel her purring, and it relaxed me a bit.

The handsome guy in the comedy wizard's outfit, who was still kneeling beside me and looking very worried, placed a hand on my shoulder. With this gesture, something jolted, kind of jumped sideways in the back of my mind and then ran forward like a dog bounding after a ball in a park on a windy day.

"Violet? Violet Goldbark?" I said, as though the words had come not from me but through me, somehow. I did recognise the voice that spoke them as my own, though; here, finally, was a cornerstone I could build on.

He smiled at me. He had really sharp-looking teeth. Very clean and neat though, and they were framed by an open, friendly face.

"Yes," he said softly. "And you are Earthfield Rockwood, but you prefer Ernie, or Ern for short. Remember?"

"I — I don't know. Maybe." I closed my eyes and tried to con-centrate. I turned my gaze inward and began to search, but felt a bit like someone who's lost their keys, turns the entire house upside-down, stops trying, decides to make a cuppa to see if that helps, then finds their keys in the fridge and cannot for the life of them explain how they got there.

"Don't force it, Ern," Violet said. "There's a lot of new inform-ation in there and it needs time to arrange itself. Well, it's not new information, it's old information, it's just sort of, ah — been on holiday. Well, bits of it have. You'll understand soon." He looked at me like a golden Labrador who's just eaten some-thing he shouldn't have and wants you to be as proud of him as he is.

"What in Earth's name are you talking about, Vi?" I snapped.

He grinned at me. "She'll be back to her old self in no time," he said, and looked at the cat.

"Who will?" I said.

A wave broke over me then, and I had to lie back on the cush-ions until the nausea had subsided. It was the sort of wave that hits you when you've been swimming in the sea and you're tired and making your way onto the beach when it sneaks up sud-denly and knocks your legs out from under you. Next thing you know, you've got a mouth and nose full of saltwater and your less clumsy loved ones, who by now are on the beach and gracefully towelling themselves down, are looking at you with kind confusion, wondering how on earth you managed to find yourself in this situation.

I remembered the train journey to Clifford's Bay three days earlier, and the narrow escape from the Spirit-Mage at the station. I remembered sitting in the pub an hour or so before that, and turning to see that Vi, who I hadn't seen in five years, had just said hello.

A second wave broke and almost drowned me. The fuzziness I'd got used to whenever I sent feelers back in time and teased at the blurry edges of the DNR'd patches of memory, or when my mischievous mind tried to probe them of its own accord in dreams, dissipated like mist cleared by a rising sea breeze. And I let it. It was all suddenly, painfully clear. All the magical memories came back, bringing along the mundane ones too entwined with them for me to risk remembering until now. All the layers of study and experimentation and experience I'd turned away from, leaving only placeholders that felt artificial, now surfaced.

I remembered my Initiation decades earlier, and the party afterwards. It was great fun, even though I did end the evening upside-down in a wheelie bin. I remembered flashes from different stages of the training that led up to it, such as my tutors at the Academy being excited by my rare combination of Earth and Mineral magic but having to stand behind protective screens lest I melt them by accident. I remembered many kisses behind the broomstick shed with my first girlfriend, Lily, who would later become a powerful Spirit-Mage. I wished we hadn't lost touch; she was brilliant. I remembered, in vivid detail, all those early days, before any of us discovered who we really were, before the incident in the playground and my fateful, year-long stint at the Correctional Centre. I'd been forbidden from practising anything barring the most pleasant magics during my time there: herbal tinctures and blended teas, mostly, and magically-reinforced bird and bat boxes. I was happy to remember all that worthy work, but less so my ill-advised association with the young Richard the Grey and how we'd worked together for a while before I realised what a prat he is.

I steered my mind away from his intrusion and turned toward the memories of peripheral, connected stuff coming back, the stuff adjacent to the difficult bits of my training. I remembered the night when, after a big exam, Vi had persuaded me to sneak out with him and come to watch his band play. I laughed when the name came back to me: Lab Coats for Jesus, a punk band made up of young predominantly-Earth Mages who all Changed into Labradors of different hues. Most of their lyrics consisted of woofing and howling. They should have been huge. It was during these gigs I first met Wilbur, who trounced Vi's lot once in a local Battle of the Bands by playing oceanic-sounding prog that would be technically impossible for anyone with fewer than eight arms. Wilbur had a suitably ostentatious bank of synthesisers and drank me under the table after the show. I smiled, then remembered that my friend was dead. I needed a few breaths to centre myself.

Okay, I thought a couple of minutes later, maybe I can accept this. Then I remembered meeting Elias at a winter Solstice gathering and the magic we made together and, unable to keep from crying, I let myself collapse into how much it hurt. And it kept coming. I wiped tears away with the satin cloth that covered my body and then remembered what it was: my Skin, green and brown like my Change-Form, presented at the Initiation ceremony to mark that rite of passage.

After the first big surges, everything else began to fall into place reasonably quickly and with less shock and pain, though it would be some time before I felt I could trust all my memories. It was like the first brush-strokes on a canvas that lay the foundation for all the detail that goes on top, but these initial daubs felt brutal, and many of them would be uncomfortable to build upon. For now, though, I just let the layers of colour, light and shadow arrive and flow to their places. I could examine everything in meditation later, over the next decade or so, and start by asking the cat to refer me to Gary's therapist.

After a while, I was certain it had all come back, except just one little detail.

"Sorry, love, but I still can't remember your name," I said to the cat.

She tilted her head to one side in a gesture that felt like the cat equivalent of a shrug. "Oh, it's fine, everybody just calls me the cat," she said cheerily. "You remember *who* I am, though, yes?"

I laughed. It made my head hurt, right down in the middle, even though I knew that wasn't physically possible. Only meta-physically.

"I do," I said. "You are a member of the Grand Council, a con-sortium of powerful Elemental Mages, and kind of our gov-ernment. So, technically, you're my boss. Well, you think you are." I laughed again.

"Here, take this," Vi said, and handed me a glass of water.

I drank. "Thanks," I said when I'd had enough, and wiped my mouth.

"Looks like you're almost back to your old self," the cat said.

"What?" I said, feeling self-conscious.

"You referred to me as 'technically' your boss."

"Yup. S'pose I did."

"I wouldn't want to meddle in Clan business, of course," the cat said. I sensed a collective raising of eyebrows of everyone within earshot. "But if you were to return, you'd have the Coun-cil's resources at your disposal."

I smirked. "What, spreadsheets?"

The cat growled softly. "Spreadsheets are useful," she snipped.

"Aw, I didn't mean any offence, cat. I'm sorry. You can keep the spreadsheets, though, but I'd be grateful to be brought up to speed on everything."

"Does this mean you, ah, you'll join us again, properly, come back to the Clan?" said Vi.

A woman swept in from the kitchen. She had long, wavy hair the colour of fire and charcoal, dark copper skin, and ruby-red eyes which flashed brighter when she saw me. I recognised her: Rennie. She grinned, showing an arrangement of wonky teeth. "You'd better say yes, you awkward creature," she said, "we've all missed you very much."

I looked at my three friends, knowing I had one or two more out there somewhere and thinking maybe I wouldn't mind getting in touch with them again. Then I looked around the chamber, taking in the details of the home that could have been mine all along. Of course, there was nothing anyone could have done to stop me from performing the DNR; it is the right of all Mages to alter our minds in any way we wish, as long as the act is performed knowingly, responsibly and without harm to the greater good. And, back then, I felt there was no danger of the greater good suffering as a result of my action. Plenty of competent and, in some cases, extremely powerful Mages were rising through the ranks, and nobody, at that time, was concerned about instability in any of the Seven Clans. Our numbers overall were reduced, sure, but we'd put the Mage-Killer away and we were confident he'd never see natural daylight again.

How foolish we were to assume that nothing would change. We'd had a few years of peace, though: the Council and the Clans growing into their complacency and me into my depression and, meanwhile, the most notorious murderer who'd ever been a Mage had time to dig through his cell wall, or whittle away the bars, or through painstaking attrition condition one of the guards to help him. That was why the Council didn't allow anyone to remain on the staff for too long, though, to prevent that type of thing from happening. I mean, honestly, what kind of idiot wouldn't take into account the risk that a Mineral-Mage of his stature, with his superior mind-melting skills, might have a go at a bit of slow-burn coercion?

Actually, that was a damned good point. "So, how did he get out then?" I asked.

"Pardon?" the cat said. "Who?"

"You know who, you daft git. All fluff between the ears, you are. Richard the Grey. The rogue Mage I'm supposed to help you catch — again. What happened?"

The cat's eyes grew darker. Her energy hardened. "Alright," she said. "Okay. That's why I brought you here, after all." She took a deep breath, let it out.

"We were so sure none of his followers had survived after the battle five years ago," she began. "We thought it was just him, and that the layers of fortification around his cell would stop him from being able to send his mind outside those four walls on a quest for new recruits. But," she sighed, "we were mistaken."

"How many lived?"

She flinched as though reacting to an intrusive sound.

"Sorry," I corrected myself, "I know they're not fully alive, as such, once they're Heartless, since they feel no emotion, but you know what I mean."

The cat nodded. "We think that one survived and that between the two of them they managed to sustain their own strength and attract a few new followers to their cause. People who wanted to stop feeling and were prepared to make a terrible sacrifice in order to achieve it. And," she added, "be eternally subservient to their leader."

I failed to understand how anyone could be drawn to join a cause that would guarantee not only a horrible death but also unending allegiance to the Grey Dickhead, but people are full of surprises, are they not? And, I supposed, there was a kind of certainty in the finality of the ritual, if you were the sort of person who wanted no choice in anything ever again. And I thought *I* was weird.

"How many are there now?" I asked.

The cat exhaled through her nose. "Our guess is no more than six. That doesn't sound like much but, as far as the Council is concerned, that's six too many. As we've already seen, they are capable of such great destruction that they don't need big numbers."

I had no reply to this, and nor did anyone else. The room was quiet for a minute, until my stomach ruined it by letting loose a rumble of magnificent proportions. "Sorry," I said. "After three days without food, I am kind of peckish." My stomach roared its protest at my understatement.

Rennie cackled. "The rest of us are thinking the same, darling. Eric!"

He appeared at the kitchen doorway.

"I think we're all ready for a bite to eat."

We all mucked in with setting the table, thoroughly getting in each other's way. When we finally sat, Vi brought in the almost cauldron-sized stew pot and placed it carefully on its mat. I worried the table might buckle beneath it, but nobody else seemed concerned. We sat and began passing bowls to be filled with piping-hot stew and loading our side plates with bread, fruit and cheese. Now fully Restored, I could clearly recall my last communal meal. It had been a long, long time ago and in a setting far less cheery than this.

Ten minutes later, I leaned back in my chair, sated. "That was the best stew I've ever eaten, mate," I said to Eric, who beamed with pride. We sat for a few minutes before the cat brought us back to the matter at hand with typical Council efficiency. She cleared her throat and the room leapt into action again, Rennie and Vi clearing the table under the cat's supervision and me sliding down in my chair, too full to move and feeling rather drowsy.

"Ernie, be a dear and get the coffee machine going, would you, please?" the cat said.

"Good idea," I said, yawning. I heaved myself upright, yawned again, and shuffled into the kitchen. It was a suitably lovely farmhouse-style affair with terracotta tiles, oak cabinets, and a flagstone floor. Bunches of herbs hung up to dry from every available sticky-out bit, and it boasted the largest fridge I had ever seen. There were shelves groaning with books on cuisine, herb lore and poisons, and a massive table covered in what I presumed to be Eric's textbooks, journals, and laptop.

The coffee machine was on the counter on the far side of the room and I set to work. I checked the water level: too low.

"Hey, El, pass us the water filter. I just need to top up the machine," I said without thinking. The colour drained from my face and my lips went numb. I had to support myself on the edge of the worktop for a moment while the feeling passed. "Fuck's sake," I muttered to myself, and wiped my eyes. Making coffee together was one of the rituals we always shared. My Re-stored mind had slipped for the barest moment, hoping that, perhaps, more than just memories of him would be brought back.

I took a deep breath and gave the top of the coffee machine an amicable pat. "Come on, old girl, just you and me. Now, let's get to it, eh?" and, scraped raw, I took up the threads of the pre-viously-shared ceremony alone.

I filled the coffee machine's water compartment in a daze that was only broken by the aggressive aroma that rose from the jar of Boiling Hot Lava when I opened it. I came round, still teary, just as Vi sauntered into the kitchen behind me. I was glad I had my back to the door, and I gave my eyes another quick wipe with the back of the hand that wasn't holding the jar of mega-coffee. I wondered whether I'd ever sleep again after an espresso made with this stuff. Still, I was game. It would help me concentrate.

"Ah, the cat'll just have some of that lactose free cat milk stuff," Vi said, opening the fridge and removing a bottle with a cartoon-style happy cat face on it. "And a pinch of this on the side." He pointed at a large baggie on the top shelf of the spice rack. It had "THE NIP — FOR FELINE CONSUMPTION ONLY" written on it in black permanent marker.

"Understood," I said, smiling. I was facing him now.

He walked over and stood in front of me. I felt exposed, but stayed there, trying not to feel too awkward with the whole being-looked-at thing. I wasn't sure I'd manage it and offered an expression I hoped was polite and not just unsettling.

"Wow, Ernie, your hair's changing colour already," he said, unfazed, as he took a long strand between the thumb and index finger of one hand. He held it for a few seconds before letting it go and moving the hand to my shoulder, which he gave a friendly squeeze. "You're looking much better already." His eyes narrowed slightly as he took in details of my face, but, discreet as ever, and perhaps also not seeing the need to draw attention to the painfully obvious, he didn't ask if I'd been crying.

Rennie cast a sly glance through the doorway and grinned. "That cat is an absolute *fiend*," she said, chuckling at the gargantuan spliff she'd constructed for human(ish) enjoyment. She licked the paper, finished rolling, then held up her handiwork. There were several inches of it. "Any green for you, Ernie?" she said, waving it at me enticingly. "I might just be able to spare some." She winked.

"Not for now, ta," I said, feeling tempted despite my words. "I don't want to get sleepy. Feel like I've slept enough, if you know what I mean."

"Of course, darling," said Rennie. She placed the spliff between her lips, grabbed her metallic red Zippo off the table top and fired it up.

NINE

Ten minutes later, I was buzzing my tits off on caffeine and attempting to sit still on the couch. I held my hands clasped on my lap, and all of me was vibrating. The cat had settled on a cushion that was evidently her favourite since it was covered in a layer of mousey brown cat hair so thick you could fashion it into another cat of similar fluffiness. She'd arranged herself in a loaf shape with her fore-paws folded beneath her chest and her tail wrapped around the left side of her body. Her upper lip sported a thin moustache of cat-milk foam speckled with green bits from the catnip she'd huffed five minutes earlier, and her eyes were slightly glazed. I wished I could look so regal whilst stoned or speak as coherently as she was about to.

She took a deep, calm breath. "Right. I'll give you the short version. We know this much: he escaped," and she giggled, then paused, making me think that this would indeed be it, but I already knew the first part, so I waited in case there was more. She cleared her throat. "Sorry. He escaped, and our first assumption once the alarm-crows cawed was that he would first go to the stores to reclaim all the objects of power we confiscated when we took him into custody. And they were — still are, in fact — closely guarded."

"So was he, supposedly," said Rennie, saying exactly what I was thinking.

"Ahem, yes, well," the cat said, looking embarrassed, "that's by the by now, really, isn't it?"

"Not particularly," Rennie pressed. Her eyes were glowing blood red. I'd never liked Rennie in full-on scary mode, and I was glad she wasn't directing this at me. I willed the couch to swallow me, in case she suddenly looked in my direction. Unfortunately, it didn't.

The cat took another deep, calm breath, applying a technique I assumed came straight from of one of the Council's "Nipping Magical Conflicts In The Bud" training manuals. To her credit, it worked. I stole a glance at Rennie. Her eyes had dimmed to a more amiable scarlet, though her expression remained grim.

"The stores are closely guarded," the cat continued. "However, it is in fact of great significance that, as Rennie has correctly highlighted, since he can escape from a cell, he is more than capable of slipping past a heavy guard to retrieve his things and would therefore be undeterred. So, why did he not simply do so?" She looked around the room like a teacher quizzing a group of students, but nobody volunteered a hypothesis. "Our educated guess is that, rather than try to take back his old tools, he might in fact take the opportunity to get some new ones. More powerful ones. Why would he waste time now, instead of doing everything he can to achieve his objective before we can catch him again? Or, as is actually the case, kill him. That's where you come in, Ernie," she said, looking at me.

"I got that, yeah, ta boss," I said, my cheeks flushing.

She nodded, pleased that I hadn't forgotten my role in the mission. "So, assuming that this is the case, our job is to intercept him before he can pick up where he left off. Separating light from shadow is an ambitious goal, but not unachievable for someone with enough skill and determination."

"Who happens to also be a certifiable megalomaniac with a taste for murder and a handful of minions who totally lack empathy," I chipped in.

"Quite," agreed the cat.

Eric raised his hand.

"Yes?" the cat said.

"But how do we know where to go first to look for him?" he said. "There are two Makers."

The Sunmaker and the Moonseer: two beings elevated millennia ago from Mages into — well, it's hard to describe, but sort of guardians, sort of gods. Between them, they keep our world and its Elements coherent. They preside respectively over the light and shadow aspects of each, ensuring that balance is maintained, for light and shadow cannot exist without each other. However, if someone were to come along who happened to be emotionally stunted enough to prefer the idea of separation to coherence, alienation to integration, he might just want to do such a thing as sunder the bonds between the light and shadow aspects of each Element and plunge our world into a nice, unambiguous, unchanging grey. A depressed and depressing grey not unlike the one I inhabited for years and which I'd go to any lengths not to see inflicted on the world. And, for that, he would need a couple of severing weapons fashioned by the Makers themselves.

"Quite right. There are two Makers," the cat continued. "And this is a major dilemma. With a new Weapon from either of them, he'll be far harder to kill." She looked at me again, with sympathy that felt like condolences. You know, the kind of solidarity you send with a bunch of white lilies.

I gulped. "It doesn't matter then, does it?"

"Oh, don't be so *maudlin*, Ernie," Rennie groaned.

I rolled my eyes. "I didn't mean it like that. What I meant was that whichever way he goes first, the result's the same. So it doesn't matter in which order he goes to the Makers. One, two, Sun, Moon, it adds up to exactly the same thing, right? It's fifty-fifty. It doesn't matter whether we go to the right one first as long as we get to him before he's reached them both."

"Wrong I'm afraid, old friend," Vi piped up. "It matters an awful lot." He'd been so quiet I'd forgotten he was there. He was sitting by the fire pit a little way away. He'd set and lit a fire, all without me noticing, and was warming his palms. The flames illuminated his face, exaggerating his kindly frown into deep shadows on his forehead. "It matters very much, I hate to say." He fell quiet for a moment. "I have a suspicion that—"

"What?" Rennie said, turning in her dining chair to look at him.

"Well, forgive me if this sounds a little over-the-top," he chuckled self-consciously, "but which extra-dangerous and forbidden working might he be wanting to perform?"

I looked around the group. Young Eric sat ashen-faced on a cushion, his shoulders slumped forward. The weight of a worry unjust to make one so youthful feel creased the skin of his forehead. I felt for the lad. He looked up at me, then cast worried eyes over the rest of the group, searching for reassurance. From the looks of us all, he wouldn't be finding any.

Rennie was deep in thought, her smouldering eyes cast downward. Her elbows rested on the table top, fingers clasped together as best she could manage with all her heavy rings of gold set with carnelian, garnets and rubies.

Vi stared into the fire, retreating into his anxiety.

The cat regarded me silently as I looked around. I wasn't sure whether she expected me to speak next, or what.

The pit of my stomach felt like it had fallen away. I understood now. "Um," I said, in a very small voice. "You mean, the Incorporation?"

This was why Richard would elect to go to the Makers directly rather than simply reclaim his old Weapons: *he* was to be part of the process to make the new versions even stronger. His Mineral nature makes his body just resilient enough that he could be part of the forging process; the energetic link between Weapon and wielder would be so strong as to make him nigh-on invincible. "What a boundless fucking prick," I said.

The cat looked pleased. "Good," she said, "I shall infer from your smile that you are looking forward to the hunt."

She had completely misread my grimace. Alternatively, she'd said that to throw me off balance as a test of my recently re-laid foundations. I couldn't tell which.

"So. What do we do now?" I said, probably failing to call her bluff.

Everybody looked at the cat, which I found strange considering the rest of us seemed to share a healthy disdain for the bureaucratic Council on whose watch the former prisoner had slipped his chains. Perhaps Rennie was loath to take charge with her usual gusto because she saw it as an Earth matter and therefore not very fuel efficient. I was reluctant to step in because I still felt decidedly wobbly. All this was still relatively new information to me, so I wanted to defer to those with more of a handle on the situation, which I took to be everybody including the most junior of our number. Judging by the quantity of half-whittled wands and staffs about the place, Eric was learning some pretty advanced Wood-magic, and doing rather well at it.

The cat sighed. "All this would be rather easier if our adversary hadn't made off with poor old Wilbur's eyes," she said.

Wilbur. Of course. They'd retired to a quiet seaside town to be near their beloved Water and live out their days beach-combing and paddling in the gentle waves before joining the greater Ocean in the beyond, but instead had ended up eyeless in a sizeable pool of their own blood. "Oh yeah," I said, "we'd be able to See him then, wouldn't we? Plain as day."

Water-Mages are expert Diviners. I don't envy them this; they're so good at Seeing what's coming and where people are all the time that life can become depressingly predictable, and, for the same reason, they're horribly prone to nervous disorders. They use a variety of instruments from rods to pendulums, cards to bones, scrying bowls to mirrors, and, in rare cases such as Wilbur's, some also use their own eyes. They're the strongest. And, as with any of us, the Weapon without its wielder is less useful — though Wilbur's eyes, being as powerful as they were, would still be good for up to a week after they'd been removed. It had been about three days, three hours and counting, so far. To kill a Water-Mage for their eyes, though, it's unspeakable. I mean, just go and have a cuppa and a chat with 'em and they'll be happy to help. Unless, that is, you want them to help you and nobody else. Wilbur was a true pearl, and I say this knowing that pearls form around grit. Water-Mages' inherent fluidity makes them non-judgemental about moral matters, so having a friend who is a good Seer is useful to any Mage, including the shadier members of the Seven Clans. It's all part of the balance. That is, until one comes along who's capable of murdering their own kind.

"So, it seems we have two urgent matters on our hands," Rennie said. "Catching an errant murderer and burying a Mage."

"Indeed," said the cat.

"Won't be happy to be buried without their eyes though, will they?" Rennie said.

"Not one bit," replied the cat. "It'll be very upsetting for the Water Element in general, which only adds grist to Richard's mill by weakening their resolve." She shrugged. "But what can we do about it?"

Nobody offered any opinions.

"I have a couple of inklings," I said.

"We're all ears, darling," said Rennie.

"As you say, cat, the destabilising impact of a Water-Mage being buried without their most powerful magical tool will be considerable. And this might lead one to suspect that it's the Moonseer he's planning to go after first, given her affinity with Water. He'll be hoping that the resultant wobble in the Element will weaken her."

"Quite a logical deduction, yes," the cat conceded.

"Well, if we're able to prevent this destabilisation by getting hold of the eyes and giving Wilbs the proper send-off, we might be able to force him to change his plans and go for the Sunmaker," I said. "And we can make sure we're waiting for him when he gets there."

Rennie gave a single, loud clap. "A race against time within a race against time? Delicious!" she cackled.

"And how do you arrive at this conclusion?" said the cat.

"Richard's a bloody great coward, at the end of the day," I said, sitting up straight on the low couch. I felt a surge in my blood-caffeine ratio in response to my increased heart rate, and was glad to still be seated; I'd definitely have fallen over, which would do nothing for my gravitas. "All bullies are cowards. The Moonseer is pretty scary, to be honest, and the Sunmaker, though intimidating, is essentially a pretty straight-up bloke. In a massive and terrifying hemigod sort of way, obviously."

The room was quiet for a minute but for the sound of the fire crackling.

"As for Wilbur's eyes," I continued, "he'll be needing to use them ASAP. And," I added, smirking, "they'll not be too chuffed about that either. I knew Wilbur and, though very Watery indeed, they did have a strong sense of justice. So, he won't find it as easy as he'd hoped, using them as a short cut to either Maker or as a way to anticipate our moves." I leaned back, grinning. A part of my mind was sure I was being too cocky, that I'd overlooked something vital, but I didn't want my companions to see any self-doubt in me. "And since he can't use the Paths without setting off the alarms and giving his plan away, he can't be far away. He'll be hiding out somewhere around the town, most likely, lying low, biding his time."

"Until when?" asked Vi.

"Until Wilbur's been buried."

"What's so important about that?"

Rennie grinned. She'd cottoned on. "Was Wilbur an Earth-Mage?"

"You know as well as I do they were as Watery as a Water-Mage could be," I said. "Therefore, if they get buried in the wrong Element..."

"Bad things will happen," said Eric.

"Yes, they bloody well will," I said. "Our first job, then, is to give our old mate Wilbs a proper burial and resettle the Element of Water. Then we can go to the Sunmaker ourselves and head off our enemy. I hope."

Ten

The cat's eyes lit up. "That's great, Ernie!" she said. "Assuming you're right, of course. But it makes a lot of sense." She stood up, stretched, then sat back down and settled on her haunches. Despite her relaxed posture, her eyes were hunter-keen. "The first thing is going to be to keep a close watch on things here while the preparations are made for Wilbur's funeral. We'll need to stake out the funeral parlour, the beach, and one or two other spots where we might overhear conversations and rumours about where our enemy might be lurking. Any other ideas?"

"Pubs, obviously," I said, smiling. "Anyone who wants to know what's what in a place, they can't do better than to prop up a few bars and just sit and listen to the locals' gossip."

"Trust you," said Rennie and gave me a wink.

We had a fling once, years ago, Rens and me. Way too tempestuous for my liking, and it was short-lived. However, though our physical relationship was long in the past, there was nothing wrong with a bit of flirting. "It's a great idea, though," she continued, "but we will have to be Veiled all the time, of course."

I wasn't looking forward to the physical or metaphysical headaches of keeping a Veil about me, which I hadn't needed to do in years, but I nodded assent. "I'm sorely out of practice with Veils," I said. "I could do with some re-training."

"I'll help," said Vi.

This was good. I'd seen first-hand how adept he was, what with the Shrouds he'd cast in the pub and at the station. If he could handle covering two of us, he could definitely give me a refresher on how to cover just myself. It could have been the Boiling Hot Lava still rampaging its way through the china shop of my endocrine system, but I felt a sense of strength and potential I hadn't felt in a long time. Which, of course, soon felt uncomfortable. Unfamiliar. Undeserved. I needed to take the edge off.

"Don't suppose you've any ale about the place? Must be a civilised hour for a tipple, don't you reckon?"

"Any waking hour is a civilised hour for a tipple when it comes to you," Vi said.

I shrugged. No point in denying it.

"Still, though," I said, "I am a bit thirsty, and all this talk of death and danger is making me nervous."

Eric nodded. "That heather stuff's ready," he said and disappeared into the kitchen.

"I'm just going out for some air," said Rennie.

Vi Changed and trotted along behind her into the garden.

The cat and I watched until the door closed behind them after giving us a brief glimpse of the high summer dusk that was falling outside. I heard happy barking a moment later. It warmed my heart.

Eric appeared from the kitchen with two stout ceramic flagons. He handed one to me, then placed the other on the floor beside the cushion he had occupied before. He fished in a pocket in his robe and brought out the baggie, which he shook gently, arching his perfect eyebrows at the cat.

"You know me too well," she said.

The young Mage-in-training sprinkled some of the dried green leaf onto the cat's small silver tray, and she promptly buried her face in it, purring ecstatically.

I took a sip of heather ale and wiped froth from my upper lip. "Bit of a monster for the old 'nip, isn't she?" I said to Eric.

"It's home-grown," he said. "The absolute best. She always has some whenever she visits, which she does even when there's no important Council business to attend to. Weird coincidence, eh?" He smiled.

"Ah, so you're the green-fingered one? Very impressive garden, that is. I had one at my old place, but I neglected it, I'm ashamed to admit. Could have done with a bit of your expertise."

Eric beamed proudly, showing large white teeth being persuaded into straighter lines by metal braces and wire.

As the cat rolled around on the floor in the throes of her trip, Eric and I drank our ale and whiled away some time in conversation. I learned that he had been orphaned as a young boy and spent miserable years in children's homes and reform centres. I was pleased he'd resisted institutional brainwashing, having been educated for some time in the ordinary world and emerged relatively unscathed and spiritually intact. Not many who pass through the system are so fortunate. He'd simply stumbled through the garden gateway one day, taking Vi and the cat quite by surprise, and never left.

"They said if I'd found this place it was obviously meant to be," he told me. "And I had no family or friends to miss me, so I stayed. It's been two years now. I'm really happy here."

I could see that. The place had a pure, calm vibe and, despite a little clutter here and there, looked admirably well cared for. We drank a toast to serendipity and worked our way through the heather ale while the cat snoozed on her cushion.

Rennie and Vi came in from the garden. Vi was still dog-formed. He curled up beside me on the couch and fell into a contented sleep.

"How are you feeling now, Ern?" asked Rennie.

"Better after a bit of beer," I said. "Always calms me down."

"I meant after the Restoration, actually."

"Oh." I let out a guilty laugh. "I think the holes have mostly been filled in now," I said, "but there's still some tidying to be done around the edges, if you know what I mean. One or two things still to find homes for."

"Yes, that's to be expected," she said.

We looked at each other for a moment.

"I'm glad you're back with us, Ernie, darling. Really."

I gave another awkward little laugh; I was never good at accepting compliments, especially from current or former lovers. I wanted to change the subject. I pretend-yawned and made a show of looking around the chamber curiously from my seat.

"Anyone gonna give me the grand tour, then?"

"Sure," Eric said. "Come on, I'll show you round."

Rennie smiled in a way that said she was aware of my evasiveness, but wouldn't press further on this occasion.

❧

The sleeping rooms in the House were every bit as lovely as the Hearth room, and I claimed one of them as my own immediately I walked in. I just knew; it had an atmosphere about it. A low, wide bed lay beside a huge window on the far side of the room, which gave onto lush gardens that stretched down and away to wide, empty fields. The walls were made from trees and twisted vines that reached up overhead to a ceiling that glowed the same peach-pink as the dusk outside. It felt perfect.

I walked over to the antique wardrobe and placed my hands on its worked metal door handles. Before twisting them open, I hesitated. A weird feeling had crept into my guts. Not residual nausea from the Restoration — this was something else.

Rennie appeared in the doorway behind where Eric stood. Both had strange expressions on their faces, for some reason, but neither said a word.

I shrugged, turned back to the wardrobe doors and opened them.

Rennie shouldered past Eric and darted forward to catch me as I collapsed backward. She supported my back with her chest, wrapped her arms about my waist, and brought me down gently onto the woven reed floor. "We didn't want you to see this so soon," she said.

"It's alright," I said between sobs. "It's alright. I'm glad it's all here."

I was looking at a wardrobe full of clothes, books, and other things, all of which I knew intimately and had expected never to see again. I'd thought them as dead as their former owner, but here they were, plain as day. Elias's clothes and gear. All of it. I hadn't been able to bear keeping hold of any of it after he'd died and, in any case, what would have been the use of keeping things that would help me remember, when all I wanted was to forget? And, putting emotion aside, it posed too much of a risk to the effects of the DNR: even a sniff of something of his packed away somewhere in my house would have threatened the integrity of its effects, and that disintegration would have been too dangerous for me to go through alone. It hadn't occurred to me yet, as my memories came back, including all my memories of him, to enquire as to the whereabouts of his possessions. There was no need to now: here they all were. "I can't do this," I mumbled.

Rennie cradled my head in her arms and stroked my hair and, while fireflies brightened to golden lamps that glowed against the indigo of the ceiling, I let fall the last of that day's tears. Eventually I stopped and, in the fullness of dark, comforted, we bade each other good night and she fell asleep with her arms around me.

Eleven

In the morning I lay still for a while, enjoying the huge, comfortable bed. Rennie must have moved me there the night before. It was a far cry from the thing I'd put up with during the years of my absence: a mattress whose springs dug into my body whenever I moved and a headboard that threatened to come loose and crush me to death in my sleep at any moment. I'd thought countless times about fixing or changing it, but a combination of deep inertia and the laziness that comes from growing accustomed to something — even if it happens to be crap — conspired to prevent me.

Rennie had got up and left a while before, and I was glad of the time alone. As I lay there with my eyes still closed, listening to the sounds of the rest of the House waking up and preparing to meditate together before breakfast, I realised that if it weren't for Vi's rude interruption of my liquid lunch several days previous, I would be waking up in precisely that crap bed and not questioning anything. I had come to know that house so intimately: the two broken stairs I had to step over; the light switches in the living room and kitchen that weren't safe to use during rain showers; the spongy patch on the bathroom floor; the attic trapdoor I never dared open. I'd framed these features as endearing idiosyncrasies, signs that the house and I were allies, united by our brokenness. But the truth was that what felt like a safety net had ensnared me. As much of a fuss as I'd made about it at the time, I was beginning to feel grateful that Vi had cut me free. I'd been living in the kind of comfort that lies to you, and I was done with it.

After a while longer, I peeled back the covers and worked my way to the edge of the bed, luxuriating in how far away it was. Room for several more people in here, easily, I thought to myself with a smirk.

I yawned and stretched and walked naked to the full-length mirror on the far side of the window, where the morning sunlight shone in and blessed everything, making the greens brighter and the browns richer. Even if there had been drapes to pull across the window, I would have left them open so that when I got up I could study the textures of morning as they played in the sky and the garden outside.

Looking at myself in the mirror, I noted with delight that my hair had returned to its natural ninety-five percent black, and some of the worry had lifted from my face and body. I was back to early middle-age, with just a few strands of steel grey in my hair and the beginnings of softening in my skin. I stood straighter and felt taller. The effects of my mental jiggery-pokery had worn off entirely then. The accelerated ageing had been my price for the luxury of forgetting, and I had been happy, at the time, to pay it. It had also been a useful disguise; it'll take me a couple of centuries to age that much naturally.

I took a few deep breaths and walked to the wardrobe. As I had the night before, I rested my palms on the metal handles that had been worked into the shape of laurel leaves, letting them nestle, cool, in my palms before I let go, turned the key and pulled the doors open.

The smell of Elias lingered about his things, but so faintly that I fancied only I and others he had been close with would be able to tell it apart from the ambient fragrance of the wardrobe.

I rifled carefully through his clothes until I found what I was looking for: a green dress that was one of his favourites, which I often borrowed when he wasn't wearing it. I pulled it off the hanger to examine it and was pleased to discover it wasn't moth-eaten. The fabric felt as soft as I remembered, and when I put it on it hung in the same way, draping itself over my body in a gentle embrace. I smiled at my reflection in the mirror and wiped away the tears that ran down my cheeks. I walked bare-foot to the chamber door and, as I reached out to open it, I heard the vines that had closed over it in protection draw back to let me pass through.

"Ah, good morning! Sleep well?" the cat said as I entered the Hearth room and inhaled the aromas floating from the kitchen: freshly toasted bread, fried mushrooms, tomatoes, and Boiling Hot Lava. She perched on a chaise longue, primly grooming her face and whiskers.

"Morning," I said. "Yes, I did, thank you. Really well." I rubbed my eyes and yawned again as I walked through into the kitchen to pour myself a coffee from the full pot on the terra-cotta tiled worktop.

Eric was at the sink, washing frying pans.

"Hiya, Eric," I said.

He raised a hand to wave hello without turning away from his scrubbing.

I poured my coffee, grabbed my plate of food from the side where it had been left for me, and went back into the Hearth room. I ate at one of the low couches around the fire pit, where logs crackled. Nobody spoke over breakfast, each alone with their thoughts.

A copy of the local newspaper lay on the couch across from me and, once I had finished eating, I fetched it over and sat down to enjoy some small-town scandal about goats escaping from a field and eating somebody's prize petunias, or whatever. I leafed through its pages, dismayed to see them mostly filled with adverts. I stopped near the back when I saw that the Births, Marriages and Deaths section carried an obituary for Wilbur, announcing the details of their memorial service and burial — which was weird, since they had no family apart from us, and we like to keep our business to ourselves. The announcement was tucked away in a little box in the bottom right-hand corner of the page. I'd almost missed it because it was covered by my hand as I held the paper, but when I moved it to turn over the page, there it was: a short, functional utterance outlined in narrow black.

"Seen this?" I called to Rennie, who was at the dining table, her flame-festooned head deep in concentration on the oil painting she was working on.

"Hmm? Oh, yes. Must have been written by someone at the Golden Sands," she said. "Only a professional could produce something quite so devoid of emotion."

I nodded and read the announcement again. "Burial in two days," I said. "That's pretty soon for a mutilated corpse, don't you think?"

"It is indeed," said Rennie. "Really rather hasty, darling."

The cat stopped her grooming; she had progressed to her flank and was giving great sweeping licks of her striped fur, occasionally interrupted when she paused to dislodge some irritating particle or other from her skin. "Which is especially interesting considering the fact that the body was missing certain important somethings," she said.

"Absolutely," agreed Rennie. She was twirling a paintbrush in the fingers of her right hand and her eyes were vibrant with sparks of red and orange in the irises. "So, either the coroner was sufficiently stupid not to notice that the deceased's eyes had been ripped from their skull, or our fugitive had time to weave a powerful glamour on his victim before he fled."

"Not possible," said the cat. "I was there not five minutes after he'd gone, by my reckoning, and a glamour to fool literally everyone for a few days, taking into account temperature changes and possible autopsy intrusion, would take far longer to fashion. So that means—"

"Someone at the morgue is either utterly incompetent, or they've let it slide, possibly with a little backhander by way of encouragement," I said.

Rennie stopped twirling the paintbrush and placed it on her palette, which lay on the table beside which she had erected her easel. She folded her arms, resting her elbows on the table, and leaned forward, her gaze even more intense than usual. "So, either they were paid off, or they're on the other side, and I don't mean in a death-and-beyond way."

"Therefore, we have a possible traitor in our midst, or maybe just an easily-bought invertebrate," the cat reasoned. "All the more cause to keep an eye on the death-house."

I'd been leaning back on the couch, listening to the other two lay out their theories. I sat up and crossed my legs. "For whose benefit, though?" I asked.

"What do you mean?" said the cat, her head tilted to one side in interest.

"Well, don't you find it strange? All the pretence of publicly announcing the death? No offence to their beloved memory, but who'd give a shit about this person nobody knew?"

The cat tutted. "They did have *some* non-Mage friends, Ernie," she said. "They were quite the whizz at the local Bridge Club, despite the fact that they won every game owing to un-canny foresight. I expect that lot'll all want to say their good-byes, won't they?"

"True," I laughed. "Lucky they didn't opt for cremation, then, I suppose. I mean, it is safe to assume that burial at sea is a tad unorthodox in the mundane world for people who've never been in the Navy. And if a crew of Wilbur's own Clan elected to take matters into their own hands and fins and tentacles, it might look a bit weird, right?" I imagined it: an eclectic bunch of mostly other-than-human folk rowing a little boat out to sea with an oddly shaped lump wrapped in sheets, while the local morgue's alarm goes off and the staff report one of the cadavers has disappeared. Mind you, though none of us were of the scaly, finned, many-armed, or tentacled persuasion, that was pretty much exactly what we'd have to do to get old Wilbs back to their predominant Element. If we didn't, things in the world of Water would soon be seriously out of balance, and this would be bad for all of us.

Rennie's eyes flashed yellow. She chuckled. "Can you imagine it though, the *volcano* of steam that would erupt if they were cremated? Whooosh!" She threw back her head and laughed, and I heard a forest fire in her voice. This is one of the things we used to argue about, back when we were involved; I found the forest fire laugh a bit close to home, considering my Change-Form, even though my Mineral content makes fire-play totally safe. It just doesn't float my proverbial, though there are plenty of other things that do. I let myself daydream for a moment.

The cat dampened Rennie's laughter with a cough followed by a stern glance. "So," she said, "we have some reconnaissance to do over the next few days, it would seem. I'll take charge of the shift rotation," Rennie and I looked at each other and simultaneously rolled our eyes, "and it should all go smoothly."

The cat jumped off the chaise longue and padded to the tall dresser that was built into the tree-wall behind where I was sitting. I turned my body to watch her, resting my elbow on the back of the couch. The dresser sat in a deep recess between two of the struts that supported the high-domed roof and had a set of shallow open shelves displaying turned wood dishes of varying dimensions, a deep oaken platform holding tall vases and vessels filled with bursts of edible herbs and flowers gathered from the gardens and, below it, wide, deep drawers whose handles were wrought iron rings which awakened a desire within me to open all of them in turn and try to clamber in.

The cat reared up onto her hind legs, resting her forepaws on the edge of the shelf, and leaned forward, opening her mouth. She clamped her teeth around the corner of the clipboard that lay there between a couple of green glass vases with cheerful yellow and white daisies and daffodils painted on them, and pulled it towards her. She lost her grip and it clattered to the floor.

"Drat!" she said.

Rennie and I could not help but exchange a glance behind her back.

"Bureau*cat*," I mouthed to Rens, silently, and we shared a breathless giggle, covering our mouths with our hands.

Eric came from the kitchen upon hearing the clatter of the falling clipboard and picked it up. He carried it over to the chaise longue, and the cat leapt up, placed a paw on the upper-most sheet of the various papers that were clamped to it by the holder at the top, where a pen was also held conveniently in place, and took a moment to read what was written there.

"Yes," she mused. "This should work just fine."

Rennie, Eric and I looked at each other and shared a collect-ive raising of eyebrows. Eric's were still the best, by several country miles.

I sipped the last of my coffee, including the grit that had settled at the bottom of the cup, and used my tongue to sweep the bits from my mouth. "Come on, then," I said. "Let's get to it. In a bit, though, after I've had some more of this stuff to get me going." I stood, picked up my coffee cup and went to the kitchen to refill it with silken bitterness.

TWELVE

I savoured my second coffee, brushed my teeth, and did some practice. My breath and body routines used to take me two hours, back in the days before the forgetting. Needless to say, it felt shit for the twenty minutes I prised out of myself that morning, even after two Boiling Hot Lavas, and I grumbled and swore, but by the end I felt successfully earthed. The feeling in my head after the Restoration was something akin to the one that lingers after you've come off an acid trip: some of your circuits have been re-routed and other entirely new ones created. It was a strange but not unpleasant sensation.

When I'd finished my practice, I washed in the stream that ran through the garden outside my bedroom window, laughing at how bracing the water was. I stuck it out for a few minutes before I admitted defeat and went to the bathroom for a nice warm shower.

When I sauntered into the Hearth room in a paisley dressing gown of Elias's that I'd never liked when he wore it but that I'd developed an inexplicable, sudden affection for, I found that the next couple of days' activities had been planned out in detail.

The cat and Rennie were sitting at the dining table, poring over maps and calculations on Rennie's laptop, the cat's clipboard beside them, for reference.

The cat looked up when she heard the patter of my bare feet on the floor. "There you are!" she said. "Feeling alright?" She looked me up and down as she said this, appraising the gown. She frowned. She'd apparently concluded from one garment that I was beyond redemption, a lost cause.

"Yes!" I couldn't resist laughing. "I'm fine. What's the plan, dear cat?"

The cat nodded satisfaction that I'd deferred to her — and the Council's — authority on the matter.

I drew the paisley robe closer about myself and tightened the turquoise cord of belt. I was aware of my naked sternum, with its vertical line of inked runes so long ago scraped across the area where the skin is thick but the flesh is thinnest. The tattoos had aged pretty well, considering: just a slight fuzziness around the edges and a bluish tint to the ink.

"Well?" I said, "If I'm gonna bother getting properly dressed, it'd better be for a good reason."

"Indeed," said the cat. "Today's errands are purely in the information-gathering vein. No antagonism, no fisticuffs or wandicuffs, no drawing attention to ourselves, got it?" She stared over the rim of her glasses at me, then at Rennie, and we both laughed like people who'd been found out.

"Oh, like I ever would!" Rennie said with an ostentatious swish of her arm, which was clad in the deeply vented sleeve of her gorgeous ruby red velveteen gown. "Darling, I don't like to draw attention to myself; you know that." She gave a flutter of her purple eye-shadowed eyelids and winked at the cat.

The cat did not take the bait. "Rennie, you Veil yourself and go to the beach, please," she said. "Rent a deckchair, outwardly wear an appropriate and inoffensive garment or garments of some kind, and just people-watch. Yes?"

"I can do that," Rennie said.

We all knew that she would go there, including the walk from the House, stark naked, and use the Veil to convince the mundane world that she was wearing — well, anything at all — but we knew also that the Veil she cast would be so strong that she would appear just like any other beach-goer to even the trained eye, and that the disguise could be trusted not to slip.

"And you, Ernie," said the cat, "leave separately, and rent one of those bikes that tourists like to pedal about on, looking at things. You know the sort."

"*What?*" I almost shouted, "Me, ride a *bike*, not likely!" This was not what I had wanted to hear. I experienced a rush of shiny new flashbacks: falling, traffic, hailstorms when the battery went in my cheapo headlight and I found myself cycling in the profound darkness of a midwinter morning. I swore I'd never cycle again after that. There was already enough suffering in my life, ta very much.

"You *can* ride a bicycle, can you not?" said the cat.

"Well, yes, it's just, it's been a while."

"So, you don't need stabilisers; you can fake a convincing impression of someone who is just an innocent out-of-towner riding around, except you will make a point of doing a little circuit around the town, let's say once every forty-five minutes to an hour, and let's also say you just so happen to go along the street where what passes for a Coroner's Office in this town just so happens to be located. Alright?"

I nodded as I considered her suggestion. I'd have to dig around and find some suitable attire. Unfortunately for me, Elias had been so partial to wearing frocks that he possessed that, unless he had a secret stash of Lycra clothing I didn't know about, absolutely nothing that would be practical for riding a bike, and my Veil-skills were nowhere up to Rennie's standard. Going commando was not an option. It wouldn't be comfy on the saddle, anyway.

"The town is very flat, at least," the cat offered, a conciliatory tone fleetingly edging the officiousness from her voice. "And there's a chest of drawers in one of the guest rooms that will have some clothes you can borrow. Leggings and such."

"Okay," I said. I decided to take what I needed from the chest and leave behind my old purple jumper and tracksuit bottoms — if they survived the washing machine, of course. I was sure some itinerant wizard could make good use of them. Now I was clad in flowing green paisley, they just didn't feel right for me anymore.

"That concludes this morning's briefing," said the cat.

Rennie closed the lid of her laptop. She looked me up and down. "You look really well, Ernie," she said. "It's good to see you getting back to your old self."

"I have mixed feelings about it, to be honest," I said. "I wish I could have just taken the memories I wanted back and left the gnarly stuff."

Rennie smiled. A wave of melancholy passed across her face and was just as swiftly gone, lingering only in her eyes. "We both know that's not how it works, darling," she said quietly.

"Aye," I replied. "That we do."

❧

I readied myself for the day's mission. The chest of drawers I had been directed toward contained an extensive selection of leggings in every conceivable colour and design. I opted for some black ones with full moons and howling wolf faces on them: suitably serious, I thought. I nabbed a few other pairs to keep in my room: one with leaf patterns in the bright greens and yellows of spring, another with the same print but in autumnal hues of red and brown, and a couple in plain black. In the other drawers I located some plain tunics and vest tops I liked, and an array of sexy yet practical underwear.

I carried my armful of swag back to my room and hurled it all into one of the empty drawers at the bottom of the big wardrobe. I changed into the moon print leggings and a long grey vest top that covered my hips and wouldn't ride up while I was cycling, feeling the muted tones suitable for a bit of subterfuge — quite the opposite approach from the one Rennie was sure to take. I smiled to think of her walking starkers to the beach but Veiled in a pair of shorts and a t-shirt. Or perhaps she'd go for something less dowdy, like a yellow halter neck sun-dress and straw hat. Either way, she'd fit in on the outside. And I had to do the same and not let the mask slip. I felt nervous, but with my relatively unassuming choice of clothing it should be less effort to keep my Veil up. Perhaps, when I'd had a bit of practice, I could be more daring and go out in some of my fancy new undies, but that could wait for another day. I needed to start simple.

When I went back into the Hearth room, Rennie had already left, and the cat was installed proprietorially on one of the low couches beside the fire pit. "You've just missed her," she said. "She was keen to get a good spot on the beach. It's almost eleven already."

"I'd best be going too, then, hadn't I?"

"Not quite yet. We need to be sure your Veil-skills are up to par before we can let you out into the world."

I listened for any sign that Vi might be on his way to help, but heard none. Anxiety fluttered in my abdomen. I wanted to stall until he got here. "Actually, can I have five minutes? I'm a bit anx—" but the cat cut me off.

"Great! Okay now, don't rush it, Ernie, and remember to breathe steadily."

This was my first bit of proper magic in five years. I mean, I had effectively Shrouded my house, in a mundane way; the result of never having the windows cleaned or washing the curtains for as long as I lived there, plus the laminated sign I'd stuck to the door that simply said: "No Visitors." I'd been tempted, when I first moved in, by "Piss Off," but that seemed a tad unfriendly, even by my standards, and had the added risk that some people might find it amusing and knock anyway.

The cat cleared her throat and gave me a gentle tap on the arm with a forepaw, derailing my train of reflection. "Come on. You can do it. I'm here."

But Vi wasn't. I wondered where he'd got to. Never mind. Maybe he'd arrive any moment. I'd have to get on with it for now. I steeled myself, took a deep breath, exhaled long and softly. I gave the cat a little nod to signal my readiness to try, closed my eyes and turned my gaze inward. There it was. Swimming in my solar plexus, oscillating, turning, round and round, round and round. I moved to the pool's edge and reached down into the water, gently, keeping my breath soft. That was it, the way my personal Veil had always felt for me, like satin against my fingertips. I took a gentle hold, not grabbing, not forcing. At the moment of contact, the Veil surged up as a soft, dark flow of energy. This was the crucial moment: I needed to create a strong, clear image to project outwards, and I must not doubt it for a microsecond. But what did I want to appear as? I hadn't thought of that. I wavered and lost my grip.

"Shit!" I spat. "Damnit!"

"It's alright," the cat said. "That was excellent for a first try. You're just a bit out of practice, but the knowledge is there. Trust it. Yes?"

I puffed out the breath I'd been holding. "I just hadn't expected it to be waiting there for me after so long. Give me a minute and I'll try again."

"Good. Now, one more time, and just keep steady. Think carefully about what you want to project through your Veil, visualise it clearly and stick with it. That's the key to keeping it up."

I suppressed hurt thoughts about why Vi wasn't helping me with this like he'd said he would, shifted my weight from side to side, and placed my feet hip width apart. Closed my eyes. Slowed down. Went inward. This time, I was already kneeling at the water's edge with the satin fabric of the Veil lightly held between my fingertips. And I had a clear image in my mind's eye. As I exhaled, it took shape upon the fabric and spread to envelop me. I held it there for a few minutes, taking great care that my breath stayed steady, then let it go. I opened my eyes. "Well?" I said, "What did you see?"

"A perfectly innocuous, doughy-bellied tourist, wearing beige chino shorts and a pale blue polo shirt," she said. "Totally, perfectly unremarkable. Except maybe lose the neon-pink bum bag and go for a nice muted olive man-bag or something; you'll draw less attention to yourself."

"Nice!" I said, pleased with my work. "Looks like I'm about ready to go outside."

THIRTEEN

The cat walked me to the garden gate. With each step, I grew more apprehensive. By the time we arrived and she turned to bid me goodbye, I felt less like the arms of adventure were opening out to embrace me and more like I was staring into the sticky web of a large and hungry creature with unrelatable eyes and far too many legs. I considered feigning illness to wheedle my way out of it.

"Are you feeling alright?" said the cat, regarding me with concern.

"Umm," I mumbled, "as a matter of fact—"

"Don't worry. Just a bit of nerves. You'll be fine."

"Uhh," I coughed and sniffled, but it was too late.

"Just remember what I said. Keep calm. Breathe. It'll be over before you know it."

The cat's brusqueness took me straight back to the Academy nurse, who would say precisely these things before presenting me with a cup full of weird purple stuff and expecting me to drink it. Any sign of anxiety was whisked away, tidied up like the empty wrappers of forbidden sweets.

"Yes, miss," I said, before I could stop the words leaving my mouth.

"Hmm?" The cat looked at me.

"Nothing," I said sheepishly.

"Hm. Anyway, there's a treat to look forward to when you get back," she said. "It's Vi's turn to cook today and he does an excellent roast."

"I shall look forward to it." I still felt like an idiot, but marginally more hopeful for having an incentive to come back in one piece. Whenever danger loomed too close out there in the world of risk and strangeness, I resolved to recite to myself: "there's no place like Yorkshire puddings and gravy."

"Good luck," said the cat. "And remember, the bicycle rental place is one of those charming old wooden beach huts by the seafront. You can't miss it. Just go back along the Old Path and turn left, and it's a couple of hundred yards along when you get to the end. Anything — and I mean *anything* — suspicious, you tell me as soon as you get back, yes?"

"Understood." I almost saluted, but resisted the urge lest she think I was being disrespectful.

"Don't risk trying to send any information here psychically; the airwaves are most definitely unguarded outside the safety of the House. Face-to-face is best. Got it?"

"Got it. It'd be too much on top of keeping the Veil up anyway. It's only day one."

The cat narrowed her eyes. "True," she said, then she turned and padded away. "Off you go, then. I believe in you," she called over her shoulder.

I watched the tip of her fluffy tail bob left and right with her steps, until I felt a rush of energy behind me. I turned.

The garden gate stood open. I gave my Veil a final tweak, took a deep breath, grounded myself and walked through the gateway, leaving the cool, herb-scented garden behind. Here, once again, was the Old Path. Truth be told, I was reluctant to walk it alone. What if I got lost? What if it twisted and turned like before and sent me mad, or I ended up somewhere entirely unexpected? I took another deep breath, and began to pick my way along the narrow path. After a few paces, I looked behind me. This was just as much of a mistake as it had been the last time. I couldn't see the gate, just a solid wall of trees and ominously dark and thick undergrowth. Feeling sweat bead on my brow and my heart quicken, I turned and began to walk again, but not twenty paces later I found myself at the edge of the churchyard. I was shoved off the Path by a business-like gust of wind, and stood there feeling that bereft feeling of having been kicked out of a pub that had done something as audacious as closing so the staff could go home and get some sleep. It was well out of order. Nevertheless, here I was, back at the boundary with the mundane world, on the path I had to follow to get to the bustle of the seafront and my impending two-wheeled errand. Lukewarm, salt-flecked air met me, and I drew up my Veil, feeling its satiny texture envelop me, changing my skin for anyone but myself. To any stranger, whether their gaze slipped across my presence or lingered there, my hair was not long, black waves but close-cropped and blond, my skin not golden and lightly freckled but a pasty pink-white with flares of sunburn on my shiny nose and pudgy cheeks, and my sartorial instincts had utterly deserted me. I took the opportunity to practise walking in a manner befitting the person I was Veiled as, mostly for my own benefit, so as not to jar with the illusion I had conjured.

I'd forgotten how odd it felt, knowing I looked completely different on the outside to how I felt on the inside. I remembered how strange it felt when I first learned the technique. It was as though the real me was hiding behind a screen or a wall, controlling the strings of a puppet that was also me but clad in other skin. I got used to it after a while, but now, the first time Veiled in so long, I felt like a novice again. I knew, though, that the feeling would threaten the magic if I wasn't careful, and I didn't want to risk ruining everything so soon when the others had been so kind and welcoming. I felt guilty enough already about having to be rescued, on top of the grief. I reminded myself that the key was not to get stressed out and just to go with it, but that could be tricky. It's as paradoxical as *trying* to relax. I minded my breath, and kept my walking pace slow, which was a sensible decision in any case: bloody hot out, it was. I had a proper sweat on.

At the end of the path, I paused to look around me. Nobody was about, save someone walking a dog a bit further along the side street and, the other way, I saw gaggles of bright-shirted day-trippers sauntering with dripping ice creams clutched in their chubby hands. The dog made me think of Vi. Where was he?

I felt a nudge at my calf and almost jumped a mile into the air before I turned in an affected lumbering fashion that suited my disguise. There Vi was, dog-formed. He was also covered in mud, which explained where he'd got to.

He glanced up and down the street. "Can't smell anything amiss for now," he said, and nodded. "You're good to set off. I wanted to help with your Veil back at the House, but by the time I'd finished my bath you'd already left. The cat keeps a *very* strict timetable," he added in a whisper.

"Thank you. Is it — does it work?" I looked myself up and down, and couldn't tell. I'd not yet honed the art of separating projection from reality.

"It's solid," he said, his voice back at its usual volume, which was still pretty quiet. "Just keep it up. You'll get tired in an hour or so, and I don't just mean from the cycling, so make sure you come back when you start to feel it fading; you'll be vulnerable. No need to take any stupid risks at this stage. Okay? There'll be plenty of opportunities for that later," he continued as an afterthought, almost under his breath, but the words hung in the stifling air like a rancid fart.

I reached down to ruffle his ears, which were only a little muddy, and he licked my hand. I took a mental snapshot of the moment, for posterity. His appraisal of my Veil was reassuring at least, though I still felt horribly unprepared.

"Right," I said, a little shakily. "I'd best get off."

Vi trotted away and I turned to face the surreality of a small seaside town.

꩜

With each step I took that drew me nearer to the seafront, the outside world turned the volume up. The sun blazed overhead, making everything look bleached even through the lenses of my aviators. The grass in the churchyard was crispy and dehydrated; I prayed for no lightning strikes whenever the next wild summer storm hit the coast.

I couldn't believe I lived out here, in this world, for all those years. Well, that is, if "lived" is even the right word. I'd existed, sure enough, but I wouldn't go as far as to say I'd really been living. As I lumbered closer to the seafront in my temporary body, I heard music blaring from shops selling all manner of gaudy souvenirs, chatter and laughter, and underneath it all, beyond the milling of people and their chaotic thoughts, the sea. A pleasant shiver spread up my back and cooled my skin.

I stepped off the pavement to circumnavigate a crowd of people gathered at a shop window and carried on for a bit at the edge of the road. When I spotted the bike hire sign a little way along, I crossed over, having to wait for several cars to crawl by as their occupants fruitlessly assessed the likelihood of parking in any of the spaces on the main strip.

I saw the bike I wanted straight away. It was propped up outside as if just waiting casually for me to happen by, chewing gum and smoking and leaning on things like it was a teenage tearaway with great hair in a film from the 1950s. It was exactly the same as my old one, but a newer model. Bottle-green metallic paint, twenty-one gears, road tyres but not the posh kind, and dropped handlebars. Stunning. I didn't give a shit that my corpulent Veil-body would look awkward perched on the narrow saddle; I needed this piece of comfort to ground the real me, and I mentally elbowed aside all unpleasant memories related to cycling. It took some effort.

The proprietor of the Cycle Shack sidled over, looking me — well, the Veiled me — up and down with an air of snotty condescension.

"Yeah?" he sneered through thin lips above which a scratty moustache clung for dear life. "Sure you want this one, mate?"

I unfolded the crisp tenner I'd pulled from the neon-pink bum bag — I'd managed to sneak out without the cat seeing this little adjustment and telling me off, and was quite proud of myself — and held it out.

"Fair enough, mate; whatever," he said as he plucked the note from my fingers. "Back by half three, yeah? Closing early today." He chewed his gum at me with his mouth open and looked me up and down again before he turned his back on me and went to the cash register. He squeaked back across the shack's boarded floor with my change and a fake smile and I wanted to punch him. I wished him nightmares of bodily disintegration, which I had a feeling he was plagued by anyway, given his attitude, and left it at that.

"Sure," I said, and wheeled my shiny temporary steed away, fighting my urge to go back and let him have an earful about body positivity.

I walked the bike through the worst of the crowds. Once there was more space, I moved to the kerb, guided the beautiful thing down at the edge of the road, mounted, and set off. I had to fiddle with the gears a bit, but they clicked easily into place in response to my touch on the controls, and I soon forgot any worries I'd had about cycling again.

The breeze was refreshing on my face, giving some much-needed relief from the sun's heat and the effort of maintaining the Veil. I was grateful that the air could get through it. The effort of keeping up the illusion plus the exertion of cycling for the first time in years, even on this flat road, was making me sweat buckets. I carried on, past the grand Victorian townhouses, past the pebble-dashed modern buildings that looked like piles of brownish grey vomit by comparison, and inhaled the smell of the seaweed exposed by the low tide. I'd left the crowds behind and the *click* of mussels being dropped by seagulls to smash their shells on the pavement's hard, pale slabs rang in my ears.

The funeral parlour was on the street off to the right, almost on the edge of the town centre, as the houses of death tend to be. Most people like to be reminded of mortality on their own terms by sentimental fictions rather than feel the warmth of the cremation oven in their midst as though it were a hearth, and I can't say I really blame them for that.

It was eerily quiet off the main strip, as though even the turning of the world had paused and everything had closed in around me. All I could hear was my breathing and the gentle rotation of the bike's wheels. I found comfort in the mechanical whirring of the gears and the grip of the tyres on the tarmac.

The building reared up ahead on the left, lit by the strong midday sun. I squinted into the hard light, newly aware that if anything were amiss, I couldn't see well enough to fathom what it was — or, worryingly, avoid riding straight into it. I pedalled on, swallowing the anxiety that rose, and hoped my Veil was sticking.

When I saw that nobody was hanging around outside the three-storey building, I calmed down. Keeping my eyes on the road, I scanned the main entrance, the parked cars outside, the little strip of lawn and flower boxes, and found them all empty. The place had a strange vibe, but I put that down to its function as a corpse processing plant — harsh, but fair — rather than any supernatural shenanigans of a more than expectably untoward nature. I mean, all these places are haunted. It goes with the territory.

I rode on by, making an additional effort with my Veil just in case anyone sensitive were watching. Once I'd gone a few hundred yards further, I pulled in again to catch my breath. Hard work, this was.

A buzzing started in my ears — a sign that either I was drastically unfit and on the verge of passing out, or my Veil was under attack.

"Oh, for fuck's sake," I muttered, mostly to my green metallic steed. I took a few deeper breaths, rested for a minute, and the feeling subsided. I cast a glance about me and, seeing nothing, set off again. I could see the tip of the church tower a mile away over the roofs of the bland seaside estates, and it reassured me. I followed the road away from the seafront and took the next available turn. It was a dead end, terminating in a crumbling red brick wall liberally hung with razor wire that someone had evidently tried and failed to pull down at some point and which nobody else had bothered to re-attach. I braked hard and peered at the wall. Faded graffiti read "H3X0RZ" in three-foot letters inexpertly sprayed in primrose yellow. But that wasn't what made me look. Something was shimmering in the air just in front of the wall.

I stilled my breath and checked to make sure nobody was around. There were modest small-town business premises on both sides of the street: a carver of headstones on one side and a picture-framing workshop on the other, and neither had windows that gave onto this stubby little alleyway. I waited a moment. No, I was sure. A strong feeling had overcome me. I decided then, perhaps recklessly, to test another of my long-neglected skills.

I looked past the paint, the wire, the bricks, and gingerly felt around for the thing that had prodded at my sixth sense.

I dismounted and lay down my steed on the warm tarmac so gently and quietly that hopefully it wouldn't blip as an unattended vehicle on any potential bicycle thief's radar. I crept towards the wall in a similar fashion, barely disturbing the clouds of insects that hovered and flitted around the nettles and cow parsley that pushed their way through the dirt. I wished for rain, for Earth's sake, then pulled in my focus and crouched down, holding my breath. Something was there. I was sure of it. Too late, I turned and looked over my shoulder.

A tall, shadowy someone stood behind me, solid barring an empty space where a heart should have been. I felt a rush of fire-hot air and a blow to the side of my head.

In the split second before my lights went out, I began to fall sideways in slow motion, and I saw them spin away from me and take off down the street. They looked very much like they were in a hurry to get somewhere.

Fourteen

I woke up flat on my back on the tarmac. My throat was parched and the side of my head ached where it had been thumped. I groaned, coughed, turned onto my side, then eased myself up to a sitting position. With my eyes closed, I gently examined my head for swelling. Just a bruise to the spot in question. I was also relieved to note, once fully upright and with my eyes open and looking in the right direction, that the bike hadn't been nicked. I'd have deserved it; I was a bloody idiot for leaving it there like that. I crawled the six feet to where it lay exactly as I'd left it, the skin of my fingers pressing hard into the hot, dusty tarmac as I dragged myself along. I grabbed the bike's handlebars and stood it up, then used it to pull myself to my feet.

The bike bounced on its fully-inflated tyres as though it was glad I was paying attention to it again and impatient to set off on another adventure. Departure, I concurred, would be wise. The light had changed and I guessed that about an hour must have gone by. Only the Makers knew what could have happened in that time. I felt a surge in my blood pressure, and my head started to swim when I realised that my Veil had slipped while I'd been unconscious. It hadn't just slipped: it had disappeared completely. I was nakedly myself. I looked around fearfully; there was no sign of anyone about. I closed my eyes and took a few deep breaths.

"Shit," I whispered. "Come on, Ern, it's just there —" I concentrated hard, my mind grasping for the feel of satin. It eluded my touch. I slowed my breath further and felt a cool shiver respond to the movement of the warm afternoon breeze across the skin of my arms. I tried again. Yes. There it was. As soon as my fingertips connected, the Veil rose and covered me once more.

I decided to retrace my steps, or rather, wheel revolutions; I had to take the bike back to the shack anyway, from where I planned to head straight for the House even though I had piss-all to show for myself but a sore head and an empty stomach, though I supposed the others would be interested to learn about what had happened in the alleyway. Fire-Mage, by my reckoning, and definitely not on the side of good and justice. I mounted my steed again and set off at a modest pace back the way I'd come.

As I turned left out of the dead-end alley, the sight of the sky over the ocean almost took my breath away. I'd have allowed it to, but for the fact that the consequent lapse in mental focus would have compromised my Veil again. The early evening sun — I'd evidently been out for far more than an hour — was a bloated orange disc crowned with a halo of pink cloud, and the sky glowed turquoise between and beyond everything. The tide had come in and most people had left the beach, though some had moved their towels and wind-breaks higher up its slope to catch the last of the day's rays.

Pedalling leisurely down the street towards the seafront, I let the light and sound wash over me and got so distracted I almost didn't notice the two drunken blokes having a fist-fight in the middle of the road. Not much to do around here, granted, but this seemed like a lot of effort to go to for some entertainment on such a hot day. They swung and swore at each other, scarlet-faced and sweating, staggering across the baking tarmac, and I had to swerve to avoid them. My Veil wobbled at the same time the bike did. Luckily, the blokes were too distracted, and all I got was a "watch where yer goin' ya fuckin' weirdo!" bellowed at my back as I pedalled away. Not the first time such words had been directed my way, and I'd been called far worse. I let them bounce off my Veil and kept going. Nothing could deter me from my mission now. My stomach rumbled, and I near-drooled at the thought of the promised meal.

I got to the end of the street without further incident, turned left and headed for the Cycle Shack, but I could see already that it was boarded up. When I got closer, there was no sign of its proprietor, so I decided to hang on to the bike rather than leave it for a thief. I was glad of the extra speed it lent me and I accelerated away in the direction of the church. I felt the wind in my hair and could almost taste the roast dinner I'd soon be scoffing.

I turned into the side street that led to the path beside the churchyard and braked hard. The bicycle squeaked to a stop and my heart leapt into my mouth. It was about the same size as a large piece of roast potato, and I wasn't sure how I should feel about that.

A Shrouded patch of air shimmered about thirty yards away. I glanced around. A few gaggles of people strolled on the seafront, but none of them were looking this way. Even if they had been, they wouldn't have seen the bloody great whirling ball of orange flame hanging about ten feet in the air — which I supposed was fortunate. The thing spun like a burning dervish, its heat scorching lichens from the leaning headstones and charring the long grass that grew on the humped earth of the graves. For a moment, I froze to the spot. I'd come off the saddle and put my left foot down when I braked to a stop, but kept the other on the pedal in case I had to exit the scene in a hurry. It was very tempting.

I knew I was no match for this, so I stayed as I was, eyes wide, fingers vice-like on the handlebars, knuckles white. I was more concerned that my presence there would draw unwanted attention, that people might see some tourist bloke hanging about, staring at mid-air — so I made a pretence of reading the inscriptions on the headstones nearest me, just in case, while I thought about what to do.

I was spurred close to action when, from within the spinning mass of flame, I heard a voice I knew — and it didn't feel like its owner was winning the fight. Flecks of dark shadow moved in the flames, and every attempt Rennie made to string a Word or two together was sliced to fragments that spun uselessly outward, their power diffused.

Her sudden, piercing cry was impossible to ignore.

"Rennie!" I yelled as I swung my leg over the crossbar and threw the bike to the ground.

"Ernie!" she shouted from within the suspended fireball. Her voice roared as though it was made of living flame, which it was at that moment, to be honest.

The skin on my face and arms grew uncomfortably hot. I couldn't risk going any closer without knowing whether I could use magic to protect myself. My Change-Form would work, but it was out of the question. There was the smallest flutter of leaves within me, but I quickly suppressed it, according to long-established habit. I stood there uselessly as the swirling mass of flame spun quicker and quicker, and I thought of Vi's fight back at the pub. I'd not been any good then, either.

"*Ah, fuck it!*" I muttered to myself. I cast about me for something I could use as a weapon. "A-ha!" I grabbed a fist-sized piece of chipped headstone from the ground nearby and flung it with as much force as I could muster into the middle of the fireball. It didn't occur to me until it was too late, that I might hit the wrong person. Luckily, it found its mark.

The Fire-Mage shrieked, her flames dimmed, and Rennie took her chance. With her adversary distracted, her voice rose quickly higher than the roar and rush of the inferno and could not be interrupted. She loosed a string of Words, and grey ash rained harmlessly to the ground. Rennie and her opponent separated and descended about ten feet apart, facing each other.

The Fire-Mage raised her arms. She began a furious invocation, and bright red lights glowed in her palms, protected by the bony cages of her long, skeletal fingers, which curled like the legs of dead spiders.

Rennie, unshaken, raised her right arm and drew a spiral in the air with the tip of her index finger. A lasso of orange flame shot out and wrapped itself around the cloaked figure — three, four, five, six revolutions — then Rennie raised her other arm, held her hand aloft, and swiftly closed her fist. The rope of flame became a net that tightened around the Fire-Mage and cut her body to pieces. Bits of it fell softly onto the crisped grass, where they melted into the ground. After a minute, only an unpleasant brownish oily patch remained, exuding a nasty smell.

Rennie placed her hands on her broad hips and grinned. "Job well done," she said. She wrinkled her nose at the smear on the grass. "All in an afternoon's work. Ashes to ashes, as it were, ha ha. Oops, sorry," she said, and bowed to each of the singed gravestones in turn. "You'll be fine after a bit of rain." She turned to me and gave a shrug of pure innocence, then wiped sweat and ash from her face, pushed her hair back, and sighed.

"Dunno about you, Ern," she said, "but I'm *ravenous*." As I'd suspected she would be when she left the House, she was stark naked; unsurprisingly, her Veil had dropped while she'd been fighting.

I felt a shiver of cold and looked about me, nervous that the commotion would have attracted an audience, but nobody was around. Maybe they were all too busy watching the fist-fight I'd almost collided with a few streets away.

"Let's get back, then," I said, and picked up the bicycle, of which I was now technically the thief. Rennie swept away towards the path, leaving a trail of grey-white motes like tiny ashen fireflies behind her. I watched as she walked; she left no footprints, and the ash sort of evaporated as it touched the ground. It was a shame about the damage to the cemetery, but with any luck people would assume it was local vandals. There were, after all, plenty of them about. The next rain would wash the ash and the remnants of the defeated Fire-Mage away, and the grass would recover soon enough. The lichens would take longer, but there was nothing we could have done to help that.

I stopped myself: no, you're wrong, mate, I thought to myself; there *is* something you can do. Ignoring Rennie, who was waiting for me some distance away, looking stern, I knelt down to apologise to the spirits of the damaged plants and quickly sent them some healing energy that would speed their regeneration. The deceased Mage's residue I sent further down into the Earth with the intention that it be transmuted and put to better use. That done, I joined Rennie and we hastened to the trees.

When we got to the place that led through the undergrowth to the garden gate, Rennie turned and looked past me. Her brow furrowed in concentration as she peered back along the path.

"Hopefully there aren't any more of those about," she said. She didn't sound convinced, and neither was I. I hoped the Fire-Mage she'd bested was the same one who'd whacked me in the head. If there were more lingering nearby, we were in trouble.

We exchanged a look and swiftly made our way. The Old Path behaved exactly as it had the day I arrived, except for being a little wider to accommodate my new bike. It twisted and turned and closed its door of dense green behind our backs, and we went with as much speed as our legs and tyres would allow. I didn't feel safe until the gate had closed and locked behind me, at which I sighed in relief, and laid the bike down on its side on the grass.

Vi came bounding joyfully through the garden. "You're back —" he began to say, then stopped when he saw my face. "What happened? Is everything alright?" He trotted to me and I bent to stroke between his ears. He stood up on his hind legs and licked my face, which was a bit weird, because I didn't let any of my other friends do that unless under the influence of mind-altering substances. I supposed I could make an exception for an actual dog, or as close to one as it was possible for a person to be.

"Oh, mate," I said, exhaling heavily. "It's been a right old time. Rennie's just had a scrap with a Fire-Mage and I had a bit of a to-do near the funeral place, possibly with the same one. Oh, and I've accidentally nicked a bike."

"So, I see," Vi said, peering past me.

"It — oh, never mind. Anyway, the Heartless Ones are keeping a tight watch on old Wilbur's remains, it would seem. Well, the rest of them anyway, minus the parts that could have done the watching for themselves." I thought of empty eye sockets, and shuddered. "I really need a drink," I said. "Is there any of that heather ale left?"

"Certainly," said Vi. He trotted into the House. A minute later he emerged, man-formed, holding two unlabelled brown bottles. I could see from the condensation on the glass that whatever they contained was delightfully cool. "I could do with one myself," he said. "We've had an interesting time here, too." He handed me a bottle. "All the heather stuff's gone until the next batch is ready," he said, "but there's heaps of this to get through. Elderflower pale. It's really quite good."

I took a sip. Floral sweetness slid down my throat. "Mmm. This'll do nicely," I said, then drank a long draught. The bottle was half empty when I lowered it from my lips. "Not as strong as my usual preference, but it's a great brew," I said when I'd wiped the drips from my chin.

Vi took some less greedy sips from his bottle. "Glad you approve," he said. "Come on, let's go in and sit down. Food's nearly ready. Let's eat, then we can talk."

We went inside. I helped Vi set the table, and Rennie and Eric brought through dishes bearing mountains of steaming hot food.

The cat picked her way across the table top between the serving dishes, sniffing at each one in turn and wrinkling her nose. I clocked her having a sneaky lick of the butter, though, as she passed it.

Eric brought her a porcelain platter of poached white fish and set it down beside her placemat, a laminated one with little smiling unicorns on it.

"Bit childish, isn't it?" she said haughtily.

"Sorry," Eric shrugged. "All we had left." He shot me a cheeky smirk and went into the kitchen. He came back with two bottles of red wine, one of which he'd uncorked. "Help yourselves," he said.

We ate quickly and with little conversation; the food was too good to waste time talking over it. I noticed that Vi looked at our faces as we started to eat, lingering long enough on each one to make sure his cooking skills were adequately appreciated.

I'd nearly died for the third time in as many days just hours before, so I savoured my dinner (the cat was right: Vi was a mean cook) and relished the company. At the time of my decision to work the DNR, forgetting had felt the only way to relieve myself of the emotional weight I carried. But we all carry such weight, do we not, and is it not also our choice how much we allow it to make us heavy? What better way to honour what we've cherished and lost than to try, especially when things get really fucking difficult, to find some lightness, even in small things, even as we crumble?

"Bloody great, that," I said, patting my belly. "Not had a decent roast in years."

Vi looked nervous.

"What is it?" I scanned the rest of the group. Eric looked apprehensive too. Something was clearly up.

My eyes met Rennie's, and I was surprised and dismayed to see an anxiety in her expression that approached my own.

"So, what happened out there?" the cat said.

Rennie sighed deeply, then took a sip of wine. "Everything was ship-shape on the beach," she said. "Well, at least it seemed that way at first. I'd Veiled as a sixty-year-old Cretan woman in a long, white beach dress with a metallic green mermaid print swimming cozzy underneath. I must say I looked fabulous. I was carrying a wicker tote bag, wearing a broad-brimmed sun hat. Little picnic. Bottle of fizz. Book to read. Enormous sunglasses. Easy-peasy. So, I walked at a suitable ambling pace down to the seafront, turned left, and went along for about a quarter of a mile until I saw a lovely spot right at the far side of the bay. There were a few others around, some families, young couples, a group of friends hanging out and drinking cider, all the good stuff you'd expect on a gorgeous summer's day."

The cat listened with interest, her paw hovering over the touch screen of her tablet. "Okay," she said, "so, just to be sure, no sense of any Elemental magics being worked anywhere, nothing in the air, the sky, the sand?"

"Nothing whatsoever," Rennie confirmed. "Just the lovely warm sunshine and the sight of people relaxing on the beach with their loved ones. Until — Oh!"

Vi leaned forward and rested his elbows on the edge of the table. "What?" he said.

"I forgot something. I'd got an ice cream on the way."

"What flavour?" I butted in.

The cat glared at me. "That's *hardly* relevant."

"I'm painting an evocative picture," Rennie corrected her. "All the details are important, even the inconsequential ones."

The cat's whiskers twitched, but she didn't argue. "Go on, I'm listening," she said.

"So, I'd got this rum and raisin double cone. Really effing good, it was. I intended to take my time with it so as to savour every single lick properly. But, as I was ambling to my chosen spot, which I'd seen from some way off, as I said, something — ran into me. It's weird." She shook her head, took a sip of wine, put the glass back on its coaster and pushed back her chair. She bent to inspect something. "And I have a bruise on my leg exactly where I felt it hit me. Hm. Curious."

"What ran into you?" Vi asked.

She thought for a moment. "You know, I have no idea. I dropped the ice cream and it smeared all down my leg — well, my dress, for anyone watching — and I got distracted looking for tissues in my bag so I could wipe it off. When I looked up again, I didn't see anything moving and the weird feeling had just melted away. Like my poor ice cream as it lay on the sand in the glare of the sun. A tragic loss." She tossed her hair dramatically.

The cat tapped her screen a couple of times. "Then what?" she asked.

"I just carried on walking," Rennie said with a shrug. "Nothing else I could do, if I didn't want to be noticed. I wasn't worried about the Veil, of course, but it would have looked amiss if my body language had suddenly changed. Anyway, I did have a strange feeling then, until I'd settled beside the cliff, but maybe it was just embarrassment I felt seep through from my Veiled identity. I can't say for sure; I'm not really used to it."

"Embarrassment is so not you," I said.

She smiled. "Exactly. So, I just wrote it off, I suppose. The day was pleasant and warm and everyone around so happy, and I couldn't feel anything too untoward after that strange little shove I'd got. I assumed someone's dog had run into me whilst chasing a toy or something. Everything was fine after that, until I decided to go into the water."

The cat's eyes intensified. "The water? That is interesting."

"Taking a swim to cool off felt like an appropriate thing for my Veil-identity, so I left my stuff on the beach. The couple having a picnic and a smoke next to me agreed to keep an eye on it; they seemed trustworthy. I got up and wandered down to the water's edge, all the while looking about me as subtly as I could.

It was a bit difficult, because I'd left my sunglasses too, so I was squinting. Anyway, I waded in and swam out a little way. Then I dipped my head under the water—"

Everyone at the table leaned forward simultaneously, rapt with attention.

"— and I heard this *sound*." She paused with her head tilted to one side, thinking. "I can't describe it very well," she said, "but it sounded almost like the water was crying."

"It will have been," said Vi, matter-of-factly. "Wilbur was a Water-Mage. The water of the sea, their specialism within their Element, is mourning their death."

"Hence the urgent need to be returned to it," the cat said. "And why the Grey and his Heartless army want so much to prevent this. They want to break the connections that hold our world together, sunder the bonds within and between the Seven Elements. Permanently fragmenting the body of a Water-Mage as powerful as Wilbur weakens the whole Element in a way that, though apparently small, has a knock-on effect. A seed of doubt planted at the right time can grow into something terrible, and Wilbur's most powerful divination tools being laid to rest in the wrong Element would confound extra-sensory perception for any Mage they've ever worked with, making Water as a whole extremely vulnerable to attack. And there's another reason why they took Wilbur's eyes."

"What?" I said. "I thought they just wanted them to make it easier to find and threaten the Makers."

The cat nodded. "Correct. But they're also useful for Seeing one or two other things."

"Such as?" Rennie said.

"Well, us, for a start," said the cat, "and also Wilbur's magical equipment, which my guess is they haven't found yet. They must have thought that the eyes would help them see where it's kept — but Wilbur had one of the best safes I've heard of. Mineral- and Fire-Mage pal of mine knocked it together for them and added a little Earthbinding to fasten the lock mechanism. I used to mock them for it, you know: 'who needs that hecking fortress in a sleepy little place like this?' I'd say. Paranoid old so-and-so was right to be so cautious, though, eh? Ha!" She tapped at the screen a few more times, shaking her head and chuckling.

I was glad someone was so amused. "So, what happened next?" I asked Rennie.

"I got out of the water and decided to patrol rather than lounge on the beach any more. I just felt so sad and strange after hearing that weird crying. I walked around for a while on the beach and up and down the esplanade. I got another ice cream from a different van, mint chocolate chip this time, and then I thought, stuff it, I'll just go back to the House. Then I ran into the Fire-Mage — she rushed me from behind one of the headstones in the corner of the graveyard. She was a feisty one; wish I could take credit for having trained her myself. Anyway, I'm glad Ernie arrived when she did. If she'd been earlier, the Fire-Mage might have gone for her, and — no offence, darling."

"None taken," I grumbled, remembering the moment when I had frozen on the spot, completely forgetting that all my most powerful magic had recently been Restored, helpless to do anything but look a bit surprised that I was likely about to snuff it. Rennie had said many offensive things to me prefixed with this over the years. I couldn't say I was inured to it, exactly, but I knew her well enough to know such observations were merely blunt rather than malicious. And, more to the point, on this occasion the observation was accurate.

"But you're so newly back among us. You're a bit of a liability until you've had some more practice and got used to being fully yourself again. You know?"

I smarted at this, but she was right. If the Fire-Mage had been the same one that hit me, she obviously passed me over for a more worthy adversary. I was probably just in her way rather than being an actual threat.

"That's fair enough," I said. "I've not had to do any proper fighting yet, have I? I feel like my old strength is there, but it's lurking somewhere, out of practice. I've had no cause to use any blades to shear any bones yet, and I need to be sure I can handle myself when I catch up with a certain dickhead so I can Earth him out of existence." I clenched my fists, feeling a throb of anger mixed with a flutter of something else. Something that took pleasure in the causing of harm. By the Makers, was a sinister part of me actually *looking forward* to fighting him? Bravado is easy when you're not staring death in the fangs, though, isn't it?

Vi gave me a sympathetic smile. He knew how much I'd enjoyed a good scrap, back in the day, but something in his face warned me to be careful what I wished for.

The cat cleared her throat. "In actual fact," she said, "once we've heard what happened to you out there earlier, Ernie, before you got to the churchyard, there is something you can be of use with."

"Oh?" I said, regretting having set the intention of being more useful. I wasn't ready for battles yet, not now. I'd only just eaten and there was wine still to drink. It would be criminal to leave it, and myself, un-drunk. "How's that?" My voice quivered around the edges, and my fingertips gripped the lip of the table top to stop them from trembling.

"It's about Wilbur's stuff," the cat said. "Well, just one thing actually, and it's in their safe. So, we need you to go to their flat at the first available opportunity, find the safe, and pick the lock."

FIFTEEN

Just like that? Just stroll on in, whistling a merry tune, break into a crime scene — a *murder scene*, no less! — and crack a safe?" I let out a hearty laugh that I hoped still conveyed the deep cynicism I felt about this plan.

Rennie and the cat looked at each other, then turned to regard me with a mix of patience and exasperation.

"Essentially, yes," said the cat. "That is almost exactly what you will do."

"Bloody hell; didn't take you long to devise a plot to have mincemeat made out of me, did it? Just when I was starting to feel comfy, and all." I sniffed and folded my arms defensively across my stomach. "Very nice. Pluck me from obscurity, support me just enough so's I trust you, encourage me to get my old powers back — and, *and*, and this is not the least of your offences, I might add, manipulate me into an emotional attachment to this lovely space and that room where all of El's old stuff is. Show me just enough to like you and this life and then land me with this. Fucking typical. I should've bloody known."

The cat looked apologetic. It didn't suit her. "Ah, yes," she said. "I suppose, um, I can see how it might look that way to you."

"Ha! A confession!" I tightened the cross of my arms and turned my head to the right, with a suitably offended flourish, to look over my shoulder. I hoped this was giving the correct impression of how annoyed I was at being made into Grey-bait within days of arriving here, and also that it would have the intended effect quickly — it was physically very uncomfortable.

The cat continued: "Ernie, please hear me out."

I sighed and turned my head back the other way to look at her. To her credit, she seemed genuinely contrite.

"Go on," I said. "Since I've been drinking your wine and beer, and my belly's been enjoying the best food I've had in ages, I owe you that much."

"It's *your* wine, your everything, technically," she said, "but never mind. Now. Listen, we're not throwing you into danger so carelessly as you think. You won't be going in alone, for starters, and, secondly, there's no way they'll catch you."

"I wish I could be so sure about that."

"Even a Heartless assassin can't take that many risks so close together. They have to regroup periodically too."

It all sounded a bit too dangerous to me. "I'm sorry," I said, "I still don't see how I can just wander nonchalantly into the building."

The cat smiled, glowing with self-satisfaction. "You won't be *walking* anywhere," she said.

"Eh?"

"I know it's been a long time since you Changed, Ernie."

Uh-oh, here it was. I suddenly felt very sick indeed. "I swore I'd never do that again. I swore! I wanted to be human-formed forever, it's best for everyone that way. I can't Change. It's been too long. And, in any case, what good will I be as a bloody great tree? Am I supposed to reach in through the window with a branch or something, whilst the enemy bombards me with explosives?"

Glances were exchanged around the table, which told me that my companions thought this idea actually sounded worth a try.

"No," I said, shaking my head slowly and giving each of them a chastising glare. "That was not a serious suggestion."

"Ernie. Please listen."

I scowled, but couldn't help but be interested in whatever crazy proposition the cat was about to make. Her voice was so soft and lovely. I thought of what a great interrogator she must be, with that silken tone and those claws.

"Eric has been getting really good at quite a few magical techniques, including Veiling, Shrouding and Shifting."

"Go on," I said. He had a little Spirit in him too, then. This was interesting. The more talented of those guys can change anything into anything, at least temporarily.

"Therefore, we were thinking it would be good practice for him, and for you actually, if, for the second round of patrols, he could Change himself and Shift you, and you could sneak in together."

My heart was pounding. Shifting was the opposite of what I could do; I found it fascinating and had never had the opportunity to experience it, what with my repertoire being limited to: Rock-Hard Tree. I'd always had a hankering to fly. My mind raced as I thought of what it might feel like to be a butterfly or a bee, a bird, or even a bluebottle. A smile forced its way through a crack in the wall of my grumpiness.

"We thought you could be, oh, a cockroach or something. They're resilient and fast. Lots of skittery little legs too, and most people's instinct is to run away from them."

The bubble burst. "You've clearly thought this through," I said drily.

"Or," the cat said, reading my expression, "Eric is particularly strong in Corvid form. He could fly in as a crow, carrying you as a worm." I looked from the cat to Eric. He had arched his eyebrows in my direction; this did not portend well.

I couldn't believe what I'd just heard. "A worm? I mean, I love worms, honestly, but they're a bit delicate, like. What if we get into trouble? What if Eric's hurt and I can't protect myself?" I shook my head in disbelief. "A cockroach I could deal with; at least they're quick on their feet. But — oh! And on top of the noodle-body, with him as a crow, how do I know he won't just bloody eat me?!"

Eric looked crestfallen.

"Please be assured, his integrity is unshakeable," the cat said.

"Yeah, it is, actually," Eric said, "but I might just happen to drop you instead and you could get snapped up by a hungry blackbird before I could fend them off." He leaned back in his chair and smiled broadly.

"Hnnnff," I grumbled.

"If I may interrupt," the cat said, "Ernie, we have it all worked out. For him to be on wings is the quickest and most precise way we can get you both in there without attracting any attention. You can watch from a tree, high up, you see; his eyesight will be faultless. And, at the opportune moment, you'll be swept up and borne over the roof of the Golden Sands and in through a window that's always left open in the upper storey of the building."

"What kind of window?"

"It's the second-floor staff toilet."

"Nice," I grimaced.

The cat ignored me. "He'll Shift you back to you again as soon as you're in through the window," she continued. "You won't be in that particular room more than a few seconds. All we need to do is observe closely for any movement of the enemy. And we have the rest of tomorrow and the following day, too, don't forget. We've established that this town's modest little morgue is guarded too, but all that's there is the rest of Wilbur's body, and that's not going anywhere just yet. It's far more important for us to get to the safe in their flat before Richard's lot find an unscrupulous safe-breaker and beat us to it."

"Very good point," I said, nodding. "There are a few of those about, one of whom was my Magical Security Methods teacher, actually, back in the day."

"Quite so," said the cat. "Consequently, time is very much of the essence." She tapped at her screen a few times and pushed her glasses up on the bridge of her nose. "The plan is this: you'll start out in the morning on patrol again, Ernie, but in a different Veil this time, of course."

"What do I do about the bike? I can't very well just brazenly ride stolen property around such a small town, can I?" This was me admitting to myself that I had zero intention of returning it to the Cycle Shack at this point, even though it probably would have been fine with a sufficiently gushing apology and a dose of faked old-lady forgetfulness.

The cat sighed. "Hmm. You can try a modest Shroud to cover the bike, too — if you feel up to it? You'll be touching it, after all. Shouldn't be too much additional effort to include it."

"Oh yeah! I didn't think of that." I swelled with pride at the feeling of both having a shiny new bike to ride around and getting my own back on that guy at the Cycle Shack into the bargain. "I'll try before setting off, just to be sure, but I reckon I can cover it. Won't take much more effort to include something I'm sitting on. Only issue is if I have to dismount and leave it somewhere."

"In that case, just make sure you leave it well out of sight," the cat said curtly, and tapped at her screen again.

I raised my eyebrows.

Eric half-smiled in a way that told me he was looking forward to Shifting me into a worm.

"Fine. Alright then," I said. "And what if I happen upon Rennie embroiled in another little scrap?"

"Just ride by, darling," Rennie said. "You can't intervene anyway, really — so just head back here and raise the alarm if anything goes skew-whiff."

I sighed, dissatisfied with the idea of leaving a friend in danger, but she was right: there was nothing I could do to help her without being burned to a crisp and, being so newly back to the fold, I was reluctant to blunder into such a fate so quickly.

"You'll be watching the sea and the funeral parlour alternately, Rennie," the cat said. "Change your Veil in the public loos each time you've done a round, if they're not busy."

"It'll be fine," Rennie beamed. "Most people don't notice what's right in front of them, do they?" She laughed wickedly.

"Don't do anything too risqué, Serenity," the cat warned. "I know you must be terribly bored here doing routine surveillance work."

"Far from it," Rennie said, grinning. "I can try more ice creams that way. And besides, I'm really damned nosey."

"Isn't that the truth?" the cat said, flat-voiced, before she tapped once more at her screen.

"What about me?" Vi said.

"You go with Ernie," said the cat. "In whatever form you choose."

He nodded, smirked enigmatically, and said no more.

Sixteen

That's how it came to be that Vi and I went out the following day, first Veiled and Shrouded as a leather-clad biker couple on a Harley, then as an elderly lady pushing her bonnet-wearing Scottish terrier in a pram and, finally, as a thirty-something woman with long braids tied up in a bun and a toddler in a child seat behind her on her vintage push-bike, one of those ones you sit on really upright. I had full awareness, though, that I was still riding the plunder gained from my half-accidental theft from the Cycle Shack, and I made sure that our respective disguises all stayed strong throughout our circuits of the town. It was hard work, and I sensed that Vi was shoring up my strength at certain points, such as when I got flustered at junctions and traffic lights, or had to stop myself from swearing at idiots who wandered into the road to cross without paying attention. On the whole, though, I was happy with the improvement in my practice.

Each time we changed our appearances, I took us round on different routes, hoping our meandering would be random enough not to awaken suspicion. We rode through a couple of brief rain showers, and I enjoyed the feeling of water on my face, cooling my skin. I made sure our journeys always took us along the broad esplanade for its full length, so we could taste the salt air and smell the seaweed and the water and look out over the expanse of blue to see freighters in the distance and imagine, beyond everything, faraway shores as bands of promise draped over the curvature of the earth.

The first time we passed the Golden Sands we saw nowt but a couple of old dears outside on garden chairs in the shade, sipping tea, reading newspapers, and casting critical eyes over the handiwork of the gardener who picked over the flowerbeds. The ones dotting the lawn contained an array of pansies and the like, and the ones tucked close to the wall boasted varieties of rose. The observers gestured and projected their voices at him, and I swear I caught one of them telling him he'd missed a bit. I hoped for his sake he was wearing earplugs, but perhaps he didn't need them. Selective hearing is a great skill to cultivate.

The second time, about an hour later, the gardener was still there, working on a different flowerbed, but the old dears had gone, the chairs they had occupied sitting empty. One had tipped over sideways and now leaned drunkenly against the other. The sky had darkened, and sporadic drops of rain were falling, so I assumed it was that that had driven them indoors, but then I saw something in the shadow under a balcony and concluded that a weird shift in the energetic climate must have prompted the old dears' retreat. It was a new addition to the rose bed, tucked right in the corner and tall enough almost to reach the first-floor windows. It was wild-looking, dark-barked and sort of wispy, with a hollow in its centre. This Wood-Mage definitely wasn't on our side. I kept my gaze on the road, but released my grip from the left handlebar, reached back, and poked Vi gently on the leg.

"See that?" I hissed under my breath.

Vi looked to the right, then turned his head back in the other direction, doing an excellent impression of a dog casually look-ing about for interesting things, but not too interesting.

I took a right turn at the end of the road, carried on for a bit, then pulled into a quiet alleyway between two houses.

"Yup," Vi said. "I saw. I'd smelled something was off."

I gulped. "What shall we do?"

"Let's not pass by here again for a while, in case whoever it is gets wind of us," Vi said. "Rennie will have everything in hand, anyway; no need for a too-many-cooks situation, eh?"

I ruffled the fur on Vi's neck. "Come on then," I said, "let's go a bit further, have a rest, see a bit more of the surroundings, eh? Might be a nice country pub we can go to, with a garden."

The rain spotted for a while then stopped. The sky looked as though it didn't want to spend too much all at once and was saving up for a really big shower at some point later on.

I took us beyond the town's boundary, thanking the Makers for flat roads. A couple of miles further out, we spied an attractive little inn set in rambling gardens. Perfect. I looked about us, then accelerated into a long driveway that led to the farm buildings I could just make out about a mile inland. Once out of sight of the main road, it was safe to change our Veils again.

We sat for a few minutes, testing and tweaking them, then exchanged a silent look.

"Dunno about you," I said, "but I could do with a proper drink."

"Waaaa," said Vi, in character as a toddler.

"Very funny," I said, "but don't you dare make a habit of it, mate."

Five minutes later, we were sitting at one of the pub tables on the lawn outside the inn, watching the world go by. The world, in this particular place, consisted of insects and birds that flitted around the trees and the flowers, each talking in their own specific language. It was beautiful, even if they were all saying either that they wanted everyone else to fuck off or that they wanted a shag — or both. I'd decided against booze; needed to keep my mind sharp.

Once Vi and I had shared my glass of orange juice and lemonade, we set off. We coasted the two miles back into the town and I was grateful for the quiet road and the gentle breeze. I loved the soft sound of the bike's tyres on the tarmac and the whirring of the gears. I sank into it for a moment, meditating on the movement of small, central things. Something in my mind that had not been able to relax for a long time loosened ever so slightly.

Vi interrupted my contemplation. "I've had an idea."

"I don't like the sound of this, but go on, let's hear it."

"Well, since we're Veiled as a parent and child, I reckon it wouldn't look too suspicious if we were to go into the Golden Sands. Just pop in. You know, as if we were family visiting one of the residents. We can easily tuck the bike out of sight somewhere. What do you say?"

I squeezed the brakes and pulled us to a stop at the side of the road, in the shade of a high hedgerow. The buzzing of insect life grew louder and the air became too still and heavy.

"Oh, shit," I said, turning sideways on the saddle so I could face Vi, feeling a rush of fear but knowing he was absolutely right. "We could just walk in, the two of us, and nothing would look untoward." There was just one snag. "Okay, in theory, suppose we do this," I said. "We walk in, right, just a woman taking her kid to visit Nanna or Grampa, yeah? But who do we say we're visiting? There's no way to avoid going past Reception, and these places are like bloody low-security prisons these days with their sign-in sheets and CCTV in the lobby and what-not. And we can't very well say we're there to see Wilbur, can we. Theirs is the only name I know of any resident there."

Vi thought for a moment. "You're making it too complicated," he said, and shrugged. "The place is pretty big. I reckon we can get away with just using a first name. I'd bet anything there's at least one Jean or Joan or John or Eileen there, you know? And we can say we live far away and haven't seen whoever it is for a really long time. So, what do you say we just give it a go?"

Butterflies in my stomach flexed their wings. The skin on my face and chest tingled. "It's a risk," I said, thinking of the climbing rose in the front garden that wasn't normally there and hoping it would stay put, not seeing us, until we'd done our thing and were safely away, "but I can't fault your logic. You're a crafty git."

I patted Vi on the back and he burped loudly.

"That's much better, thanks," he said, and we laughed.

"Right," I said when we'd calmed down, "it is a gamble, just guessing a name, but I'm game. Let's change things up a bit. I'm sick of passively waiting for Fate to shine her searchlight on me when she can be arsed. My legs are getting stiff, anyway. I could do with stretching them."

❧

I rode us back to the Golden Sands in the opposite direction to the way we'd passed by the previous time. I defiantly leaned the bike against the rack beside the main entrance without so much as a glance at the garden, picked Vi up, put him on the floor, and got him into his toddler harness. We walked in, him toddling in front and me holding onto the reins, inching forward as calmly as I could manage. As we crossed the threshold, I inhaled the heady aromas of boiled food and disinfectant. To our left was the Reception desk, behind which sat a matronly woman with perfectly sculpted silver hair. I felt a tingle in Vi's aura as he turned up his Veil to maximum cute.

The woman behind the desk cooed and unrolled a stream of baby-talk in Vi's direction. She stood up and leaned over the desk, gazing adoringly down at him.

Vi gurgled indulgently.

"How can I help, lovey?" the woman said, addressing me but looking all googly-eyed at Vi.

My heart beat a tattoo in my chest. Beads of sweat erupted at my hairline. I did my best saintly-but-exhausted-mother smile. "We're, uh," I managed before my voice cracked. I cleared my throat. "Sorry. We're here to see—" My mind had gone blank. Fuck's sake, I thought. Not now. And there I was thinking I'd got my old courage back. "Violet," I blurted out.

Vi shot me a look. I felt his Veil waver for a split second and I also felt him think me a bloody idiot and chide his own recklessness for suggesting a tweak that turned a relatively low-risk plan into a potential suicide mission.

The woman at the desk — Jane, her name badge said — Jane's forehead creased as if her mind had let something slip into the well of her memory, and she was grasping for it in the dark water, splashes echoing off its mossy walls. But as quickly as the expression had appeared, it passed and was gone. She looked at me and smiled warmly.

"Violet, of course!" she said. "Lovely lady. She doesn't get many visitors; she'll be really happy to see you. Shall I call up and let her know you're coming?" She moved a hand toward the phone on her desk.

"No!" I said too quickly. "No, thanks, no need. I'd like it to be a surprise. She's not, ah, met the little one yet. We live far away, you see."

Jane nodded. "Aww. That's lovely," she said, nodding some more and grinning, her eyes brimming with sentimental tears. "Really lovely." She wrinkled her nose in a cutesy fashion at Vi. "You two darlings go on up. She's on the first floor, along to the right when you get out of the lift. Flat 107."

"Thanks so much," I said. Then "come on, you," as sweetly as I could to Vi, who burbled in faultless impersonation of a twenty-month-old human child. Honestly, this Mage had become an expert at subterfuge since I'd last spent significant time with him. I felt like I was back in training — which, in so many ways, I was.

As the lift doors closed us into its metal lock-box, I thanked the Makers that our pretend relative not only lived on Wilbur's floor but was their neighbour. She was in the flat just on the far side of theirs. We wouldn't even need to walk past her door. I felt guilty that we weren't really going to pay her a visit, and wondered whether we should, since we'd used her name to gain entry to the building for technically nefarious means. I quickly thought better of it. I could be soppy at times, and it had got me into trouble more than once; the poor woman would have no idea who we were and would likely sound the alarm. As much compassion as I felt for Violet and her infrequent social visits, I knew we couldn't call in. It occurred to me that Jane would ask her about us and our cover would then be definitively blown, but hopefully by then we'd be well past the need to venture into the Golden Sands Retirement Complex ever again.

I pushed open the double doors that marked the boundary line of Wilbur's corridor. The chemical smell was much stronger in here, levelled-up from the potency required to tackle one's common or garden stains and spills to that necessary for shifting large amounts of arterial blood. I felt nauseous.

Wilbur's door still had yellow and black crime scene tape across it at waist height. It hung like a sad Christmas decoration waiting to be taken down, and I wanted to rip it away and burn it. I stifled the surge of emotion in my chest, reached out a hand and tried the door handle. It didn't move.

"Shit," I whispered. "Locked. Arsing shitting *bastard*." I wiped sweat from my forehead. The air was so stuffy I felt light-headed.

"You'll have to pick it," Vi whispered back.

"Aaargh!"

"You can do it, Ern."

I'd have to be really careful. After all, Violet-Next-Door was ideally placed to hear a mouse fart in the flat beside hers, even more so since the place was so conspicuously uninhabited at present. I fished in my bag and brought out the twisted wires I always had on me. You never know when such things might come in handy, so I always had the wires, along with pocket tissues, a lighter, and at least one 20p piece on me, along with whatever else was lurking on my person. Anyway, here we were, about to commit a criminal act. I stilled my breath and slid the wires into the lock.

A wave of energy spread from the base of my spine, up and along my arm, and into the wires. They were really only there as a conduit to transmit the energy from my body into the lock; I didn't need to wiggle them. I whispered the First Words of Unfastening and felt the lock give. I tried the handle again and the door opened.

"Bloody hell," I said. I kept the door open with one foot while I wiped sweat from my forehead again, then I squatted down and ducked beneath the tape, being careful not to snag it. When we were through, I put the door on the latch and closed it softly. Time would tell whether Violet-Next-Door would pick up on anything. We had to move fast.

I almost lost my nerve at the sight of the dark patch on the carpet's mustard yellow. The blood had mostly gone, but a tell-tale shadow lay in its place. Whether just residual damp from cleaning, or the remnants of something more corporeal, I did not wish to know. At least the windows had been left open against any lingering odours.

All of Wilbur's furniture was still in place. This was something I hadn't considered: what if we'd successfully lied our way in here only to learn that everything had already been removed and the object we sought had gone to a house clearance place or been chucked into a landfill? Thankfully we wouldn't have to find out.

I glanced around. "Where d'you think the safe is?" I whispered.

I felt Vi lower his Veil, and I placed him on the floor. Dog-formed and with his olfaction undiluted by the effort of maintaining his disguise, he sniffed the air. "Try the bedroom," he said, softly.

I stayed Veiled. I didn't want to allow for the possibility that I would not have the strength to raise it again if I let it fall. I turned and opened the door behind me that led into the bedroom. This was the room that adjoined Violet-Next-Door's place; I'd have to be extra, extra quiet.

As soon as I stepped into the room, I saw a little mahogany corner cupboard on the far side, tucked beneath the window. I girded my Veil, took a deep, still breath, and tiptoed over to the cupboard. I felt Vi come into the room behind me.

"Yes, that's it," he whispered, excitement thinning his quieted voice.

I knelt and held my right hand over the cupboard door.

"What d'you reckon, Ern?" whispered Vi from beside me.

I rested back on my heels. "I can have a go, can't I?"

This would take a lot more than twisted wires and a few simple words to crack. I rooted in my bag and found what I was looking for: one of those little jars that baby food comes in, that I'd bought and emptied down the sink. I couldn't quite bring myself to actually eat the contents, and it was a shame Vi hadn't been there in dog form because he probably would have loved it. The jar was the perfect size to store just a little of the Ancestor Dirt I'd gathered at a funeral prior to the DNR. I brought the muddy-looking thing out into the light, feeling its power awaken and thrum into life as I held it, and I concentrated. Words came to me and I opened the jar. I placed a pinch of Dirt on the palm of my left hand, put some on the tip of my tongue, and let the depth of my Element's foundations fortify me. I licked the earth back onto my palm, then blew Words across it.

Vi nudged at my arm, making it hard for me to keep pushing my energy forward and down, but I had to maintain my concentration. I hissed at him: "*Stop it, daft hound!*"

He teethed at me then, gently, and I knew something was not going according to plan. But I had to keep going. I held my focus for another ten seconds, which was all it took for the safe door to melt inwards and for me to reach my muddied hand in and over and encircle the object within.

You see, Wilbur's scrying glass looks like crystal, but it is made of pure Water, and if I had touched it without that dirt on my hand it would have been Unmade there and then, and there would be no more than a little puddle warping the base of that corner cupboard as though some 1920s laudanum enthusiast had carelessly chucked a glass of champagne in there whilst probing for some other liquid relief.

I transferred the Water scrying-orb into my bag where it could sit beside the jar of Dirt; I knew that they were safe together, and I sensed the conversation they would strike up once properly acquainted.

It was only when I looked up that I saw a twist of rosewood grow and thicken outside Wilbur's bedroom window. Wood-Mages, like Earth-Mages, mostly can't fly. But, depending on their Form, they're fantastic at getting taller and climbing stuff. Wisps of grey smoke burst out and spun from a central, voided point, and I felt the weft of the world suck backwards.

"Aaaargh!" I yelled.

I slung my bag onto my back, and Vi and I legged it through the bedroom and back to the main door of the flat. I cast one last look around, then pulled the door open.

The windowless corridor was eerily still and quiet. The stuffy air made me start to sweat again immediately, after the relatively well-ventilated environs of the murder scene.

"Which way should we go?" I said at full volume, now that our cover was well and truly blown.

Violet-Next-Door's door opened and curls of grey smoke seeped into the corridor.

"Guess it's back out the main door then," I said. "Run!"

We pelted along the corridor, crashed into the double doors, and fumbled with the handle before I noticed the green push-button with PRESS TO EXIT printed on the asylum-grey wall above it.

I yelled the shortest curse I could bring to mind, then slammed my palm into the button. The doors had to think about it for a bit, of course, and then they opened more slowly than Wilbur's bloodstained floor was drying. I could barely contain myself.

Getting the lift felt like the way to certain death, but since death is certain anyway, one way or another, I pressed the call button. The lift was still on this floor, and the doors opened immediately. We leapt in, and I punched G.

The lift doors drew open onto a mostly empty lobby. Someone was at the Reception desk, talking to Jane. A uniformed security guard. He frowned at us and pressed a button on his walkie-talkie. This was not good. I stood there, frozen, grinning like an idiot. Vi bit my hand to get my attention.

"Side entrance," he snapped, and we ran to the left along a corridor and all the way to its end. The PRESS TO EXIT button was no match for me this time, and we burst out into a beautiful garden filled with mature shrubs, well-curated flowerbeds, and, behind it all, a high red brick wall festooned with creeping vines. I ran and leapt, then reached an arm down to grab Vi by the scruff and hurl him over the wall. Once we were both on the hard tarmac, we wasted no time in bolting. I felt a wrench at leaving the bike behind, but it had never been mine in the first place. We ran on, Vi leading me through short-cuts until we came to a road I knew, and then I strode ahead and took us back along the path beside the churchyard and to the twisted undergrowth that led to the House.

⁎

The gate swung closed behind us and we collapsed onto the fragrant grass.

I closed my eyes and lay there awhile to let the breeze dry the sweat from my face and neck. Presently, my breathing slowed to normal, and I began to notice the feeling of green beneath my body, and Earth beneath that, and I felt better. I rolled to one side and sat up. Vi lay panting on the ground beside me, all four paws held skyward.

Eric thundered out into the garden in a gangly, teenaged way. "What happened?" he said as he helped me to my feet and dusted bits of dry grass off me.

I picked up my bag and held it to my chest. It vibrated with the energies of Earth and Water: having a right good chat in there, they were. I was heartened. I knew it would be alright for me to use the scrying-glass now, since it knew it was safe and with allies and friends of its murdered Bearer.

Vi Changed, righted himself, and came to standing. A series of expressions passed across his face: apology, defiance, pride, relief. "Ah," he said, "please don't be angry, Eric, but there was a little bit of a change of plan. You won't need to practise your magics tomorrow after all." He grimaced. "I'm sorry, I know you were looking forward to it."

"Not really," Eric said. "I need a lot more practice in here before I can do it out there." He nodded and pursed his lips grimly. "We'd better go inside, I suppose," he said.

Vi and I exchanged a look.

"Oh heck," I said, trying to make light of it, but I knew as well as anyone else that we were in the shit, good and proper.

"*What?*" screeched the cat when Vi informed her of the aforementioned — and now afore-happened — change to the plan she had so carefully orchestrated.

Vi bowed his head, but I could see one of his eyes from the side and, even from where I was, I detected the mischief of a puppy.

"Yes," he mumbled, "sorry, it wasn't on your spreadsheet, but you said we weren't allowed to send any comms when we were out in the field."

The cat hissed, sprang from her chair, and swiped Vi across the face, making him reel backwards, clutching his cheek. She landed on the floor and stood up on her hind legs. I felt the Change begin in her, then, and wondered whether she might let us see her in Mage-Form — human — but it wasn't to be. Her energy settled, and once more she was pure cat.

Vi winced and patted at his cheek. He lowered his hand and looked at it. The cat had broken the skin, but there was no more than a row of tiny red beads along the line of the scratch. I found myself in awe of her restraint.

"There is no need to berate the Council's system," she growled. "It works very well if you are capable of sticking by it." She dropped back to all-fours and looked down at the floor. "Nothing wrong with being organised." She bent for an impromptu groom of her flank, and I felt a warm rush of sympathy.

"Thing is, cat," Vi said, "alright, well, it was my idea. I take full responsibility. What happened was I had a brain-wave about just going right in to the Golden Sands, you know, since we were Veiled as a mother and child."

"I'm listening," said the cat, her eyes dark and intense.

"I thought we could just say we were visiting one of the residents and have a little peek at Wilbur's place."

The cat shook her head. "Of all the rash, stupid, ill-thought-through schemes. Trust a dog! No offence," she said, staring at Vi.

"No," I butted in, "it wasn't like that. The responsibility is mine, too. And, well — just —"

The cat sighed in exasperation. "What?"

I took my bag off my shoulder and opened it. I reached in and closed a hand around the cold globe of Wilbur's scrying glass.

The cat's and Eric's jaws dropped when they saw the thing. It could be Unmade only by extremely powerful sorcery, or, if it chose to do so, could simply disintegrate of its own accord. Water-Weapons are especially clingy and possessive of their Mages and are prone to suicide should anything befall them. I had taken a poorly calculated risk, but the fact that the scrying glass hadn't either melted itself in a fit of grief, or exploded in scalding steam out of sheer spite at the touch of my skin, bode well, and also, I admitted to myself, said something about the return of my long-forgotten skills. It was my hunch that, as long as

Wilbur's eyes were in the possession of their murderer, the Water crystal — Wilbur's metaphysical eye — would remain intact and able to See. And, with a bit of luck, it might just agree to help us.

SEVENTEEN

The cat came round to the new plan pretty quickly, for a bureaucat. She tapped at her screen for a full hour, muttering, with only momentary pauses to preen her whiskers, and when she finally looked up to address the rest of the room, she narrowed her eyes in a manner befitting a feline who had fully considered a matter and was now satisfied.

"The Council, though unimpressed with your deviation from the agreed schedule—"

"*Agreed?*" I mouthed to Eric, who shook his head and gave me a knowing look.

"—has found your actions to be of benefit, in the grand scheme, since you have moved everything forward by a full twenty-four hours. This, we are sure, will play to our advantage."

"How?" Rennie said, as she sauntered into the room, dripping ashes.

"Bloody hell, where'd you get to?" I said. "You look a right mess."

"I had quite an entertaining afternoon, in the end, between the Heartless utter shit that ambushed me and the other one at the Funeral Home, topped off with a downright unbearable traffic warden. I had to hide for a bit; shake them off my tail."

"That would account for your dishevelled condition," said the cat, looking her up and down.

"I quite like it, actually," Rennie crooned, "very post-apocalyptic." She held out her long, tattered skirts, unleashing a rain of delicate grey ash that evaporated as soon as it hit the floor. "We all burn in the end, darling. I'm going to shower and change. Excuse me," she grinned, and swept out of the room.

"Right," said the cat. "As I was saying, now we have the thing we were going to take by rather more convoluted means, we can proceed with our plan apace."

"What plan?" I said. "The funeral is still going to be in two days, so even though *we* may have changed something, we still have to wait for the big day."

"No, we don't," said Vi. "The cat is right. We've got time to steal the body now and give it a proper burial at sea, before it can be interred."

"And what of — you know, the rest?" I said, lowering my voice.

We all sat back in our chairs at that point, nobody knowing what to say. We'd already dallied so much while the Grey Dickhead forged a path to his new Weapons; sat here twiddling our thumbs. Nobody had any suggestions for the time being.

Ten minutes later, Rennie walked back into the chamber, clad in a flowing dress of saffron yellow. She had something in her hand. She walked to the table and placed it softly on the table top.

"Here you go," she said to the cat.

The cat leaned forward and sniffed at the small leather pouch that Rennie had deposited in front of her. Her eyes widened. "I know what this is," she said. "How in all the Makers' infinite dimensions did you get your hands on these?"

"Nicked 'em, didn't I, mate?" Rennie said in a loose parody of my accent, which she garnished with a well-observed nonchalant shrug. "Turns out that the murderer, as tired tropes advise, is coming back soon to gloat over his crime." She tutted. "Such a poor stereotype, really, to fall into that pattern, but there we have it. I mean, as we are all extremely aware, Richard is a shit, and shit, as they say, does have a habit of sticking."

The rest of us were dumbfounded. We looked at each other, unable to speak. A cold stress-hormone flood spread through my guts.

The cat frowned. "And how, exactly, do you know this?" she said, suspicion grating in her voice. She fixed Rennie with an authoritative stare.

Rennie sighed ostentatiously and waved a hand in the air in a gesture of dismissal. "So good to know you trust me, darling, after I put myself in mortal danger for your cause."

"It's all of our cause, Rens," I said. "You may not feel affected yet and, much as it must pain you to even consider the possibility, you're vulnerable too."

She harrumphed and shot me a sober look. "I need a Fireball."

Eric got up and went to the kitchen, returning with a tumbler and Rennie's favourite whiskey. Well, one of them.

"Thank you, sweetheart," she beamed. "Now I can tell you the whole story."

"Please do," said the cat. "First, though, Eric dear, would you put our little gift in the fridge?"

Eric creased his face in disgust.

"Don't worry," the cat said, "they won't rot until they're reconnected with the rest of their owner, but I don't feel comfortable with them. I feel like they're looking at me." She coughed awkwardly, and Eric gingerly picked up the pouch containing Wilbur's gouged-out eyes and carried it at arm's length into the kitchen. He came back a few moments later, wiping his hand on his robe.

Rennie gave the cat a look of chastisement. "You can thank me whenever you want," she said, then poured herself a good slug of Fireball and downed it in a single gulp. She roared in pleasure — I was surprised not to see flames coming out of her mouth — and poured more whiskey into her glass. She made do, for now, with simply inhaling the fumes from the second, also very generous, measure. "So, what happened, in a nutshell, was that I saw and heard an opportunity, and took it."

"I don't suppose you'd care to elaborate?" said the cat. She was furiously taking notes, paw-pads tapping away at her tablet screen.

I smiled. No doubt the Council were in apoplexy, what with two unexpected deviations from their plan in the space of as many hours.

Rennie settled back in her chair, Fireball in hand, and took a sip. "Ahhh, that's the stuff. I didn't see anything untoward on my first pass. I'd Veiled as a young skinhead guy walking a spritely brindled Staffy, so I was able to go by at a good pace and do another sweep a few minutes later, going the opposite way."

"M-hmm," said the cat, her voice low.

"Patience is a virtue, darling," Rennie said. She took a deep breath and another fortifying slug of whiskey. "Anyway, where was I? Ah, yes. So, on my first patrol, I noticed the guard, but he was just floating there and not doing much, so I assumed nothing was going on inside. Felt like he was about to doze off, truth be told. So I walked past and headed back towards the seafront. I stood for a while and looked out to sea. There was a violent squall offshore, looked really dramatic against the blue of the sky. Disappointing lack of lightning, though," she said, momentarily dismayed. "I watched it for a few minutes, then went to the public toilet and changed my Veil." She took another sip of whiskey, then another, emptying the glass.

"What to?" asked Eric.

"An older lady with a walking stick," Rennie continued. "What do you think the benefit of that disguise was, our talented young Mage-in-training?"

"You could walk by more slowly and get a closer look?"

"Quite right! That's exactly it. This Veil allowed me to shuffle by and study the scene a little more. I also thought to Listen and use the Sight and have a little eavesdrop and a peek through the windows too, though I knew it was risky. But, you know me," she smiled. "So, on my second pass, I went really slowly and quested out with my Hearing and my Sight, despite the fact that it made me a beacon to any magical being, friend or foe, who may have been lurking about the place. But maybe that was good, because that's when things got interesting."

Vi was on the edge of his seat, man-formed, wide-eyed and biting his nails.

I felt almost sick with nerves but couldn't tear myself away. "Or otherwise put," I offered, "that was when you decided to *make* things more interesting."

Rennie grinned and wagged a fingertip at me. "Maybe," she said. "No matter now. What happened was — and, please understand, this transpired over the course of no more than two minutes — I Heard a conversation taking place in one of the office rooms. A group of coffin-polishers was sitting round a desk, talking shop, and one of them said the R-word, except he called him by his affected name. Aldrich, pah!" She scoffed and shook her head.

"Anyway," she continued, "so, I stopped walking and listened harder. Heard one of them say that he'd been hiding out nearby, waiting to come and pick things up before he could execute the next phase of his plan. Then immediately afterwards, I Saw Wilbur's, ah, you know, they reached out to me. I was surprised; I hadn't expected that they'd be anywhere near here by now, but I got a sudden, very strong feeling and decided to act on it while the opportunity was there. They wanted me to get them out of there immediately, or it'd be too late." Her voice had quickened with excitement, and her irises were scarlet flame.

"I see," said the cat, sounding like a weary judge who'd rather have had a few more after-lunch brandies but had to go back to the courtroom and snooze through a succession of petty cases. "Could you take us through what happened next, step by step, so I can assess current risk, and the Council can decide the appropriate course of action?"

Rennie rolled her eyes. "My Sight and the eyes, they kind of *joined together*," she said. "I'd never felt anything like that before. Quite apart from the shock of learning that the murderer had evidently left them there to come back to, I also had to make sense of this new spiritual experience. Amazing!"

Vi coughed his polite cough. "That's quintessential Wilbur," he said. "They always were such a gifted Seer and are evidently able to avail themselves of others' powers even from a mortuary refrigerator. And perhaps leaving the eyes for now was a judgement call on Richard's part. He'd be easier to detect travelling through the Unseen realms with something like that on him. Leaving it until the last minute, probably, until he makes a dash for one of the Makers."

"I did suspect as much, yes," Rennie agreed.

"What happened next?" I said.

"I turned, walked through the door — speeding up, because the instant I had started to use my Senses in a more deliberate manner, my cover was shattered. So, I wasted no time in going to where I'd felt the call from. It was one of the offices, and the pouch was just sitting there on a table, can you believe it? There were several people in there, the ones I'd Heard, I guessed, and they were so shocked to see me just brazenly walk in," she had put her glass down on a coaster and was gesturing wildly with her arms "that they just watched me open the door, cross the room, pick up the pouch, turn on my heel, and walk out again. Well, I ran out, but you know what I mean." She laughed with abandon for a full thirty seconds, while the rest of us looked at each other, agog.

"As I came out of the building, an Earth-Mage attacked me," she continued, once her laughter had died away.

I shuddered at the idea of an Earth-Mage without a heart. Mind you, I thought, in another life that could have been me.

"Strong, that one," Rennie continued, "but I managed to get free, let go of my Veil, and I pelted along the road for about a quarter mile."

"You bloody great idiot!" I said, slapping the table top. It hurt my hand. "You're so reckless!" Then, more quietly, "I'm glad you're alright, Rens, but by the Makers!"

"Were you followed back here?" asked the cat.

Rennie shook her head. "I don't think so. But it's not safe to go out there again for now."

"We're gonna have to, though," I said. "We've got a body to snatch."

"Ah," said Rennie. "Yes, that is true. It's quite exciting, actually. I've never broken into a morgue before, and today doesn't count, since the door was unlocked. Burned one or two establishments down by accident during my training, though..." her words tailed off into a wistful smile. Nobody pressed her for further detail.

The cat finished tapping at her screen. She took off her glasses and rubbed at her eyes. "Ernie is quite right," she said. "We still need to retrieve Wilbur's body, reunite it with the rest of them, and give them a proper send-off in accordance with their Element. We'll have to use the Generalised Rites, of course, since none of us are Water-Mages, but we cannot avoid the necessity for the ceremony to be aquatic."

Vi, dog-formed again, whined softly and wrinkled his nose.

Fair enough. It was far more sensitive than anyone else's in the room. Being as I am, so thickly Earth, the process of decay doesn't scare me, even though it's a bit stinky, but I couldn't blame anyone else for being squeamish.

"I'm assuming," Vi said, "that the guard around the funeral parlour will be heavier now?"

The cat nodded. "I dare say so," she agreed. "This will be quite an operation. And with Richard due back on the day itself

— that is, if he hasn't decided to come back a little earlier than planned following today's little turns of events."

"Shit," I said. "Shit, shit, shit." I had not prepared myself for the possibility that I might have to face him before this week was out. I'd wanted to ease into things a bit more gently than this.

"Quite," said the cat. Her tablet made a bell chime sound a bit like a cheery death knell. "Ah! Let's see what the Council has to say about all this." She put her glasses back on and prodded at her screen. She read for a moment, her frown deepening, then looked up and took her glasses off. "Um," she said.

Rennie narrowed her eyes and took a gulp from her third glass of Fireball. "What?"

The cat's expression was hard to read but, if I'd have had to guess, I'd have said it was somewhere between incredulity and embarrassment. "The Council, ah —"

Flame-irised eyes brightened with curiosity. "Yes?"

"We're to decide for ourselves the appropriate course of action now, given the sudden changes to the plan."

Rennie cackled with delight. "Oh, that is just *precious*. We're on our own just when things are beginning to get really hairy, you mean?"

The cat lowered her head and took off her glasses. She licked the lenses in turn and wiped them on the tablecloth. "I suppose you could say that, in a manner of speaking," she said quietly as she performed the practised routine. "I could call for reinforcements, but their arrival would make the enemy surer we're planning something. So, yes, for now at least, we're on our own."

"Good!" Rennie said. "Just the way I like it. Freedom to act on behalf of my Element without interference from grey suit wearers and spreadsheet fetishists. No offence, cat."

"None taken," said the cat, her voice sounding, despite her words, distinctly offended.

"So," said Rennie, "let's get to work."

Vi barked happily, then leapt off his chair and zoomed about the room for a bit before trotting out into the garden.

Rennie looked at me. "Sorry, darling. I kind of leapt in and took charge there, didn't I? You're the boss of this place," she said with a sideways glance at the cat, who was busy, or at least doing a very good job of pretending to be busy, grooming herself. "I should let you lead the mission."

I shrugged. "I'm still pretty new to all this, really. Dunno that I'm ready to lead anything yet, or whether I ever will be. Always been more of a hang back and bring up the rear type person, you know me. Bit slow to get going sometimes."

"Yes," Rennie said, "as long as there's a decent pub at 'the rear,' as you put it, eh?"

"Well, ah." No, there was no point in arguing. She had my number, good and proper.

"We can be a sort of committee, if you like," she said, her eyes sparkling. She looked at me, then at Eric. "Yeah?"

I nodded and shrugged at the same time. "Alright."

Eric smiled broadly, revealing his rows of braces and wire. "Okay!"

"I'm sure Vi will be fine with that arrangement, too; he's a reasonable sort," Rennie reasoned. "Cat?"

The cat looked up from her grooming. Her tongue was sticking out. "That'th acctheptable," she said, and went back to her task.

"Right," said Rennie. "The first thing we need to do is intensify our own defences."

"On it," said Eric. He strode to the fire pit, took up a poker from the rack beside it, and used it to draw some symbols in the cold ash at the hearth's edge. Then, he put the poker away and walked across the chamber to one of the many cupboards built into its wall, where he opened a door and took something down off a hook. It was a gong, which he struck with the mallet that had been lying on the sideboard next to the cupboard. I'd been wondering what that thing was for and expected a memory to come back, but evidently that one was still finding a home. He put the gong away, shut the cupboard door, returned to his seat, and folded his arms, looking like something important had been settled.

"That it?" I said, "Looked like great fun, but what was it in aid of?"

Eric arched one of his perfect eyebrows at me. Ouch. I considered myself told. "Just wait and see," he smirked.

Vi came in from the garden, man-formed. He looked alarmed. "What was that massively loud noise?" he said, looking around as if expecting to see that some kind of battle had erupted. "I thought we weren't meant to draw attention to ourselves?!"

At that moment, an energy sparked to life in the fire pit and rippled outwards, covering everything. I experienced it as something similar to a static charge, but bigger and more ambitious. My hair follicles tingled and my skin felt electric. The air smelled of soil and rosemary for a moment, then the aromas began to fade away, but the energy stayed in the air, strong and green and pungent. It made me remember what, or more accurately, who, the gong was for, and a folder's worth of memories found their proper places. This was a working too advanced for most Earth-Mages, even those as competent as Vi, and lay outside the bounds of what most would need in their lifetime. Despite the extraordinary circumstances that made it necessary, I found myself thrilling with excitement.

The cat had finished grooming. "Young Eric has been learning defensive Earth-workings," she said, glowing with pride. "He's the best in the cohort. Best for decades, actually."

Vi smiled. "So, nobody will have heard that gong but us, then. Right?" He looked around at our faces for an answer.

Eric smirked again. "I wouldn't say *that*."

Vi frowned. His ears were so much more receptive than everyone else's that he must have heard the strike of the gong as loud as a thunderclap, one of those that, when the storm is directly up above you, you're so startled you almost separate your skin from all your bony and meaty bits. Poor guy. I could never deal with the anxiety that must come from being so receptive to every sensory signal. "What do you mean?" he said.

Thud.

"And what, in the heck, was that?" he added, looking and sounding as though he was on the verge of panic.

Thud — thud — thud.

The sound came from underneath the chamber, as though someone were knocking on the underside of the floor. I had that weird sensation you get when you learn that something isn't quite as solid as you had previously assumed — and it's not a sensation I enjoy when it pertains to the ground beneath my feet. The air began to ring with a deep, low vibe, the humming of tap root veins and the secret language of the world beneath everything.

Eric got up and went to a place on the floor. He pulled back the rug, reached down, grabbed something, and pulled upwards. A trap door opened. I hadn't been expecting that, though with this being the House of Earth it did feel fitting that it should have at least one door down into the ground. I don't know why I hadn't assumed it'd be there from the off, to be honest. In my slightly wine-sozzled condition, I congratulated myself for adjusting so quickly. Perhaps I was beginning to accept the return of my knowledge and powers.

I listened and watched with great anticipation as a faint shuffling of many footsteps climbing stairs grew gradually closer and louder, and then saw a multitude of Earth-Nymphs emerge from the trap door. This first sight of them was another gong being struck in my head; one of my mental filing cabinet drawers slamming open so hard it almost came off its rail thingies, making my teeth rattle. I wouldn't have been surprised if the others had heard it even though I knew it was an exclusively internal sensation, but nobody said anything.

The Nymphs pouring out of the floor were a mix of Root and Soil. Root-Nymphs are made from twisting fibrous strands that can knit together with great strength anything that needs, well, knitting together, and Soil-Nymphs are like little dust-devils made from earth. They spin until they find their place to rest and, when they do, they settle into an impossibly dense matter that cannot be dug or shovelled by hand or machine. Their effectiveness diminishes with depth, since they're gradually slowed by the existing soil particles and eventually run out of digging-steam, but their range extends a couple of storeys underground, which in many places is good enough to get right down to the bedrock, or close to it. Boggy ground is a notable exception: neither Root nor Soil is able to maintain their composure with all that Water around. There are various Elementals that excel in wet environments, but they are the wards of Water-Mages, and therefore not for the likes of me to interfere with.

The Nymphs flooded out through the open door and along the garden path to the gate. There, they separated: some went up the gate and into the trees at the boundary, some sank into the ground, and others went left and right along the border between the worlds. I felt a slow diminuendo in the vibes as their energy sank down and up and over and a pleasant locking feeling as they met behind me on the opposite side of the House's many gardens and quietly connected everything within their circle even more strongly than before.

The cat began tapping at her tablet screen again. "Excellent work, Eric; they really like you!" she said once Eric had shut the trap door, pulled the rug back over the floor, and smoothed it down carefully.

"I like them too," Eric said with a radiant smile. It was no mean feat, mastering Earth-Working; I'd never known a Mage under seventy years old who had. This lad was a good 'un.

"Uhh," I said, not wanting to interrupt, but feeling like I had to.

"Yes?"

"Okay, so I'm duly reassured that we're safe in here, but what's next out there?"

"So," said the cat. "Our guard is strengthened now, which means we're safer to bring Wilbur back here once we've, ah, liberated the larger part of their remains so that we can reunite them with the, uh, smaller parts." She creased up her face, tabby stripes darkening and ear-tips dipping slightly downward, and glanced distastefully towards the kitchen.

"I'm guessing you won't be performing the Rites yourself, then," Rennie said, "even though funerals technically fall under the Council's jurisdiction." She gave a playful smile.

The cat looked nauseous and prodded fervently at her screen. I'd no idea why she bothered, since it was clear to everyone in the room that she simply felt too uncomfortable. Or, in actual fact, that was precisely the explanation. Some folk will do anything to avoid admitting they don't feel up to something, eh? Mind you, I wasn't one to talk, with my five years of self-inflicted oblivion.

"There's no need for any official paperwork with this one," she mumbled. "So it's, um, we can just —"

Rennie laughed, which brought me back to the room. "It's quite alright!" she said, still smiling, fire dancing in her eyes. "I'm not one for squidgy corpses either. Plus I probably shouldn't touch them anyway, in case they end up toast." She held up her hands and wiggled her fingers and little flames erupted from her fingertips. She blew the flames out and tendrils of grey smoke snaked into the air as she lowered her hands. "See?" she said with mock innocence.

"Fuck's sake," I said. "I can do it. And you all bloody well know it, too." As an Earth-Mage, I wasn't ideal to perform Wilbur's Rites, since they needed burying at sea and would not be happy to end up as maggot-snacks, but at least I wasn't capable of incinerating them with a mere touch. "Someone else'll need to come up with the actual plan, though; I'm still new here," I added. "I'll need some help carting the body about, too. Oh, and where are we going to put it? It's bound to, er, ripen pretty quickly."

"It can go in the big fridge," Eric said. "There's loads of space, and I cleaned it while you were out. It won't be in there for long anyway."

I chose not to mount any kind of challenge. I deferred to the facts that he'd dwelt here far longer than I and that his fridge-cleaning skills were doubtless far superior to mine. We needed to get old Wilbs back to their Element very quickly indeed, and we just about had the capacity to make their final journey respectful, as well as tactical.

"That's quite right," said the cat. "We've space to store the body while we make the final preparations. We can get things started for the Rite now, can't we, at least? Well, you can," she said, signalling that I needed to get to work.

"Right then," I said. "I'll fetch my gear."

EIGHTEEN

I got up from the dining table and went into the bedroom I shared with Elias's remaining worldly possessions. His clothes were the fabric hangover from his life.

I pulled open the bottom drawer of the bedside table on the far side of the room, next to the big, gorgeous window that almost covered the wall. My holdall was in there, cowering at the back and looking rather like a neglected, sagging lung. Poor thing. Been with me through the lowest of lows, it had. It was probably sulking because I'd been ignoring it while I hung out with my fancy new and old friends, but the worn-out article would always have a place in my heart. Even when I started using a new bag to carry my gear, as I inevitably would, I'd not get rid of it.

I took the bag carefully out of the drawer and carried it to the centre of the room, where I laid it on the rug at the foot of the bed. I was apprehensive about picking through its contents, as though my fingertips were scalpels and my belongings were warmly pulsing arteries carrying the precious blood of life. One careless nick of a blade, and there'd be so much lost.

I remembered this feeling from long ago. It was the anticipation that would always build inside me during the run-up to an important ceremony: a combination of excitement about the outcome and anxiety about getting it wrong and everything blowing up in my face — sometimes literally. I knew, though, that in this tattered old bag was everything I needed. I could perform the Generalised Death-Rites for Esteemed Mages with all the correct tools, ones you would expect an Earth-Mage to keep close at foot: pentacle, jar of Dirt, favourite lump of obsidian, two pairs of thick emergency socks.

It was a fair while since I'd performed the Rites, despite the fact that my new old memories were trying to trick me into thinking that the most recent had been only last week instead of five years ago. This left me awash with big feelings: new guilt about my time away that added to the stale stuff that haunted me throughout it, plus new feelings of grief layered atop the mourning I'd been doing for all this time. Therefore I felt a powerful need to take extra care and time over the preliminaries. The only problem with this was that I didn't have that long to piss about with the usual preamble. I had to just bloody well get on with it.

I sat down cross-legged beside the bag and almost laughed at the state of the thing. Unzipping it felt redundant, since it was visibly disintegrating and I could have just enlarged one of its little holes and reached in, but I went through the motions: a morsel of comfort for both of us windblown, well-travelled things. No need to accelerate the inevitable. I reached in. Ah, there it was. I closed my fingers gently round the pentacle and moved it into my palm so my fingertips could grab the jam jar of Ancestor Dirt from which I'd filled the baby food jar I took with me to Wilbur's.

"Perfect," I said as I examined the jar for cracks. "Not a blemish."

I grabbed a little ornamental dish from the dressing table. It had a couple of pairs of earrings in it, but I tipped them onto the dressing table's polished wood surface, giving a few words of apology, and carried the dish to where my gear waited on the floor. The vines had closed over the far side of the bedroom door and I thanked them for the privacy they lent this part of the Rites.

I sat down and tried to think of the saddest thing that had ever happened. It wasn't difficult to find with so many reminders around me, and fresh tears sprung from my eyes. I kept the emotion coming, and surges of raw pain expressed themselves anew in body-warm salt water. I cried for a few minutes, conscious of time's urgency, then came back to myself and opened my eyes. The dish now contained half an inch of my tears. I placed it on the floor. My hand was shaking, and I had to steady it by grabbing my wrist with the other hand. I dug my fingernails into my skin and swore at myself, once for almost dropping the dish and again for being unkind to myself in such a difficult moment. Once the dish was safely laid down, I took a deep breath, opened the jar, and carefully sprinkled about a tablespoon of the Dirt onto the liquid. The effect was dramatic and instantaneous, better than I'd dared to hope. It can take a bit of persuasion for Grief and Memory to integrate and agree to work together, since they often have such different ways of seeing things, but this was *my* grief and *my* memory; I wasn't trying to marry recalcitrant strangers. The two substances felt my essence in each other and took a mutual liking without any need for arbitration from me. They were Bound within seconds.

I smiled away the last wave of feeling and felt it retreat just out of sight to where I knew it would wait in the gloom, keeping company with cloying Self-Pity and sharp Existential Malaise. It could stay there for now; I had more work to do.

I carefully stood, holding the dish, and immediately sensed the vines unclasp and peel back over the other side of the door. I then carried it, cupped in the palms of both hands, slowly to the Hearth room.

❧

The others were sitting round the long dining table, which had been cleared of dinner plates and dishes that had been replaced by coffee cups. Rennie and Eric were playing a card game at one end of the table, betting for dried chickpeas, whilst the cat had her nose buried in some paperwork that covered the other end. Vi was curled up, dog-formed, snoozing on a couch, with a well-chewed toy bone beside him.

I wanted to stand in the doorway for a while and just watch them all, enjoy the experience of entering a room and knowing other souls were in there. I'd had this luxury a bit at the old place with Gary the cat, whose name I hadn't known until a few days ago, but that was such a sporadic thing that I never mistook it for a relationship, and especially couldn't now I knew he'd been sent to spy on me for the Council. There was no time to linger, though, so I permitted myself only a brief pause before I continued my approach.

Rennie looked up from the betting game. Her eyes were bright and intense as she scrutinised me over her red horn-rimmed spectacles. "Ernie, darling, how delightful to see you!" she gushed, and smiled a little too forcefully. Her eyes gave away something unusual, and I leapt on it.

"Ey up, Rens. Losing, are you?" I said, and winked at Eric.

Rennie's face was thunder.

Eric, glowing with pride, began to gather up his winnings. "S'pose we should pack it in anyway," he said. "I need to put all these on to soak for tomorrow's houmous."

Rennie sighed. "Yes, I suppose," she said, and stuck out her bottom lip, sulky as a spoilt girl denied a fifteenth go on the carousel. She was doing it for effect, of course, and we all burst out laughing. Except the cat, that is.

"Eric!" she snapped, "while you're in there, fetch something strong and airtight for Ernie's concoction."

When he returned from the kitchen, he held in his hands a metal box with the first stanza of the first section of the Rites graven into it. I couldn't have thought of anything more perfect. Eric opened the lid to reveal sigils of Earth etched in a repeating pattern all around its interior, interspersed with little jewel-eyed skulls.

"Where'd you get this precious thing?" I said, as I tilted the dish and let the paste of dirt and tears find its gloopy way into the box.

The cat coughed. "Never you mind."

"Why?" I retorted, indignant. "I know I'm new back, but if you really want me to be back among you properly, why not tell me, eh?" I looked up at Eric, who I now realised as we stood close to one another was a full foot taller than me.

"It was left behind in Richard's cell," Rennie said.

Instinctively, I let the box go and pulled my hand away in horror. Luckily, Eric's reflexes jumped to life and he caught it only a few inches into its fall.

"Thanks, Rennie," the cat sighed. "I didn't mean you to find out quite like that, Ernie, but yes, it was among the things he left behind, which as it happens were all of his little trinkets."

"That doesn't explain why you brought it here," I said. I felt a Change behind me and then a hand on my shoulder.

"His cell was cleared after the escape was discovered," Vi said softly. "We took everything. Some things we destroyed, some we could not, and some it was not our place to. There was this and a few other bits left that he'd collected over the years, taken from Mages in other Elements, or won in bets, or stolen."

"And this is your main Element, plus it looks cool with all the skulls and stuff," said Eric.

I nodded. "That it bloody does," I said. "It's fit for my purpose, that's for sure. I hope its original owner, whoever that was, won't resent us the theft." I made a mental note to pay extra close attention to my dreams over the next few days.

"Right," the cat said. "Now we're prepared, what say we get going?"

"Yeah?" I looked around and saw facial expressions in several shades of trepidation. "There's an actual plan of some sort, then?"

"Bah, who needs a plan?" Rennie exclaimed. "Let's just go in, guns blazing, as it were." Her eyes flashed. "Only joking," she said, grinning.

"If I'm not mistaken," I said, "we need to get to the funeral parlour, break in, remove a full-size actual fucking *corpse*, bring it here, perform the Rites, then bury said corpse at sea before our enemy can take advantage of Water's temporary energetic wobble. Did I miss owt?"

"You did," said the cat. "We need to not get caught and/or killed in the process." She peered meaningfully through her reading glasses. "Do you think you're ready for something like this?"

"Nope," I said. "Not sure I ever would be. But here I am, about to do it anyway."

"Good," said the cat. "Well, there's nothing more to say. Over to you, Rennie."

Rennie nodded grimly. "Okay, guys. Listen very carefully. This is how it's going to work."

NINETEEN

T he plan, such as it was, was decent enough considering our severely limited time and resources. The first part of what Rennie led us briskly through would be relatively easy, but it was the second part I was most worried about.

Half an hour later, I found myself in a stinking drain we'd accessed from the tunnels beneath the House. A party of especially feisty Root-Nymphs had been instructed in advance while I'd been preparing the first part of the Rites, and we found that a person-sized hole in their wall of soil and impossibly dense twisting fibres had been opened up in perfect time for our arrival. We squeezed through, Eric having the most trouble since he was the tallest of us by some margin.

Once the sole of Eric's right boot had cleared the gap, it began to close and knit together again, until there was no evidence of it having ever been there, and not a sniff of it in the air. I found a little courage, though I wasn't sure from where.

We came along a path similar to the Old Path, that compressed the geographical distance between the House and the bit of the town we needed to get to, and crouched in the dank tunnel just below street level, breathing through our mouths to try and avoid the worst of the stench. I coughed a few times and tried not to retch; the airborne odours tasted solid and altogether too fruity for my liking.

"*Quiet!*" the cat hissed.

"*Sorry,*" I whispered, then mouthed a mild curse.

"I heard that," she said under her breath.

Eric passed me a handkerchief from one of the inside pockets of his coat. He'd sensibly left his long robe behind; the hem would be a nightmare to clean if it trailed in this lot.

I folded the hanky into a square, covered my nose and mouth with it and breathed the stinking air with a hint of the essential oil blend Eric had fragranced it with. It was lovely. I picked up patchouli and hints of other stuff I didn't recognise. I nodded thanks to him, and he nodded in reply and smiled.

Rennie, who had gone through first, moved from where she had been leaning against the tunnel wall and into the centre, where the filthy water was almost knee-deep. Her irises glowed the orange of sodium street lamps in the gloom. She jabbed a fingertip into the darkness along the tunnel twice, then pointed vertically, indicating that we were to follow her along a short way and then ascend to street level.

Here it was: the part I was dreading the most. This was where it could all go wrong. It felt wrong already, to be honest, and we'd barely begun.

We crept along the tunnel until we found ourselves beneath a manhole cover, where we crowded in a little gaggle with our grubby faces turned upward at the deep, invisible night above.

"We're at the back of the building, in the yard," Rennie said in a voice that made her sound like an uppity schoolteacher. "It's protected by a high wall and a really nasty-looking security fence, so this door is rarely locked."

"Rarely?" said the cat. "Those don't sound like well-calculated odds to me. The Council would have—"

"*Shut up!*" said Rennie in a loud whisper.

Vi, man-formed, picked the cat up from her spot against the tunnel wall, and she gave a single, quiet purr.

"Thank you," she said.

"I'll get back to it, if you don't mind?" Rennie said.

The cat rolled her eyes.

I was staying out of this one. Eric and I exchanged a sneaky glance in the blue half-light that filtered through the grille on the drain cover.

"Now," Rennie said, "I'm pretty sure we'll just be able to walk straight into the building. When we do, we need to go along the corridor to the big room opposite the office I went into, you know, where I grabbed the eyes from. Wilbur's in that big room, in one of the fridges. There aren't many, so we should find them easily. Then we just grab them and dive back in here as quick as poss. Yeah?"

It didn't sound like the best-laid plan to me. I mean, what the bloody hell were we supposed to do if there was anyone Heartless, or multiples thereof, in the room as well, keeping guard?

Vi read my mind. "We'll just have to fight anyone or anything we see, Ernie," he said patiently. "It's the only way to get Wilbur back to their Element before their energy can be fully appropriated."

My heartbeat quickened. I'd not had a chance to use any of my combat skills since I'd arrived. None of us were bothering with Veils, because we'd collectively reasoned that who else but us would be breaking into a morgue to steal the cadaver of a murdered Water-Mage, so there was no point in disguises. And we'd elected — unanimously, once the cat had been persuaded — to conserve our fighting spirit for actual fighting as opposed to wasting our precious resources on skulking around pretending to be other human or non-human folk.

Rennie looked at each of us in turn, her fire-bright eyes searching our faces.

"Ready?" she whispered.

We all nodded to signal that we were, or rather that we weren't, but were here anyway for the cause and for our departed friends.

"Right," Rennie said. She slowly reached up with both hands and placed her palms on the underside of the metal grille. I'd been expecting it to be heavy for some reason, but when she lifted it, it moved easily and she pushed it aside, taking care not to scrape it on the tarmacked ground.

Rennie pulled herself up with the grace of a gymnast, then helped the rest of us out of the malodorous hole. We left the drain cover where it was and tiptoed to the door.

All the lights on this side of the building, both ground and first floor, were off. I almost fooled myself into thinking that this was a good thing, but there was no way the place would be undefended and, in any case, many Mages can see in the dark. My skin went cold, and I don't just mean the bits with horrible drain-grime on them. My ears started ringing. I took a few deep breaths.

Rennie tried the door handle. It turned. She pushed the door open and stepped into the darkness.

We followed in single file: Vi, carrying the cat; Eric; me. I nervously glanced over my shoulder before I let the door close behind me. I saw nothing there, but knew from experience that this by no means indicated that there *was* nothing there. I put my hand into the messenger bag I'd borrowed and closed my fingers around the handle of my bowie knife. Bloody terrifying, this thing, and it had seen me through one or two scrapes in its time. I'd had its Maker infuse it with Words that would emanate from the tip of the blade and join their strength with that of my voice. It all seemed a bit showy and dramatic for this mission, but I felt like I needed the comfort of overkill, since I'd had no opportunity to use my voice yet. Well, you might soon, came the unwelcome thought as I snuck along the corridor at the rear of the group.

A light came on in one of the rooms further along: harsh white diffused through opaque glass door panels.

I heard the strains of an angry voice from behind the door.

Rennie raised a hand to indicate we stop. We froze in place and held our breath.

The voice rose and fell a few times. It sounded like an argument, though I couldn't hear what was being said or how many people were involved. We stood there, still as sentinels. After a couple of minutes, the voice quietened and the brighter light was turned off. The corridor darkened once more, but not completely. Must be a desk lamp on in that same room.

Rennie led us on until we stood outside the door directly opposite the one where the voice had come from. The corridor was
wide, not quite hospital dimensions but ample enough in its
small-town way. It was spacious enough for a trolley with a
corpse on it, at least.

I felt it close in on me just then, at the exact moment that
Rennie opened the door into the room we'd come to pillage. I
didn't have to see ahead to know what was about to happen.

Richard the Grey rushed at us out of the shadows. He'd been
waiting. Unsurprisingly, I froze, useless. A part of me had
thought I could somehow get away with never having to actually encounter him, certainly not this soon, and I was as thrown
as it's possible to be.

Rennie screamed and leapt into a raging exchange of blows
and Words with the murdering bastard, with the cat, Eric and
Vi aiding her.

I heard the door of the office behind me open. I turned to
face it, glad, like the brave soul I am, to turn away from my enemy. Someone burst out, and I thrust a hand into my bag for
the knife.

As the others yelled and screeched and struggled behind me,
I engaged in my first fight in years. My opponent threw off his
office worker Veil and revealed himself as an Air-Mage. Not as
strong as the one Vi had fought in the pub, fortunately for me,
but he began to twirl on the spot and I felt a punchy little tor-
nado start to form. He struck first, and I sliced through cloud
with my enhanced blade. Though short, the thing was effective.
I pulled my attention away from what was going on behind me
and focused on the task at hand. It felt good to use my muscles
again, as sore as they'd be tomorrow if I got through this test in
one piece, or as close to it as I could manage.

We fought a while and, to my surprise, I had the advantage.
Every time he moved, I anticipated the direction of his lunges
and feints, stabbing and slashing and pulling my arm back just

in time. I felt strong as I moved my body this way and that, balancing with more grace than I thought myself capable of even in my healthier days. I felt a glow of elation rise in me, as though I might begin to levitate. Everything was in slow-motion, cinematic. But not for long. My attention faltered when I heard Richard yell behind me, making my head feel like it would split open and causing Rennie to roar like an erupting volcano. Distracted, I turned away from my fight for a split second, giving my opponent the chance to land a lucky blow to my head. I staggered and fell, dropping the knife and clutching my forehead as blood ran between my fingers and dripped onto the polished floor. I rolled onto my back, blinking blood from my left eye, the other one wide with surprise. My illusion was shattered.

Eric, who'd had his back turned on my fight while he helped in the far more important one, stepped calmly over me and produced a book from one of his pockets. He opened it, spoke some Words over it, and it became a network of Root-Nymphs. He spread them out like a loosely-woven blanket to the width of the corridor and flung it onto the Air-Mage. It shrunk down instantly, slicing his body into fragments. Eric placed the little bundle back in his pocket, produced a lighter, and wasted no time in setting one of the fragments on fire. It fizzed and sparked, then caught light and burned with a sickly green flame. We both coughed as acrid smoke filled the corridor.

"Need to burn more of it," Eric said between coughs, then held his lighter to another piece, then another. Each of them ignited in the same way, adding to the foul miasma that had by now triggered the fire alarm.

"*Shit!*" Eric shouted over the cacophony, then spluttered as he bent to put a flame to the last fragment. He straightened, waved his arms about to dispel the smoke, even though it had nowhere to go, coughed again, and reached down to help me to my feet.

My head felt terrible, and I was bleeding profusely from the cut on my hairline. Half of my face was sticky with blood. I could hardly stand and lurched from side to side, my free arm held out for support that wasn't there. I felt like an extra from a 1970s zombie film, something I'd have been proud of under different circumstances.

The screaming in the fridge room stopped, but the fire alarm continued blaring at its ear-splitting volume.

"Shitting hell. Fire brigade'll be here soon," I said, slurring my words, then burst out laughing. This made my head hurt even more, so I stopped. I fell down again, slipping in the puddle of my own blood that lay in the middle of the corridor. I landed on my face, adding a bruised nose to the head injury. I was picked up again, and stood upright. Someone's arm was around me.

"We need to get out. Now!" said the cat, from beside my ear.

"Vi!" I cried.

"Yes," he said. "Come on, I've got you."

He pressed me along the corridor towards the back door, the cat digging claws into my shoulder and his.

When we got to the door, I grabbed the handle and pulled it open. Fresh cool air hit my face, reviving me a little.

Vi urged me on. "Go!" he said, and walked me the last few steps.

He more or less pushed me straight into the drain, and I landed on hands and knees in the foulness. This was too much. I voided my stomach into the disgusting stuff, then pulled myself to standing. Vi and the cat were behind me. I heard voices above, one of them deep and male, and turned to meet my doom.

"It's Rennie," Vi said. "She and Eric have Wilbur. We don't have long. Go!"

I staggered along the tunnel path to the place where we'd joined it. The Root-Nymphs had nearly made the opening for us and, as soon as it was vaguely me-sized, I hurled myself through and crawled a couple of paces forward. I could barely see and had no depth perception because of my blood-coated eye, but I heard Rennie and Eric approach, and I helped Vi pull Wilbur through the gap. I held their limp, cool body close to me while the others came through, and we all watched the Root-Nymphs seal the gap behind us.

"Come on," Rennie said. "Let's get to the water before it's too late."

TWENTY

The thudding started when we'd got most of the way along the tunnel that led back to the Hearth room. "What the fuck?" Eric said, his eyes wide and white in the earth-shrouded gloom.

"It's him," Rennie said.

We must have looked ridiculous, all of us, carrying a dead body as quickly as we could through a space whose ceiling was too low for us to stand at full height. Especially Eric. He was stooping deeply to carry his share of the load, while the rest of us were only bent over a little. I was uncomfortable, but he looked to be in pain.

We picked up pace and the thudding continued behind us with metronomic regularity, every five seconds.

We reached the foot of the wooden spiral steps, hauled our cargo up and into the House, and carried the load to the dining table. It felt disrespectful without a nice coffin to put them in, but it was better than the floor and we had to put old Wilbs down somewhere and take a few moments' rest. My arms and legs were burning and, though I knew I was less physically fit than the others, I saw in their postures and facial expressions that their bodies were protesting, too.

"How did he know where we'd gone through?" I said, between deep, dragging breaths.

Rennie grimaced and rubbed at her lower back. She shook her head. "I don't know," she said. "He must have been close behind us and seen the light of the tunnel fade as the Nymphs thickened the earth of the wall."

"By the Makers," said Eric. "We were really lucky he didn't grab one of us then."

Rennie sighed. "Yeah, we were," she said. "Took all I had to stun him. I knew we wouldn't have long, but I didn't think the bastard would come round so quickly."

I nodded. "Well," I said, "we're all in one piece now. Barring our friend there," I added with a nod towards the table. "Sorry, I forgot about you, old chap. Oh! Speaking of, where's the rest of 'em? We should probably perform the Rites now, shouldn't we?" I hurried into the kitchen and made for the fridge.

"They're in the door," Eric called in. "Top shelf."

"Ah," I said as I spied the little engraved box. I picked it up and returned to the group of my living and dead friends.

The loudest thud yet resounded from below ground. It was persuasive.

"No time to lose, indeed," said the cat. "Let's get Wilbur back to the Water and make our enemy's job harder."

"Best way to the beach is through your bedroom window, Ernie," Eric said, "then down through the gardens, and there's another gate at the bottom that opens near the top of the cliff on the far side of the bay."

"Perfect," I said, though I knew I couldn't assume that we were safe behind our layers of defences, not from him. "Hopefully, he'll be held up trying to get through that wall for a bit. Worth a try, eh?"

"A reasonable assumption," said Vi. "Do we have everything we need for the Rites?"

I stowed the box in my bag. "I'll grab the rest on our way through. Let's go."

As we hoisted Wilbur's warming body onto our shoulders, the thudding continued, growing louder. I could have sworn as we carried the corpse through into my bedroom that I heard cracking sounds, as though something were giving way.

"Wait," I said breathlessly. I bent my knees and lowered away from my part of the load so I could get my pentacle and also grab a cloak from the wardrobe to use as a shroud. I picked up my ceremonial dagger with the emerald and sapphire-inlaid handle from the bedside table, then slid the window open on its runner.

The wind had picked up. Sad, delicate storm clouds wove lace-like across the sky. The new moon was a grey lamp that hung in the darkness. I quickly hailed Her before I put the remaining bits of equipment in my bag and returned to my pall-bearing duty.

As we stepped out into the garden, the first drops of rain fell. It was perfect. The moon, the rain, all coming together at this exact moment to aid Wilbur's passing. We moved as fast as we could without slipping on the damp grass and bore Wilbur over lawns and beneath trees to the boundary gate that would lead us down to the sea, their grave.

Eric dropped out of position and went to stand at the gate. He raised his hand, and it opened. He returned to his place, and we continued, pressing on, the wind at our backs. We were on open ground, and the grass rippled like waves on a bright green sea. Lightning flashed in the distance, over the deep, dark water.

I could see the edge of the cliff now, feel the change in the air where it fell away.

"Slow down," I called, and the pace slowed to a brisk walk. We were all breathing hard.

"There's a rowing boat at the foot of the cliff," said Eric. "Straight down, just follow the sheep track over the edge."

I gulped. Never been one for just walking off cliffs, me, especially in the dark and the rain, but as we neared the edge, I saw, in a flash of lightning, that a narrow path dropped down and led to the foot of the cliff in an unexpectedly benign manner.

We went over the edge. The ground was slippery and threatened with every step to give beneath the combined weight exerted through each individual foot. The phrase "dead weight" doesn't come from nowhere, I thought, letting out a bitter cackle. Several times, one of us almost went over, but we held each other's shoulders, just like the pallbearers in the fancy hats do, and lost neither our footing nor our burden.

Eventually, we almost tumbled from the bottom of the cliff onto yielding sand flecked with dry seaweed and countless eroded chips of rock from ancient landslips. It felt strange after the crumbly earth of the cliff.

"The boat's just ahead!" Eric shouted.

A clap of thunder shook the sky. The storm was on us now, the rain pelting down and all of us piss-wet through.

I could see the rowing boat, the pale curve of its hull where it rested high up on the beach above the tide-line on a ledge of sun-bleached and sea-licked broken shells.

We pushed onward, reached the boat, flipped it over; and hurled our cargo on board. I winced at the lack of dignity, but we were pressed by need. Together, we pushed the boat down the slope of the beach, which on this edge of the bay was steep, and soon reached water. I felt a surge of hope when the sea took its weight, and the vessel started to bob like a buoy on the surface. It reminded me of the stolen bike, eager to set off in pursuit of adventure. We jumped in.

"Hey!" I shouted over the wind and the thunder. "Who else can row apart from Eric?"

Eric took up one oar and Vi the other, giving the cat a second to jump off his shoulder first, and they set to rowing us out.

Waves broke over the prow, and Rennie and I had to bail out water with our hands. The cat clung to my legs, digging her claws in. I'd normally have cried out, but the pain helped me focus. Between ejections of cupped handfuls of water and my laboured breaths, I went over the Rites in my head. The memory bubbled up like clear spring water, and the words came easily and in the correct order. Wilbur's body rocked in the bottom of the boat, looking perfectly at ease with the situation, while the rest of us edged along a high board towards the dive into panic.

As soon as I started scanning for a place to hold the burial, I saw it a few hundred yards ahead: a lightning bolt hit it and an aquamarine glow lingered in the water, showing us the way.

"There!" I screamed over the wind and the slapping of the waves against the hull. The choppy sea was throwing us around, and Rennie looked like she was about to vomit. A Fire-Mage with a decent set of sea legs must be a rare thing indeed, I supposed. I resisted the urge to poke fun at her; I'd get plenty of chances later.

We came to the spot. Since we had no anchor, we would just have to hope we didn't drift too far off our mark, but I knew that Wilbur's Element would accept them gladly wherever they touched it.

The wind dropped away like the end of a final breath leaving a dying body, and the boat stopped rocking.

"It's time," I said. I got all the necessary bits out of my bag and placed them on Wilbur's chest. As I did so, I began the Rites, speaking the words in a low pitch, below my normal speaking voice, which is quite deep to begin with. These words were not for anyone else to hear but Wilbur and the Water.

As I finished the second stanza of the thirteen I needed to recite, an almighty shriek rent the air and, simultaneously, a flash went through the storm clouds. I followed its direction back to the top of the cliff, exactly at the point where the funeral party had begun its descent. Someone was standing there, arms held aloft.

"It's him!" Rennie yelled.

I continued with the recitation, though my heart and lungs felt like they had been dropped into a vat of liquid nitrogen, and the words did not come easily for a few breaths. Then, I heard the fucker's voice on the wind.

"Errr-niiiiiie," it called, piggybacking on the whispers of air and water but stabbing through them like a blade.

That was enough. I sped up my recitation of the Rites, enunciating with great care nevertheless, and, as I reached the antepenultimate stanza, I opened the box containing Wilbur's eyes, took them into my hands, and stuffed them back into the sockets they had been ripped from. They were squishy but also weirdly hard. I did not like this mix of sensations at all, but cast my selfishness aside and sent Binding energy forth with my words as I pulled the makeshift shroud back over the cold, lifeless face.

The Mage-Killer's voice came at us again, stronger. I felt it as a low-frequency pulse, a shock wave, and worried that it would capsize the boat, but it reached the edge of the glowing aquamarine area a few vital feet away from us, and its energy was quelled.

I looked at my companions. Vi and Eric held their oars out of the water and both stared at me, faces rigid with shock. Rennie knelt on the other side of Wilbur, her hand resting on their abdomen, and she looked at me too, unusually quiet. The cat hunkered down in the bottom of the boat, covering her eyes with her forepaws. I didn't blame her. I looked again toward the clifftop. The Grey Dickhead stood with his arms held high, pushing Mineral intent from his palms. He fired quartz-hard beams of energy at us, making the air ripple. The boat rocked and shuddered, but when the magic met Water's protective boundary, it could go no further. Our hull held fast — for now.

"Hurry!" shouted Vi. "Finish it!"

I turned back to my task and recited the final stanza of the Rites, inviting the others to join me in the few simple bars of the Ending Song to bring the funeral to a conclusion.

When we were done, I stood up, and I felt the Water hold the boat as steady as Earth for me. I gave thanks for this most generous favour and signalled to Eric and Vi that the time had come.

They picked up Wilbur's body, now restored to completion, and dropped it into the sea.

All of us stood or sat there awkwardly for a moment while nothing happened. Then there came a flash of azure light that illuminated the whole ocean for as far as we could see, before it faded through sapphire, to indigo, to total darkness. Above the flash and dissipation, a scream scraped at the air and the sea, trying to take hold and gather something to it — but it was too late. We had safeguarded Water, at least for the time being, and Richard would not be able to weaken it. Not soon and not without gargantuan effort, anyway. Not that this would discourage him for long.

The figure on the clifftop turned and marched away.

The wind picked up again and soon we were bobbing on the sea in a way most unbefitting a very earthy Earth-Mage. I started to feel sick.

"It's done," I said. "Let's go home, I'm bloody soaked."

Wordlessly, Eric and Vi took up the oars again, turned the boat, and rowed for the beach. We dragged our sodden selves wearily from the vessel and trudged up the cliff path, our energy too spent to register whether we felt good, bad, or indifferent after the success of our mission.

We reached the top of the cliff and walked through the long grass to the boundary gate, glad to be nearly home. But when we passed through the gate and it closed behind us, I smelled smoke on the air and saw the orange glow of flame.

The House of Earth was burning.

TWENTY-ONE

The House of Earth was burning, and my heart burned with it. I felt an implosion in the twisted knots of my entrails as I saw something important and expensive go up in a pall of lime green smoke.

"Noooo!" Eric cried out in anguish, and he broke from the group to run at full pelt up the gentle slope of the gardens and through the window of the room I had claimed as my bedchamber, the axis of the life I should have been living all along.

Rennie and I looked at each other and simultaneously took to running, following Eric at our more modest pace.

Vi Changed and bounded ahead. He caught up with Eric, and they leapt together through the open window and disappeared into the building, as towers of shifting orange-yellow flame climbed skyward.

Rennie and I reached the window ledge. I stumbled and fell onto my knees inside the room and doubled over, coughing up ancient tar from the bottom of my lungs.

"What if he's still h—" I tried to say, but Rennie fell over me and somersaulted into the centre of the room. She sprang to her feet and left me hunched over on the floor, on my hands and knees, spluttering.

I heard more explosions from the kitchen as vials and jars succumbed to the heat, and I felt a warm surge of air fragranced with rare, precious herbs. I cursed Richard Grey anew, as I dragged myself to my feet to join the battle against the flames.

The Hearth room was a total mess, but not from fire damage: it looked as though he'd had a good look round for anything he might be able to use against us. I suppressed my urge to check the bookshelves to see if he'd found any of the hidden supplies — that could wait — and darted through to the kitchen, where the others were tackling the leading edge of the blaze.

Eric had deployed the kitchen fire extinguisher and was directing its nozzle towards the base of the flames, Vi had Changed back to man form and conjured a heavy blue mist that he was using as a smothering cloak, and Rennie held her arms out at shoulder height and was using some mollifying Words from her Element, though she did look a little conflicted about whether or not to let her beloved Fire run its devouring course.

Standing just inside the doorway, I considered where in the fire-fight my efforts might be best placed. I didn't have long though, before my attention was diverted by a blow to the centre of my back. I turned and saw, a few feet away, a person-sized column of Watery Earth, with a strange void where their heart should have been. So this was how the Grey Dickhead had got into the House: he had had an Earth-Mage accomplice with enough skill to breach our defences. This must be the one Rennie had encountered at the funeral home.

I screamed and leapt at this traitor to the Clan with my arms outstretched. They evaded my not-very-subtle move easily ,and I somersaulted forward, landing on a heap of discarded books and scattering them across the floor. I righted myself and quickly compacted some Words that would deflect the next attack, a beam of Water that simply glanced off and turned to powdery grit. Oh, I thought, I just did that. Okay! I'd been expecting this Mage to be, well, stronger. They were still providing an effective distraction, though, while their master got away. *Oh no*, another thought intruded, *maybe he's still here*. At that, emotion surged from me like a landslide, one of those where the side of a hill that's always been happy to be hill-shaped suddenly decides it wants to get acquainted with the river at the bottom of the valley and be washed away to become a different hill somewhere new and exciting. My opponent stood no chance as I directed the flow of Earth energy and wrapped it around them in a containing force-field.

I had a brainwave then. I'd never done anything like this before, but I thought: oh, what the heck. Though my colleagues were doing well at stopping the spread of the fire, it continued to burn intensely. And, bless Eric, for all that he looked terribly endearing wafting that fire extinguisher about, it didn't stand much chance against flames of magical origin.

I began to push the contained Mage towards the kitchen. I felt so cheeky, but had to try it, now I'd become more closely acquainted with Water. Once they were inside the room and near the fire, I closed my eyes and concentrated.

"Flood!" I yelled at the top of my voice.

Nothing happened for a couple of seconds, then there came a rushing sound like a great wave. It quickly grew louder than the roar of the flames, until I imagined myself caught up in the barrel of a breaker, tumbling over and over and over with the roar of the ocean in my ears, so loudly I could not hear my own scream, and I tasted salt: the Water of the sea and of the many tears I had cried. An opening appeared in the air in the middle of the room, just above the kitchen table. Breaking waves spiralled out, and the room filled with cold seawater that knocked us all off our feet.

I was bowled backward by the force of the eruption, and up-ended in predictably graceless fashion. I clonked the back of my head on the worktop on the way and was held horizontal with my back pressed against the wall-mounted cupboards above it, my mouth and nose full of water. In the teal haze, I saw the glow of orange grow fainter and disappear, and I had a sense of something sucking inward as the fire was extinguished. At the last moment, I heard a whispering. Words were being spoken, and it sounded very much like Wilbur's voice doing the speaking. I was awash with love for them, and sent my gratitude into the receding wave. With it went the Mage I'd been fighting; they were hoisted aloft and pulled backward through the portal. At the last moment before it closed, I heard a terrible shriek as the Mage met Wilbur's anger, and was glad not to be there to witness their vengeance in person.

With the pressure that had been holding me against the cupboards now released, I fell back down and flopped around on the floor, gasping for breath and very grateful that the evocation had worked.

The room was dark and the place silent. I was surer, then, that Richard Grey hadn't stuck around. My hope was that, after setting the fire, he'd left his acolyte to hold us up while he got away, and he wasn't hiding out somewhere in the House. I cursed his name yet again as I coughed up saltwater.

I rolled myself to kneeling, then stood up. My companions had been knocked over in much the same manner as I'd been and were strewn about the kitchen either reclining or upside-down, and all were looking rather miffed about it. I stumbled into the Hearth room and brought back a lantern. I heard a *click* of fingers as Rennie ignited it.

"Thanks, Rens," I said, and held up the lantern to survey the room.

Rennie breathed deeply a couple of times to brighten the light, and I made a full turn on the spot to take in the scene.

I smiled, couldn't help but feel proud of myself. My first proper bit of Elemental power-magic in ages. Evidently, I was still in possession of the fabled "it."

"Everyone alright?" I asked, holding the lantern towards each person in turn. My voice sounded weird in the dry air. Actually, I thought, that *was* strange, the air not being humid after that little shower. I looked around and let out a squeak of surprise.

Everything was bone dry. Everything. No warping of the wood, no water stains, and any scorch marks from the fire had been washed away—in here, at least, if not in the other affected rooms. The clean-up would take some work.

I walked to the worktop above which I had until recently been suspended. I reached out with a fingertip and ran it across the surface, then brought the fingertip to my mouth and touched it with the tip of my tongue.

"Sea salt, if I'm not mistaken," I said. I looked around the room. "And everything's covered in it."

Indeed, a thin white crust lay over every surface, sparkling in the lantern-light. It was beautiful, like the first snow of winter before its purity is marred by foot or paw prints. I smiled again, more broadly. "Be really useful, this will; let's gather it all up."

Eric stood, wobbly as a new-born giraffe. "I'll look for some clean jars," he said. "S'pose someone needs to go in there at some point and see what the damage is." He pointed at the door to the workshop, which presumably had been where the fire was started and was probably where most of the damage was.

My heart gave a flutter as I remembered what I'd been trying to say before Rennie fell over me. "What if—" I began, then Vi cut me off.

"No way," he said. "He probably set the fire on his way to the clifftop. It was advanced when we got here; looks as though it had all the time we were at sea to set in. He'll be somewhere else entirely by now, getting a head start. We need to check around thoroughly though."

Eric went into the workshop. "Too dark to see much," he called from the shadows. "I'll have to sort it out tomorrow."

"We need natural light to gather this salt up too," I said. "Don't want to miss a grain of the stuff."

A few minutes later, we were all on our feet. I'd begun to feel cold and very aware of how brackish my clothes (and likely also I) smelled.

"Let's get more lanterns and candles lit," said the cat.

"Good idea," said Vi. "Then, I don't know about you, but I need a wash, followed by a damned good sleep."

That was the closest to swearing I'd ever heard him get. Must be serious.

"You okay, Rens?" I said.

"Fine," she spluttered, wiping water from her face. She looked up at me from where she sat folded up in a puddle on the floor. She was a right picture with steam rising from her clothes as they began to dry.

We all had puddles at our feet from water dripped off our clothes and hair, which had been wet anyway from the rain and our funereal voyage before I appealed to the Element to come to our aid. Everything else though, and I mean *everything*, was perfectly dry, and the only trace that remained of Water's gesture of solidarity was the coating of fine crystal sea salt over all the hard surfaces. A parting gift.

Eric returned from the workshop looking glum. "It's a complete mess in there," he said, "lots of stuff broken, and I think some was stolen."

"That's not surprising," Vi said. "It's to be expected. He just takes from others rather than putting the work in for himself. That's his major weakness."

Of course, Vi was quite right. As strong as Richard was, his predilection for theft and laziness meant that any appropriated magics would be less likely to work for him as well as they would for their Makers. There were ways around this, though, and we all knew it, so none of us were particularly reassured.

❧

All of the bedrooms and storerooms had been spared the touch of fire, but the whole House felt markedly vulnerable and intruded upon. Though not still lurking about the place, Richard's feet had trodden our floor. He had breathed our air. And he had been through my bedroom to get to the clifftop.

Rennie had offered for me to bunk up with her for the night, but I was determined to re-stake my claim to the room I'd just begun to feel was really mine. Moving around this space was so far from slithering around that house I rotted in for five years; I was afraid I'd backslide if I didn't reaffirm my presence here.

When I got to the doorway, I paused on the threshold before entering the room. Inhaled the air. It smelt of outdoors. The window was still wide open and I could see dark stains on the floor from rainwater blown and trodden in. The rain outside had stopped, and I heard water dripping from the branches of the trees and bushes in the garden. The sound of nature beckoned me, and I paced slowly over to the window and stood on the ledge for a while.

I looked out over the gardens. The air had fallen eerily still in the wake of the storm's passing, and the world rested, but as if it had dropped dead rather than drifted into an idyllic slumber. I turned my head so that I could listen to the world outside with one ear and the one inside with the other.

"That's a tad curious," I said to myself. "There's dripping in-side, too."

I turned to face back into the room and listened again. Yes, there it was: a barely audible *drip, drip, drip*. I frowned, and looked up at the ceiling for tell-tale damp patches and trem-bling blisters that released steady drops of cold water as they grew heavy enough to break its surface tension. Nothing was there, much to my relief. I had a flashback to the old place, the pots and pans I placed on the kitchen floor to catch the rain that fell relentlessly for two days and nights one winter. I'd had to kip in the living room so I could keep to the alarms I had to set so I could empty the things often enough.

I shook off the cold, damp memory, and listened again. The sound was coming from the wardrobe. A shiver ran down my back. I slid the window mostly closed and tiptoed across the room to stand before the wardrobe doors. The dripping sound was louder. I opened the door.

"Oh, shit, of *course!*" I said and laughed with relief. I reached to the shelf above the hanging rail and pulled forward the velvet cloth in which I'd wrapped Wilbur's Scrying ball. The fabric was soaked through. "Guess we'll not See our way anywhere with this after all. Oh well, never mind."

Truth be told, I was peeved that we didn't have the thing at our disposal. Thinking practically, though, it would have been a pain to carry. I'd had a puncture wound from a shard of one of these once. It had belonged to another Water-Mage, one of the Sea, like Wilbur, so when I'd dropped the orb he'd so kindly entrusted to me, and it shattered, it threw up a fragment from the floor to lodge its complaint and stabbed me in the wrist. It went really deep, too, and, what's more, the magical glass that would return to Water upon the death of its owner was covered with salt. Really hurt, that did. The wound caused one of my many scars. I touched the place, ran my fingertips over it, then let my hand back slowly away from the caress. I wasn't ready to feel all my old hurts that deeply again yet.

Saying words of reassurance to myself, I used the wet fabric to wipe some of the puddle off the shelf, making water drip onto the long sleeves of several ornate gowns.

"Bollocks," I said. "Didn't think that one through."

I conceded that I was very tired indeed and decided it was time for bed. I could wash in the morning.

❧

Needless to say, I did not sleep at all well. I dreamed of a dark whirlpool far out at sea. I was sucked in and thought I was drowning, until I realised that I could breathe underwater. Calmed, I started swimming, not seeing the beast that stalked me through the darkness. I woke up, gasping, with some of my hair wrapped around my neck, as though it had conspired with the dream-monster to strangle me in my sleep. I pulled it away and reached for the glass of water on the bedside table. It had been there at least four days, but hadn't lost much to evaporation, and it wasn't dusty in here, so I reasoned that it would be safe to drink. I raised the glass to my lips, wet them, and took a little water into my mouth. I was soon glad it was only a little. My lips began to tingle, then burn. The skin inside my mouth grew unnaturally warm, then felt like it was being scraped off with coarse sandpaper or wire wool.

"Help!" I called out before my throat began to close up. I clutched at it, choking, and lay back onto the pillow. I could feel my eyes bulging and the skin of my face flushing blood red. I'd knocked the glass onto the floor and spilled its contents. What an idiot I was. I'd a rough idea of how long Richard must have had to nose around and lay little traps, and it wasn't long, but he was powerful enough to kill with a flick of the wrist from a hundred feet away. I should have been more careful and assumed he'd poison the glass of water left within tantalisingly easy reach of his imagination — and of my lazy self.

My throat had almost closed up. I was wheezing through a gap the size of a baked bean. I tried to cry out again, but could not. I reached out with one of my arms, reaching towards the wardrobe as though Elias's essence would solidify and come to my aid. As the gap in my trachea closed still further, I shut my eyes even tighter.

A hand grabbed mine.

"Get some charcoal powder," Eric's voice said. "You'll be alright, Ern." He held my hand, and a few moments later, shoved a fistful of charcoal into my mouth, tipped my head back, and poured a load of water in on top of it.

I coughed and spluttered and kept my eyes shut.

"Good," Eric said, "it's not serious. Probably just a drop or two of Malice."

The swelling in my throat began to subside within about a minute, though it felt longer, of course, and soon I could breathe again. Well, once I'd spat or coughed out all the charcoal all over my bedspread. It was ugly, disgusting, an oil spill. But I was alive.

"I should have bloody known," I said, my breathing still ragged.

"Hmm," pondered Eric as he shone a torch into my left eye, then the right.

"Aaaargh!" I yelled in surprise. I tried to pull my head back away from the searing torchlight, but there was nowhere for it to go. I pushed my whole body backward into the soft pillow.

"Stay still, you big baby!" Eric scolded me. "I need to make sure there's no trace left. You were lucky it was just Malice and not Meltbone, you know." He shook his head and tutted like a matron on night duty in a ward full of attention-seekers with the sniffles.

Right though he was, enough Malice can be fatal within five minutes. One of my legion of recently returned memories was of a friend I'd had as a teenager who had used it to take her own life. We'd been just too late to get to her in time, though she could have been saved. I carried that guilt for years, and now, like my other old pains, it had returned. Meltbone though, well, it does exactly as the name suggests. It attacks the bones and turns them to liquid. It can be administered in various ways, but if you decide to go for the most efficient method and drink it, it starts with the teeth, followed by the bones of the jaw and the skull. And there's no antidote. If Richard had had any of that on him, my friends would have just had to watch me melt from the inside out, and there would have been naff all they could do about it but mop up the gooey mess afterwards.

"I know, mate, thanks," I said. "Your bedside manner could do with a bit of work though." I coughed and spat more of the charcoal and saliva paste out.

Rennie leaned me forward and clapped me on the back, making me cough again. A final grey bolus flew out of my throat and splatted onto the bedspread.

"Charming," she said. "That's the thanks I get, eh?"

I glared at her between straggly curtains of sweat-slicked hair.

She grinned. "Go on," she said. "Go and wash, and we'll tidy this place up a bit. Change the sheets and give everything a bit of a clean. And get you some fresh water."

"We shouldn't have let you come back in here alone after what happened," Eric said. "Sorry. We should have checked the room thoroughly to make sure it was safe."

I shrugged and swung my legs out of bed, thought twice before making footfall on the contaminated floor, crawled across the huge surface to the other side, and climbed down from there.

"I'll use one of the clean towels in the main bathroom," I said groggily as I persuaded my legs to stand me upright. I wiped sweat-congealed charcoal dust from my face and walked naked from the room.

Taking my time over a bath or shower was always one of my favourite indulgences, but sadly one I didn't get to revel in that often. Usually, it was a three-minute shower before the hot water ran out, and the bath at the old place was a salmon pink nightmare encrusted with rings of perma-dirt no amount of scrubbing could rightfully dislodge. I had attempted to clean it once and learned that lesson quickly. My relationship to the thing was reduced to resentful stares from the rickety shower cubicle that had been haphazardly erected in the bathroom corner. It was so narrow that I could barely get in and close the door behind me. Luckily, I'm of relatively svelte build or I'd have had to acquiesce to dealing with that repugnant bath.

I sank down into steaming hot water and enjoyed the fragrance of the herbs and salts I'd poured in as the tub filled. I heard sounds along the corridor, voices of people giving and receiving instructions, footsteps, and the aggressive whine of the hoover. I stayed in the bath, reclining comfortably, for about twenty minutes, which I judged to be just enough time to avoid being roped into any cleaning.

Once things had quietened down, I stood and grabbed a towel and started drying myself off. I had a mild headache and a sore throat, but no other after-effects from the Malice. I thanked the Makers that Richard hadn't had long in the building.

At this thought, my mood shifted down a notch. He'd got in here with the assistance of a Mage who worked with my own Element. It felt far too close to home. How could they? I thought. How could anyone?

Disgusted now that the adrenaline had worn off, the full impact of the violation hit me. I hurried across the large bathroom to the toilet, knelt before it, and threw up, crying rageful tears in between the convulsions in my deepest core, until my arms and legs were numb.

TWENTY-TWO

I lay curled up on my side on the bathroom floor until sufficient feeling returned to my limbs then levered myself upright. I felt decidedly woozy. I sat for a few minutes until the feeling had faded to a tolerable background hum, then stood, staggered across the bathroom, grabbed a fluffy robe from one of the hooks on the back of the door, and pulled it on. I didn't know whose it was and hoped they wouldn't mind, but mostly didn't care. Before opening the door, I paused with my hand on the handle. I had a feeling. What was it? My stomach gurgled. There it was. The dark clouds parted: a cuppa and a round or two of toast with butter and Marmite would sort me right out.

As soon as I opened the bathroom door and the acrid smell of smoke hit me, I remembered what had happened mere hours earlier. The fire. There'd be nothing edible in the kitchen — and besides, what there was, if anything had survived, might well be poisoned like the glass of water I'd foolishly sipped from. I did have one option, though. I shuffled back to my room, which I discovered had been cleaned and primped in preparation for my sleeping in it. The window was shut and the floor-to-ceiling glass panes gleamed darkly at the far side of the chamber. I crossed the room, slid open the window, and stepped barefoot out into the garden.

I sniffed the air. The wind had changed so that the breeze now came from the north east. It felt like autumn was whispering its first words on an exhaled draught, telling the world to hunker down and keep warm. Soon, this wind would grow bitter and shear down over headlands, roar through eroded bays, and aid the sea in further grinding out their curving lines. The changing of the seasons always brought mixed feelings for me. Autumn: a time to release, to let go, to accept what has gone before and turn to dive inward and reflect. But I'd already hidden away for so long, and that hiding place was the coldest I've ever been, even in the illusory haze of the DNR. I felt ready for the strong winds of winter to blow now though, scour things out a bit. I coughed, spat defiantly onto the earth, and set off into the gardens. My robe gaped open, exposing my chest and the runes inked in a line that begins where my clavicles meet and goes all the way down, between my breasts, along the length of my sternum and to my navel. I let the ancient markings drink in the light of the stars, and the cold breeze refreshed my skin as I walked slowly down, my feet sinking soundlessly into the soft, dew-covered grass.

I strode down to the gate that led onto the clifftop. I could see it from a way off, a dark rectangle that broke the green line of high, thorny hedgerow where, if I was in luck, the first blackberries of the season would be hanging in ripe clusters beneath layered canopies of leaves, between treacherous whip-like arcs of bramble stem.

I picked one. It came away easily, a joyous ripeness, and when I popped it into my mouth it was sweet with a tart edge. Perfect. This was how life should be, I thought as I savoured it: colour, flavour, texture. I ate my fill, gathered as many berries as I could fit into the hammock I made with a flap of whoever-it-was's bathrobe, and made for home.

❧

Sleep came easily and held me in dreamless depths for a timeless while. I jolted awake as if I'd sneaked a five-minute nap on the couch after eating too much dinner.

The cat, who unbeknown to me had been lying on my chest, emitted a surprised cat sound and took off vertically, ascending several feet before landing back exactly where she'd been.

Luckily, I managed to roll to the side just in time to avoid being landed on. Not fun at all, a cat walking across your tits with dainty paws that exert a confoundingly mighty level of pounds per square inch.

"Whatchyou doing in 'ere?" I slurred, my surprise spilling out before I could muster a more courteous greeting.

"Checking," the cat said, affronted.

"For what?"

She sniffed. "Thought you might have died. I was just checking you hadn't."

I sat up in the bed, crossed my legs, and flattened my bird's nest of hair down a bit. "Would you care to elaborate?" I said, trying my hardest to sound clement. I hate being watched in my sleep.

"It can be a side effect, you know, after a Restoration. Not to mention your little dose of Malice. Just one of those things can be too much to deal with, but two? Your constitution is impressive."

"Er, thanks. Lucky me, eh?"

She tilted her head to one side, the Mage in her showing her interest in a human-like manner for just a moment before the two parts of her re-integrated, and she was once more all feline, at least on outward appearance. "Actually, for a while there, I thought you might have," she continued in a chatty and informative tone, as though she was dictating a shopping list. She began to raise a paw towards my mouth. "Your breathing became so, so light, I almost had to—"

"Thank you," I interjected, and the paw was retracted and given a little groom while I talked. "I slept very deeply. Unusually so." I tried to run my fingers through my hair, but they soon got caught in its mess of thick tangles. I gave up, slid across and out of the bed, and shuffled to the sideboard where I was sure I'd spotted a hairbrush. I picked it up from beside the heap of berries I'd left so I could share them in the morning. It was a lovely thing: smooth, polished wood with the image of an oak leaf carved into it. It had stiff black bristles and the perfectly turned handle fit the dimensions of my palm as though it had been made for me. Who knew? Perhaps it had, and I just hadn't yet remembered. The information was probably lost in a drawer somewhere in my mental filing cabinet. The one with my bank statements in it, perhaps. I walked to the big mirror and teased the knots out of my hair, effecting slow, methodical caresses and sweeps of fingers and brush.

The cat watched me until I had finished, at which point she padded across the bed, jumped to the floor, and went to the window, where she sat down neatly.

"Lovely morning," she said.

I took the change of subject to mean that she was no longer concerned I'd keel over at any second. I put the brush back in its place on the sideboard, picked up a couple of last night's berries, popped them into my mouth, then went to join her by the window. The berries had been tastier last night, air-cool and under starlight, but they retained some of their wildness even at room temperature. I used my tongue to squash them into the roof of my mouth and enjoyed the rich, spreading flavour of purple.

"Mm," I said as I looked at the nursery blue sky festooned with ribbons of high cloud. It looked cool outside, autumn coming gently from far away in a shifting of the light. Neither of us said any more for a few minutes while we retreated into separate contemplations. I broke the silence.

"What's it like out there?"

"Looks a bit chilly today."

"No, I didn't mean out *there*," I said, inclining my head towards the view we shared in the moment. "I meant out *there*," tilting it back towards the bedroom door. "What's the damage?"

"Mercifully cosmetic," said the cat. "Most of it will be easily repaired with a good clean and a coat of fresh paint. He didn't have time to cause any lasting destruction, really. My guess is he just wanted to fuck with our heads."

I gasped; I'd not had the cat down as one to swear, especially when she was acting in an official capacity — which she always seemed to be.

She looked up at me and flattened her ears until they resembled the wings of a small, furry aeroplane. Tabby Air. "I hate him passionately too, you know," she said. "I know you don't think much of my post or of the Council, but *I'm* allowed feelings about our enemies as well."

"Fair enough." I reached down to stroke her. "I'm glad he didn't do any lasting damage. To the House, at least."

The cat let out a sharp breath that carried the promise of a word, but which word she intended I could not tell. She stayed quiet after that, her gaze drifting first over the gardens towards the sea, then watching the birds following the season's call to places I had never been. The furrowed dark lines in her striped fur were set into a deep frown across her brow, the sprays of whiskers above her eyes as still as the stems of flowers locked in ice.

A great banging and clattering sounded from outside my bedroom door, breaking the stillness in the air. My heart began to pound immediately and I crossed the room in long strides. The door had opened in anticipation as soon as I turned to face it, and I marched through and burst into the Hearth room.

Eric lay on the floor, groaning. A ladder also lay on the floor, at ninety degrees to Eric. It was totally obvious what had happened, but I still saw fit to ask.

"What happened?"

Eric groaned again.

I bent to help him sit up and rubbed the backs of his shoulders.

He didn't answer my question. We both knew it was a stupid one. I looked up at the ceiling to where he had liberated a patch of firefly light from its coating of soot.

"Aww, mate," I said.

He coughed.

"Cuppa?"

He nodded and lay back down with a dramatic sigh that was a mildly Earth-ier version of one of Rennie's.

"Coming right up." I went to the kitchen, where Rennie sat at the table, smoking a fat cigar. Curls of fragrant blue smoke hung in the air. A glass of what I presumed to be Fireball sat on the table in a smeared crystal tumbler with dark lines of ash clogging the geometric gorges of its topography.

The cat was right: nothing seemed to be too lastingly affected. Bits of cosmetic damage here and there, and cleaning the place would be a right old job, but otherwise there was little amiss. The sea salt that had coated all the Water-washed surfaces had been gathered up and now filled a two-pint jar.

I filled the kettle, set it to boil, then scrubbed a couple of mugs.

Vi loped in, man-formed, from the workshop.

"Kettle's on," I said, in my second stating-the-obvious utterance of the day so far.

"Yes, please," Vi said, and grabbed another mug.

"I've got berries," I said without offering any contextual information as I squished teabags into each mug in turn, sending dark brown swirls into the boiled water.

"Huh? Are you okay, Ernie?" Vi placed a hand on my shoulder and gave a gentle squeeze.

"Berries, if you want anything to eat. Picked some down the bottom of the garden last night. I was hungry. Went wandering."

"Oh! I understand now." Vi's expression changed from concern to relief. "Well, yes, I would love to try a couple, but we can have a proper breakfast first, eh? We defrosted some bits and pieces overnight."

My stomach eschewed the promise I'd made of berries to keep it quiet and let rip a deep, throaty growl. "Oh yeah. That's a game-changer."

"That's our girl. Or, should I say, our Chief Earth-Mage." Vi clapped me on the back, making me cough, and picked up his mug of tea. He walked into the Hearth room without waiting for me to protest his use of my should-be title, you know, the one I hadn't actually accepted yet, and went to join Eric in some cleaning. I heard him whistling a tune and encouraging Eric to join in. The man was so relentlessly chipper it would have been annoying if I wasn't developing a crush on him. I caught myself blushing and decided to change the subject of my internal monologue.

I glanced over at Rennie, who had finished her whiskey and was almost done with the enormous cigar, then walked to the doorway, mug in hand, and leaned on the doorframe. The cat was directing Eric, who was back on the ladder and not looking overly happy to be there, in his ministrations to the besooted upholstery and branch work.

"Where's the food?" I said, "I can cook, if you like."

Eric pointed towards the door to the sleeping and washing quarters, which I took to mean that our breakfast had been defrosted in the bath after I'd vacated it. I returned from the bathroom with a bag heavy with cold but ice-free comestibles and got to work.

Breakfast was remarkably edible, considering I hadn't cooked for anyone but myself in a long, long time. Everything tasted of toast because of the lingering smell of smoke, and an unease hung around the place, which I guessed it would until the remnants of the fire had been fully cleared away, but the food was a satisfaction. I sat back in my chair.

"So," I said. "Now we've eaten, I suppose we need to find the Mage-Killer."

Everyone stared at me, and I shrank away from the pressure in their facial expressions.

The cat, who was sitting on a cushion, cleaning her paws, stopped and narrowed her eyes. "I think the Council will agree that this is the logical next step," she said.

Everyone looked at her, then at me again.

"So," I repeated. "Are we still assuming that, since we've secured Water and made the Moonseer much more difficult to reach, Richard will go to the Sunmaker first?" I patted my belly and burped out the taste of sausages, toast, and beans. Nobody disagreed with my assumption. "Who's coming with me, then?"

Eric spoke first. "I'm not strong enough to fight him, and someone needs to guard this place and re-build the defences. So I'll stay here and be in charge of all that, plus I've got shit-loads of coursework to do. But anything left in the workshop and garage is up for grabs for the journey." He motioned with his hand towards the door that led to the workshop and beyond.

Deathly curious, I got up straight away and went to investigate. My chair scraped back over the flagstone floor as I stood. I walked to the doorway. I hadn't been into this part of the House yet, and I met it like the explorer of an alien world who's forgotten all their safety protocols: no gloves, no breathing apparatus, no scientifically detached guarding of my idealistic heart. I got to the doorway and drew in a last breath of familiar air before stepping over the threshold.

The damage in the workshop was shocking to behold. Smashed glass and earthenware littered the floor and work benches, and the smell of charred things hung heavy in the air despite the wide-open windows. The paint on the walls was blistered and the wooden benches scorched and warped. I scanned the room, taking in the extent of the destruction. When I was done, my rage burned hotter than the fire that had been set here.

"You alright, Ernie?" Vi said from where he'd been watching me in the doorway.

I wiped my eyes with my sleeve, and nodded. "Yeah, thanks mate. I just don't like seeing harm done wantonly. It's so pointless. Isn't there already enough suffering in the world?"

"Yes, there is," he said sadly. "More than enough, I'd say."

We exchanged a sympathetic look, then I dusted myself off and made for the door through to the garage, with Vi following a couple of paces behind me.

"Fuckin' hell," I said when I saw them.

"Quite something, aren't they?"

An array of vintage motorbikes and trikes stood under tarpaulins, dark lumps revealing flashes of chrome and custom paintwork where the tarps didn't all the way cover the machines.

"Whose is all this?" I said, breathless.

Vi shrugged. "They've kind of just accumulated over the years. Most belong to Mages who've either died and left them, or struck an agreement to leave them here for the time being while they're off on some quest or other. At least four of them have been bequeathed to us though, in recognition of alliances past." He raised an arm and pointed toward the far end of the garage.

"That's great," I said, "but I don't drive. Can't. Bloody useless on anything with an engine, I am. You know me, mate; militant pedestrian and designated drinker."

Vi shrugged again. "That's true, but Rennie's fine on a bike. More than fine, in fact; she's formidable. You can ride pillion, and we've a sidecar about somewhere. I can Change and go in that."

I couldn't contain my laughter. It burst out like puke and stank just as badly when I saw the hurt look on Vi's face.

"I'm sorry. I didn't mean to take the piss. It's not a bad idea, but we don't know exactly where we're going yet, do we? And what roads we'll be taking. It'd be a damned shame to lose one of these beauties along the way. I mean, I know these beasts can handle the Unseen Paths great under the direction of a suitable Mage, but still. I am sorry though." I smiled. "You'd look cute in a sidecar."

"No harm done," Vi said, though something lingered in his voice like the smell of smoke in an empty room. I wanted to wash it off my skin. "We should talk to the others properly, really," he continued. "Make a plan of action."

We went back to the kitchen, where Rennie had embarked upon a second massive cigar and the cat was in a video call with someone from the Council on her tablet, muttering low enough so I couldn't hear what she was saying.

She finished her call. "I know I said I wouldn't dictate, but the situation is rather urgent now. We have successfully dealt with Wilbur and secured the Sea, which makes it extremely difficult for Richard to bend Water of any kind to his will — not impossible, by any means, but he'll be feeling the pressure of time now every bit as much as we are."

Rennie sipped her coffee, then took another mouthful of cigar smoke, which she sent out in a horizontal plume above the table. I saw dark flames in the smoke, a swirling blueish fire. An image of Elias bounced into my mind. He was smiling in sunshine, then the sky went grey-blue above our heads and the clouds seemed to come down and touch us. The air tasted damp and melancholy.

It was a memory of one of our few arguments. Such a silly thing: we'd drunk too much and started bickering over some insignificant nonsense, and it had escalated in the way things can when you're tired and hungry. The way his face changed — I remembered how it had affected my mood instantly, stabbed my heart with a single look. I felt I'd let him down in that moment, but it was nothing compared to my failure to protect him on the day his life was taken. I saw, starkly, a mental image of myself crumbling and collapsing at the moment I was needed most. What if, now I'd come out of hiding, I failed again?

"Ern?" Vi said, and touched my forearm gently.

I jumped. "Uh — Yeah. That's — I'll just go along with whatever the cat says, she's a professional."

"So, the Sunmaker, then?" the cat said, looking over the rim of her glasses, paw-pads paused over her tablet screen. She looked at me for confirmation, and when I nodded she looked down at her screen again and tapped at it for a minute while the rest of us remained quiet, sneaking glances at each other to test our own levels of anxiety against what we saw in others' faces and nervous tics. I'd hidden my hands in my pockets, where they were balled into tense fists.

"Okay," the cat said when she looked up from her screen. "You'll go to the Sunmaker and see if you can intercept Richard there. I've just dispatched a team of Mages from the Council to go to the Moonseer in case he decides to make for Her pool first. They'll form a circle strong enough to repel him, and all are skilled fighters. We can get him back into custody, or—"

I gulped, and hoped the cat was right about the Council Mages. I didn't like the thought of him simply being thrown back in prison. That meant he'd have the option of escaping again. I wanted a proper end to this. I wanted it to be over, once and for all.

The cat made eye contact with me and nodded as if she'd read my thoughts, which would not have surprised me in the least at this stage.

"No time to lose, then," she continued. "We'd best get ready and be off. A team of Council guards is on their way from HQ to watch over the place while we're gone and finish the clean-up. Rest assured, it'll be completely spotless when we get back, and I've asked them to see if anything needs a lick of paint while they're at it, and to help Eric with his coursework, and check the wiring, and make sure all the appliances are up to safety spec, and — Oh! Sorry. I said I — the Council — you know what I mean, wouldn't take over. Back to you, Ernie."

"No worries, cat. You're right. We need to go. And I'm sure none of us will mind the Council's help in getting this place back into shape. But I have no idea where the Sunmaker's to be found, I'm afraid, or the best way to get there."

"He likes to stay put, which makes him pretty easy to locate, if you know how to read maps that are always changing."

"Huh?"

"He makes it look as though he's never in one place, but that is exactly where he is. It's just you can't get there by any other means than a portal, and they're always shifting about. There are signposts to his forge though, for those who can read them."

"Quite right," said Rennie. "We can start at the place I last found my way to him, a few months ago. If we're lucky, he'll still be accessible from there, and if we're not, he might not be too far off. He has to move the map and the Path to his forge every once in a while, though not the forge itself. But he always leaves a clue for friends and any potential clients to find him, just in case they're not as aware of his habits as I am."

I smirked at the innuendo I saw behind "habits," and tried to catch Rennie's eye to show her I understood, but she was gazing into the bottom of her whiskey tumbler, looking like she was trying to scry in the decorative bubble of air trapped in its base.

"What's the best road to take?" Vi asked.

Rennie grinned and brought her attention back to the room. She put down her glass, crossed her forearms, rested them on the edge of the kitchen table while she thought for a moment, then leaned forward. "Not any mundane one," she said, and her eyes flashed as she put on a spooky voice. "We will travel by the nearest possible entrance to the Unseen Paths." She waved her hands about like a sham fortune teller, making her bracelets jangle, and giggled. "Seriously, though," she said in her normal voice, "that is the quickest way. The only way, to be precise, as the cat has so rightly pointed out. Much as I'd love to ride one of those bikes in there and pelt along the invisible country lanes, the best way to where we're going on this occasion is actually on foot, through the nearest portal. The path is narrow and the land where we're going will not welcome tyres. We'll be there in no time though."

Vi looked relieved. I knew what a fast and reckless driver Rennie could be; poor hound must be a nervous passenger. Bless him for suggesting the bike and sidecar.

Something in my gut shifted sideways, then clicked into place. I remembered the alleyway near the funeral parlour, the weird shimmering I'd noticed behind the graffiti-covered wall. "Am I right in thinking there's a portal just along from the funeral place? That's where I had a bit of a funny turn the day Rennie fought the Fire-Mage. Don't think I got round to telling you I'd seen something, come to think of it, since we had other stuff to talk about."

The cat suddenly looked very interested in what I was saying. "What do you mean, seen something?"

I thought back to that day: the heat, the Cycle Shack, my first outing in years under a Veil. It felt so long ago.

"Well," I said, settling into a chair, "I'd rented the push-bike, gone past the funeral place and carried on a bit further up the road. I reached a sort of alleyway, a dead end between two small warehouse buildings, and something caught my attention. I rode in, taking care nobody was about who could have followed me." I closed my eyes and brought back the image of the sagging barbed wire, the dry earth with weeds growing triumphantly through the gaps in its crack-riven surface, and the odd feeling I'd had when I bent closer to the shimmering energy that floated in mid-air. "I could tell that something was there, though part of me assumed I'd just gone barmy with the heat. So I got off the bike and wandered over to look. Then I saw someone behind me, probably the Fire-Mage Rennie ended up fighting, got hit on the head, and next thing I knew I woke up on the pavement. I guessed at least an hour had passed, given the change in the light and the position of the sun, and I made my way back here. And, well, you already know the rest."

"Hmm," said the cat. "Are you sure about where you found it? That it wasn't just a trick of the heat, the light, your nerves? It's just that's not quite where it should have been."

I considered her suggestions, though I did feel a tad patronised. It was plausible that a combination of my anxiety, the heat, and the energy of keeping a Veil over myself could have caused me to see something where there was nothing. But it didn't feel right. I got so close to the shimmer. It was real. I shook my head to dismiss her assumption.

"I can see why you're suggesting that. But I'm too Earth to succumb to a case of the wobbles that quickly. And, though I have to confess that my Veil dropped at some point, and I know I was newly back to magical skills at that point having so recently undergone the Restoration, I don't think I was mistaken."

"I see," said the cat, her voice telling me she thought I was quaint on the one hand, or paw, and mildly incompetent on the other.

I raised my eyebrows and turned a corner of my mouth down in disapproval.

"We may as well head for there anyway," she continued, without acknowledging my hurt expression. "We can use the tunnel to get us most of the way and come up to surface level from the next drain cover along from the one we used to carry out our little theft from the morgue."

"We'll be needing to grovel to the Root-Nymphs before we can go anywhere," I said. "They'll be well pissed off they need to open up a way out again so soon after repairing and binding the old gateway, and I don't fancy getting scratched to bits on the way out."

"Oh, yeah." Eric turned to me with apprehension written all over his features. A couple of seconds later, though, in a manner befitting his youth, he'd shrugged away the worry and a breezy smile lit up his face, showing his wire-clad teeth. "It's okay, they're nice really, once you figure out how to talk to them. They don't like rude people," he said, and he looked quickly at Rennie and then back to me and gave the tiniest smirk with the corner of his mouth furthest from her.

It made no difference anyway; Rennie wasn't paying attention to us. She was fiddling with one of her many heavy rings, frowning and swearing at it under her breath. The huge cut stone caught the light as she moved it around, examining its setting.

She looked up and sighed heavily. "When are we off then? I'm bored."

Irritated by Rennie's tone, I elected to leave the room to begin my preparations for the journey. We didn't have long to get ready, after all. As I started walking, Eric turned and headed for the wall cupboard housing the gong that summoned the Earth Elementals. He struck the gong, and I hoped for all our sakes that the Root-Nymphs wouldn't get uppity at being called upon again so soon.

For the first time since I'd arrived, I willed my bedroom door to stay open and asked the protective vines not to close behind me as I entered. I made straight for the wardrobe, flinging open the doors and practically diving in to start rummaging about. I'd a mind to take whatever Weapons of Elias's had survived, as well as my own stuff. I'd feel far safer with things of his about me, too, and I was looking for one thing in particular.

I found it crammed into a corner at the back of the shelf above the clothes rail, behind innumerable odd socks in various organic hues. My hand closed around the scabbard and I brought out Elias's favourite knife.

The feel of it in my hand made my heartbeat quicken, and I felt suddenly nauseous. I had seen him use this knife to stab, to slash, to disembowel. Memories surged from the drawers I'd filed them into in my mind's newly repopulated headquarters. I had to kneel on the floor for a moment while the pounding in my head subsided, and I was left with just the mental image of him with this knife, the one I now held, plunged into someone's guts, right up to the hilt. Granted, the blade was fairly short, only about six inches, but it had seen more blood and made more kills than most of the swords I'd wielded, even the really murdery ones. I carefully slid the knife from its scabbard and looked at it closely. El had lovingly called it "short-stuff," but I fancied a loftier, more serious name. Nothing as cheesy as "Widowmaker" or "Bone-Hewer," or as sick-makingly horrid as "Brain-Chopper" or "Eyeball-Popper." *Brunilda*. That was it. I mean I'm no Valkyrie, but a name with such power behind it was sure to lend me some strength in whatever battle awaited.

"I re-name you Brunilda, little friend. Nilda for short," I said to the blade, my breath misting its death-cold curve. "May we together avenge your former keeper, Elias, who watched your Making and kept you all those years and polished you so lovingly and used you to stab lots of nasty horrid people and assorted other entities. So mote it be."

I gave Nilda a reverent polish with a clean cloth and strapped her to the outside of my calf, just above where the top of my right boot would be once I'd put it on. I walked to the mirror, and changed my mind immediately. As great as I thought she looked with the green leaf patterned leggings I was wearing, I was sure everyone else would think I looked a complete wanker. So, with regret, I un-strapped Brunilda and put her in a suitable travelling bag, along with minimal changes of clothing and one or two bits of my old gear that I thought might come in handy. I put the travel bag on the bed, shoved my battered old holdall to the back of the wardrobe, and went out to join the others.

Something caught my ears and I paused just outside the Hearth room to listen. A kind of conversation was taking place, but it sounded odd. It was all high-pitched, a mix of squeaks, creaks and rustles. I tiptoed as close to the doorway as I could get without being spotted, and leaned back against the wall to listen. I heard two voices. One was the squeaky, creaky one, and the other sounded almost human, like a person trying to speak another language and doing alright had their interlocutor been suitably tolerant of their mispronunciations and errors in verb conjugation, but not so alright if they were talking to someone who happened to be a stickler for correct grammar. I heard a few more stilted utterances before I felt compelled to intervene.

I sauntered in as casually as I could manage. "Y'alright," I said to Eric, and its equivalent to the Root-Nymph he was attempting to converse with. I bowed and offered the customary greeting, using an appropriately deferential form of address, then knelt beside Eric on the floor. I imagined myself getting an old phrasebook out of a drawer, blowing the dust off its cover, and opening it. It had completely escaped my memory — until I overheard the conversation — that I knew how to speak another language. At least, I hoped I did, and that I hadn't just said something terribly offensive: "May all your branches be snapped by a light breeze and your roots drink my piss," that sort of thing.

The little knotted figure bowed in response. This was a good sign; they could be grumpy little gits when the fancy took them.

I bowed again and began the entreaty, during which I humbly requested that the good folk of Root and Soil open passage for us (again), so that we might pass through (again). I padded my sentences with copious flattery, couching the request in terms of a plea to be once again honoured by their superior skill, speed, and strength. The Nymph stayed quiet while I talked — another favourable omen. When I'd said my piece, I rested back on my heels to await the response. I saw Eric out of the corner of my eye; he was staring at me, his mouth agape.

I touched his forearm, and mouthed "*sorry*" at him.

He nodded, his mouth still hanging open, then looked back at the Nymph, who had started making soft sounds a bit like a handful of wood shavings when you pick them up from the floor of a carpenter's workshop.

A few minutes later the deal was struck. We were allowed to pass through, and the Nymphs had agreed to open and close a comfortable way for a load of big clumsy folk like us. They are duty bound to protect the House, of course, but a little courtesy doesn't hurt, does it? And it's not worth getting into any tiffs with them; they have minds of their own and they really know how to bear a grudge, as one of my ancestors found out a couple of centuries back when she went poking about in their tunnels without asking permission first. The wily little creatures weakened the foundations beneath one side of the previous House of Earth, the ground subsided, and part of the building collapsed into the ground. Caused a lot of damage, as one might imagine. Her favourite artefacts, many of which were made from very, very expensive earthenware, disappeared into the hole, and once it was filled in and the House repaired, they were entombed forever.

"Everything alright in here?" the cat said as she trotted in.

"Quite so," I said. "We can use the same exit and Path we used last time."

"Excellent! That will make things much easier. We won't have to risk being above ground for long and drawing attention to ourselves. Even if we go Veiled, there are some about who can See."

"Come on, then," I said. "Let's make a move. Rennie, you've the best idea of where he's gone, so once we get through the portal you can Incant the correct co-ordinates to take us there. Okay?"

"Gotcha," she said with a flourish of hands and a jangle of bracelets.

I grinned at this. "Damn right. The last big battle wasn't ex-actly one-sided. We nearly had 'em all, didn't we...." My words tailed off as I remembered how we'd mistaken being close to victory for being near the end. How, as I lay bleeding, Elias and I met each other's gaze, each mirroring the other's relief and triumph, and then, too weak to do more than watch, I saw an axe raised behind his head.

I came to when Vi touched my hand. "Oh. Sorry. Got a bit lost back there."

"The past is no place for you any more, Ern," he said gently, leaving his hand where it was. "Let's bury it. Let's finish this."

And with that, we made to leave, the cat, Rennie and I, with Vi bringing up the rear. We walked single-file down the spiral staircase to the tunnel that would lead us back past the scene of our body-snatching misadventure and onward to further mis-adventure. Eric watched us go, waving. I imagined he was glad to get us out of the way. The past few days had been a succes-sion of disruptive events; now he'd have time and space to get the place back to its former state — with help from the Council, of course. I had grown very fond of the cat as an individual, but it's really what those spreadsheet collectors she works with excel in: project managing entirely predictable, rigidly risk-assessed maintenance and repair work, and I'm very grateful for that.

It felt strange to be back in the subterranean tunnel I'd last travelled through carrying my share of a corpse-load on my shoulders. The air smelled faintly of burning, though the fire had not reached this far, and it poked at the parts of me that are the most susceptible to anxiety. I felt as trapped as the smoke particles that had seeped down from above on invisible, eddy-ing air currents, and a yell tried to rise from my belly, demand-ing to be released, but I suppressed it and said nothing to my friends.

We reached the gateway, which had been opened for us. I could not see any Root-Nymphs waiting to bid us farewell, but they were experts at hiding when they did not want to be seen, so I assumed they were there anyway and spoke some words of thanks in their language as I passed through, as best as I could remember them.

❧

As soon as I stepped through the hole and the sole of one boot touched the surface of the revolting water in the tunnel, something felt wrong, but I put it down to the memory of the visit to the morgue and our subsequent run-in with trouble, and carried on, suppressing my nausea.

The four of us splashed as quietly as possible through the stagnant murk, and I shuddered when it seeped through the stitching in my boots and my feet got wet, which didn't take long. Vi had wisely elected to take human form for this part of the journey to keep his sensitive nostrils further above the stinking liquid, as a kindness to the heightened receptiveness he experiences in dog form.

I turned to look behind me and saw him tiptoeing along, holding the hem of his robe out of the water. He met my gaze with forlorn, shining eyes, and I turned back in the direction of our plodding. I dreaded to think what the cat must be going through now. The light from behind us was already shrinking away as the Root-Nymphs began to stitch closed the hole in the wall.

We walked in silence, treading with care, as though our foot-falls might disturb slime-beasts that slumbered just beneath the surface. I couldn't remember it having taken this long the last time, but then I recalled that we were going further than before, following the tunnel along to the drain cover nearest to the alleyway where the shimmering portal was.

A sudden flash of light preceded a detonation that shook the tunnel. I was knocked off balance and thrown into Vi, who fell backwards into the water with a loud yelp. Rennie landed on my legs, crushing one of them and twisting the ankle. The loudest sound, though, was made by the cat: she let out a wail that started as feline and rose to a woman's shriek.

Once I'd recovered from the stun of the explosion, I wrenched my leg out from beneath Rennie and pulled myself upright. My ankle was sore but mercifully not sprained, though I wobbled on my feet and had to support myself against the slimy walls as I dragged myself along to where I heard the cat crying. In the light that came down through gaps in the drain cover, I saw blood in the water. A lot of blood. Fighting back the urge to be sick, I crouched down and reached my hands into the water, searching for the feel of fur. Instead, I found a human foot.

"Bloody hell!" I shouted as my fingers made contact with smooth skin. The foot kicked out against my hand, and its owner reached out a bloody, quaking hand. I bent down and helped her sit up in the water.

"I'm—very badly hurt," the woman said, in the cat's voice.

Twenty-Three

The woman who I knew as the cat groaned in pain. She grabbed my upper arms, pressing the tips of her thumbs and fingers painfully into my flesh, and pulled herself closer to me. I looked into her face, and saw a horrible wound on her forehead and a mess of sticky blood over the side of her face, already beginning to clot, glossy black on her skin the colour of oak bark. She was weeping, a weird mix of human sobs and feline wails.

"You're the cat. Well, normally," I said, stating, yet again, the bloody obvious.

I kept her upright as she trembled, and I had no idea what to do. Her head began to loll, and her breath was light and shallow, catching in her throat and making a sound like a needle jumping the grooves on a vinyl record. Blood poured from her head wound. Her hands released their grip and dropped down, splashing into the filthy water. I held her around the waist and rested her head on my shoulder, gently, hoping I wasn't doing any more damage.

Rennie sat up, rubbing her temples. "What happened?" she said groggily.

"An explosion," I said, showcasing my expert observational skills once more. "Are you alright? And you, Vi, are you okay?" I called along the tunnel. Mindful as I was of the need to be quiet, the situation had taken something of a turn, and I elbowed caution firmly aside.

"Yeah, I think so," Rennie said. "Just bumped my head on the wall. Not hard though. I'll be fine in a minute."

I thanked the Makers for her thick skull and prayed to them again that the cat wouldn't bleed to death in my arms.

"I'm intact, Ern," Vi said from behind Rennie. "Just a bit damp and not altogether enjoying the stink in here."

I heard splashing from behind where Vi's voice had come from, quiet at first and growing rapidly louder. All of us simply turned to look in the direction the sound came from rather than get up, or prepare for a fight in any way whatsoever. Fat lot of good we were, if this was an enemy come to finish us off. Load of amateurs. I held my breath and, in character with the particular brand of coward I felt myself to be at that moment, I shut my eyes. May the Makers forgive me for dying in a sewer, I thought, as memories both new and old flashed across my mind.

A strong hand grabbed my arm and gripped it tightly. It hurt, and I cried out, a tiny sort of whimper.

"What on earth happened here?" a young, lanky voice said. Its owner was shaking me now, using my bruised right arm as the anchor point.

"Careful! She's hurt," I said, "and I think it's bad. It's her head and face. There's so much blood."

"Oh no," the voice whispered. It was starting to sound familiar now my head had begun to clear a little — though I sensed another bank of fog on the horizon. But that was alright. The breeze, though cold, moved slowly. I had a moment to think.

"The Root-Nymphs raised the alarm and told me to get down here at once. I'd felt the ground shake, though, so was already on my way."

Eric!

He bent closer. "Oh, *shit*. I've never seen her in human form before, just an old photo in one of my Transmog textbooks. She's the best there's ever been at that. I have to get her back to the House immediately. The Council's delegation will be here very soon, thank the Makers. They'll be able to help." He crouched down, and I felt the warmth radiate from him as he leaned over me to take hold of the cat and lift her up. He did so with admirable strength and grace, putting all us old bastards to shame. I also had a burning jealousy of his clothes for being drier and less offensively fragranced than mine.

I leaned back against the wall, both thankful for Eric's quick response and heartbroken that our quest had ended so prematurely — completely selfish on both counts. I wiped streaming tears of relief and shame from my cheeks as Eric hefted the semi-conscious woman-cat onto his shoulders.

"You lot go on," he said. "I'll take care of her."

"What?" I replied. "We can't go on now. No way." I stopped myself before I could whinge about how soaked I was, as though this were a legitimate reason for abandoning a life-or-death mission.

"You have to," said Eric. "You really have to. Now just fucking go!"

His choice of words gave me a jolt; I knew he was giving me an order. Not that he needed to drop an f to make me take him seriously, but that, combined with the force in his voice, gave him an authority his youth could not belie. I wished he could have come with us; he was the best and most sorted of us all. I looked at the cat's blood-smeared skin, heard her mumbling and crying, a bizarre mix of feline and human sounds that tailed off into silence as she passed out, her head hanging back over Eric's shoulder and her ravaged face staring at nothing. I prayed to the Cat-Goddess to let her live; so devoted a subject was she who made the effort to remain always Changed in honour of the feline divine. And I knew that the Goddess was aware of the dedication required. Eric took neat, dance-like steps over Rennie and Vi and began his journey back along the tunnel. I heard him slip and almost stumble in the darkness a few times as his uneven footsteps and the resulting splashes slowly faded, accompanied by some wonderfully creative swearing.

"I'm sorry I called you a bureaucat," I said to the cat as he bore her away, and I sobbed like a child.

I felt wretched. I wanted to give up, to sit in that dank tunnel forever or go back to the House and obliterate myself with booze. Neither were good solutions to the current predicament, which I could smell on my body and in the fabric of my clothing, clogging its weave and the pores of my skin. The air, the water, everything, were a disgusting blend of slippery and lumpy, the remnants of so many half-digested meals spewed or shat out. I swallowed down my urge to puke, desperate to be somewhere, anywhere, else. Yet there I sat, soaking it all in passively, defeated before we'd even got anywhere. I noted that my ankle didn't hurt any more. That was something, even if all it meant was that I was in mild shock.

"Stuff this for a laugh," Rennie scoffed. She stood up, grunting with the effort of heaving her layers of wet clothing from the water, grabbed my arm, and pulled me to my feet. Rather forcibly, I might add, but I did not protest. I wasn't sure I'd have had the energy to stand unassisted, however roughly the help was offered. I helped her to bring me the final few inches upright, coughing and cursing.

I felt around for my bag with the toe of one boot and found a lump. "Ah, here it is," I said, bending to pick it up, but I found that someone else had hold of it too. When the someone squeaked defensively in a giant rodent-like way and shot off along the tunnel, taking my bag with it, I decided that perhaps my spare undies weren't that important after all. Then I remembered Nilda, and my heart almost jolted itself out of my chest. "Hey!" I called along the tunnel, but the thief was out of sight. It had felt so right that she could be the weapon I used to fight El's murderer, but now she was gone, just like that. I wondered how to carry on now this one stabby piece of comfort had been wrenched away. "Oh, no," I murmured.

"What's wrong?" Vi said. I looked at him. He stood quietly in the meagre light, his robe dripping water from its hem, as still as a night watchman with a jaunty sense of dress who wanted to prove he wasn't that serious all the time and whose boss didn't mind his liberal interpretation of the regulations concerning uniform.

"Oh, nothing. Just me bag's been nicked by a bloody massive rat," I said forlornly.

"Oh dear. Well, maybe it's best we travel as light as possible," he offered. He was right; I had been the only one who'd considered it necessary to bring baggage.

I nodded, feeling the gloaming pressing in around me, and said nothing.

"Anyway, what do you think that was?" he asked, tidily changing the subject. "The explosion. I mean, it was obviously Mage-worked — but what exactly was it?"

I sighed with a mixture of resignation and depression. "My guess is he left us this little surprise to intimidate us, mostly," I said. "Put us off. Kind of like an anti-personnel device for Mages. That was only a tiny piece of the Charge, a crumb at most. And I've seen this stuff go up. Not much more and he'd have blown a crater in the road, and we'd all be plastered across the cosmos in every dimension and direction. As with the fire, though, thank the Makers he was in a hurry; this was similarly rushed. Done in passing with flicks of the wrist in both cases, I reckon. It's just a shame the cat was heading us up; it wouldn't have hurt a bigger body so much. And, since her Change-field is so strong, the fact she's really a full-sized human underneath her cat's body didn't help in lessening the impact. If only I'd been at the front. I'd have got no more than a few cuts and scratches."

My words shrank down into the shadows and cowered there. What a ridiculous situation we were in: three respected Mages, among the best in our Elements, remonstrating in a sewer tunnel. I hoped we'd survive long enough to have a good giggle about this one day, if the stench ever faded from our nasal receptors. I was bitten by a nagging feeling about something, but waved the distraction away, hoping it wasn't a parasite of some kind; there must have been plenty in here.

"Come on, then," Rennie said gently, "let's carry on. We still need to stop him ,and we don't have much time."

"Don't suppose there's any chance we could nip back for a quick shower and change of clothes, is there, Rens?"

She pulled her face into a sympathetic expression her features only hinted at in the gloom and shook her head. "Time's a-ticking, darling," she said, and clapped me gently on the shoulder, which was still numb from how hard both the cat and Eric had gripped the arm that dangled from it. "Not far now until we can surface. Next one's just along there."

"Right then," Vi said as he wrung some liquid out of the hem of his robe. "No time to lose, eh?" He gave an awkward grin, his teeth flashing white in the darkness.

We trudged on for perhaps another two hundred feet. I couldn't imagine surfacing and carrying on through the portal; my legs felt heavy and a deep weariness had settled in my mind. As much cynicism as I felt about what I perceived to be the unnecessary bureaucracy of the Council and their officious obsession with the spreadsheets I so despised, I felt deeply guilty that the cat had been the one to encounter that small dose of the Charge. I hung my head, slumped my shoulders forward, and dragged myself on. I was brought to a stop when I thumped into the back of Rennie, who had stopped walking. The expletives she threw over her shoulder at me snapped me out of my daze.

"Oops. Sorry, mate," I muttered, feeling by this point extremely woeful on my own behalf.

Vi brought up the rear, his superior senses stopping him from blundering into me. I felt a steadying hand on my shoulder and it gave a reassuring squeeze. I placed my own hand on top of it and we linked fingers for a moment. I felt stronger.

"Just ahead," Rennie hissed. "D'you see where it's a little lighter along there?"

I peered past her. There was indeed a patch of pale grey not far beyond us. The light came from above, through holes in the metal grate of the manhole cover. I could see drips of water falling, whether rain or standing water from the street it was not clear, and I could make out a little detail in the greasy brickwork of the curved tunnel walls.

"D'you think there are any more traps?" Vi whispered.

"Could be," Rennie said, looking around suspiciously.

"I dunno," I said, not whispering, but keeping my voice low. "He was chasing us, remember, and we were heading the other way. Would he have had the time or the inclination to come this way first then double back? Unless there's another one of his minions hanging about somewhere."

Rennie was quiet for a moment while she considered this. "Ernie, we can't afford to hang around even if we *are* walking into another trap. Regardless, there are plenty of unsavoury beasts down here without need of lurking Mages."

At the moment she said it, I felt something bump and slither past my leg in the darkness. Whatever it was, the apex of the curve of its backbone was higher than the top of my boot. "Yep, let's get out of here, too many bag thieves about."

"I'll go first," Vi said.

I felt him Change just behind me, and a golden Lab squeezed his way past me and then Rennie, and padded carefully through the water ahead of us. I heard the splashes his paws made and his snuffles as he checked ahead for any clue that something other than sewer-water and its motley array of inhabitants awaited us.

A minute later, splashes, as made by the paws of a hound trotting through brackish water, approached.

"Right-o," Vi said. "No sign of any danger. We can proceed, I think. Well, that's what my nose says, anyway." He chuckled self-consciously and fell quiet.

The three of us looked at each other.

"Okay then," I said, "let's do the bit I'm really dreading."

Twenty-Four

ennie sighed. "Well, we won't get very far with that attitude, will we?"

"Give over," I said. "I'm not in the mood for a pep talk."

"Well, perhaps you need one, you grumpy so-and-so."

I huffed, and folded my arms. "Takes one to know one."

"What? Don't be ridiculous, Ernie."

"Oh for fuck's sa— ouch! Something bit me!"

"That would be me," said Vi.

"Oh."

"Now," Vi continued, his voice low and growly. "Will you two just *stop bickering*? This is far too important a moment for a tiff. And I, for one, would *love* to get out of this grime and stink and just get this over with. What do you say, hm?"

A collective, apologetic hanging of heads ensued and then, quietly, from Rennie and myself simultaneously: "Yes, Vi."

"Good," he said.

We dragged our wet boots and bruised egos through the last few yards of water and stopped to gather ourselves in the light cast down in geometric patterns through the metal grate that marked our exit point.

"What time is it?" I whispered, peering up at fragments of blue. "I've lost track."

"I think it's almost evening by now," Vi said, "which is bad news. It's rush hour; there'll be a lot of people about."

I suppressed a cackle about whatever passed for rush hour in this backwater of a place. So many seaside towns were the end of the line, and Clifford's Bay was no exception. It was no bad thing though; fewer people on the streets meant fewer people to keep an eye on or get noticed by.

"Let's just try not to get decapitated when we poke our heads up out of the hole in the road," I said, struggling to imagine many actual vehicles and thinking instead of a motorised lawnmower puttering along. I still wouldn't fancy meeting one of those face-on, mind you.

I took hold of the side rails of the narrow metal ladder that ran up to the manhole cover and placed the sole of a wet boot on the first rung above the water's surface. I was terrified, but the surge of relief I felt at getting one of my feet out of the infested vileness lent me some fortitude. I climbed up until I found myself with my face upturned just below the metal grate. I tilted my head to listen as well as I could to the sounds at street level and waited.

"Can't hear anything," I said, knowing full well this meant precisely nothing as an indicator of the foes, or lack thereof, who could be waiting up there. Luckily, I was momentarily feeling bold. "Let's do this."

As Rennie started to climb the ladder, I pulled myself up so that I could heft the metal grate aside with the back of my shoulder. It wasn't too heavy, and I easily nudged it up, then bumped it sideways so it slid along the surface of the road, which it did with a heavy clattering and scraping that made me wince. I pulled myself up and out, and lay down so I could help Rennie and Vi, who had Changed back to human form, through the hole.

Once we had all surfaced, Vi dragged the grate back over and it clanged into place.

The street appeared deserted. All I heard was a dog barking in the distance, probably playing on the beach. The breeze was low and smelled of nothing but air warm with late summer indolence.

I had brief flashbacks to my various recent scrapes with danger but, glancing about, saw no indication of shifting energies in any perceptible direction. It didn't mean there weren't any, of course; it could just be that they were on patrol at the moment, along the path beside the pretty church and its —

thanks to Rennie — lightly cremated graveyard. All the more reason to press on un-Seen while we could.

❧

The air was peach and yellow as the sun lowered through the degrees of late afternoon, and it brought out the colours of our irises: mine sage green, Rennie's scarlet, Vi's Brazil nut brown. Our eyes met for a split second and, in unison, we turned and made for the alleyway. We strode across the twenty feet of tarmac that was so pleasantly warm and dry underfoot, and jogged into the side street between the two warehouses. My boots were heavy, which made this difficult, and I cursed anew the stinking tunnel we'd skulked through. The heat of the road's surface amplified the stench on our skin and clothing.

The wall at the end of the alley sat in the shadow cast by one of the warehouses, its graffiti-covered letters picking up ultra-violet light and glowing surreally. As soon as we came into the semi-darkness, I became aware of how soaked my clothes were. Without the sun to shine on them, the fabric was instantly cold. My skin responded by throwing up goose bumps across every available inch of its surface, tightening over the bruised areas, and making them ache. I pushed my discomfort aside wearily, as though I was throwing off bedcovers on a sweltering night, and followed Vi and Rennie to the pavement just in front of the wall.

It was identical to last time: the stubborn grasses, the cracked soil, "H3X0RZ" sprayed in primrose yellow on the neglected brickwork that was a boundary to nothing in the mundane world, and the same ethereal haze hung in mid-air just in front of it. It looked so much like heat haze, but deeper and darker. I wondered whether any of the town's residents had sensed it at any point during drugged-up rambles through these streets. Probably, but it was likely they'd forgotten about it completely once they'd come down.

The three of us looked at each other again, exchanging slower, more searching glances.

"This is it," I said. "This is where I was the other day." I looked at the shimmer, but, though I felt its substance on some level, I could discern nothing beyond it. This was no surprise; I'm too Earth for all that wobbly stuff. I've always needed guiding through portals, even though I've read plenty about the shifty, unreliable things: one of my major irks about my Elemental alignment, that. I can't even see through 'em when I'm tripping — and I've tried on plenty of occasions.

Rennie bent down to peer at the patch of shimmery air. She brought her nose to within an inch of where it started to shift normality and sniffed. "Hmm," she said.

"What?"

"Smells a bit funny."

"Funny how?" said Vi. "I can't sense anything."

This was interesting to me, how Mages differed in the ways their extra senses manifested. Some were more visual, while others had strong clairaudient impressions from beyond the shimmer, while others, like Rennie, could sniff things out as though choosing the right whiskey or cigar for the mood. And it was curious that Vi's heightened canine smell receptors weren't picking up on anything. The last thing I needed right now was the suspicion that one of my companions may be anywhere other than at the top of their game.

"Like, it smells a bit off," Rennie said. "A bit rotten. Like something you've left out on the side and forgotten about and it's sort of curdled, energetically speaking."

"What does that mean?" I said.

"Probably nothing," she said with an enviably casual shrug. She waved a hand in the air like a food critic about to write a mediocre review. "There's a trace of something, a decayed smell lingering in the air around the portal. He probably forced his way through here and left a hint of himself. I imagine that's all."

"That seems logical enough to me," said Vi.

"Can we still get through?" I said, anxious about being fried to a crisp the instant we attempted transcendence of the realms. Many a careless or reckless Mage had met such a fate over the ages, and I had no desire to add to their number.

Rennie stood up and clapped Vi and I on a shoulder each with gusto. "Sure, darlings!" she said. "We just need to make sure we're completely dry when we go through. Or the jump will boil the skin off our bones. I can't get a hint of anything that smells like a trap, though, if that's what you're worried about. That fact alone is most promising, don't you think?"

"Oh," Vi said. "I hope you're right."

"When am I not, darling?" Rennie said. "Now, both of you close your eyes." She sounded like a kid delighting in a game where she got to put blindfolds on everyone and they had no option but to trust her.

Vi and I looked at each other and shrugged simultaneously. Nothing to say, really. I closed my eyes.

A wind blew. It was a wind as from a desert at midday, but soft, sparing my skin abrasion or burning, and instead kissing it dry. I felt the water evaporate from my clothing and my body lighten. As I inhaled, I noticed the aromas of damp rot, and only the Makers knew what else, leave me as something else was breathed in: the smell of dry sand, tiny crystals, and fossilised shells in pale hues, tumbled and smoothed through aeons. The wind died away and I opened my eyes. The scene was exactly as before, but I didn't feel nauseous, and my skin, hair and clothing were clean and completely dry. I gave a satisfied sigh.

"Right," I said, with a nod in the direction of the shimmering patch of air a few feet away from us, "how do we get through here then?"

Rennie went quiet — something I read as not an overly good sign, based on extensive previous experience. The light had taken on that eerie quality that it has when teetering on the boundary between late afternoon and full evening, glowing at once blue and pink and yellow in equal, impossible intensity.

I looked around us at the dead end we stood in, noticing the fragility of the grass stems, their seed heads swaying just the tiniest bit, and the warped hardness of the upper layer of soil. And behind, the wall itself, with the new graffiti sprayed over layers of older declarations made by successive generations of the town's bored and disenfranchised youth.

"Well, darling," Rennie said, "first you have to trust me. And I mean completely."

"Ah," I said.

Vi was looking at me intently, his dark eyes looming beneath a forehead creased with worry.

"What happens if I don't entirely trust you?" I said. "No of-fence meant, of course. It's just, after what happened—"

Vi tensed further. He wouldn't have a problem trusting her —you know, dogs and loyalty, even to those who take advantage — but he was well aware that the fabric woven into my heart was not cut from that particular bolt of cloth.

"You wouldn't want to know the details, darling," Rennie said.

"I see. And where is it you're taking us, exactly?"

Her posture grew a modicum more defensive in a squaring of shoulders and a closing of fists at her sides. "We'll try the co-ordinates he fixes to in the summer first, but he may have already woven new ones and shifted the approach to his loca-tion. As I said not long ago, if your memory is up to retaining simple facts," she said. She met my gaze, her eyes hard and fierce.

I did, of course, remember that she'd mentioned this before, but just wanted to be annoying, in case it was my last chance in this lifetime. I smiled, mostly to myself.

Vi exhaled, his breath making a whining sound on the way out. "Can we not start another argument now, please? This is not exactly the moment, either."

"Indeed," Rennie said. "So, Ernie, you need to try your very hardest to trust me."

Trust. Definitely a work-in-progress, but I was learning. "Mm-hmm," I shrugged.

Rennie turned to face the portal. She reached out her right hand and touched the hovering patch of shimmer with the tips of heavily ringed fingers. Concentric circles of red and orange light spread out from the contact points. She pulled her fingers away. "Good. It's responding normally to my touch. Now, join hands. This is going to feel a little strange."

Rennie took hold of my left hand and Vi's right before Vi and I closed the circle, locking our fingers tightly. As soon as the three of us had made contact, Rennie jumped backward, pulling us into the portal behind her. My receding view of the alleyway showed, against the wall, a climbing rose I was sure hadn't been there before. I opened my mouth to alert my friends but it was too late: the portal was closed.

The journey itself took only a few seconds, but it felt far longer. In those stretched out instants, I had the time to observe sensations at once like spinning, being lifted up, and plunging downward. My ears filled with a rushing of wind that sounded like countless whispering voices surging forward on a tide of sound waves. I tried to focus in and make out individual words, but then thought: no, don't listen, perhaps they're trying to warn you, tell you to go away, stay out.

I smelled nothing. The air in the Unseen carried no fragrance, natural or otherwise. I focused on that instead, on how odd I thought it was, and something inside me relaxed and found it fascinating and then let it in, accepted it. At that moment, I felt another tug on the hand holding Rennie's, and suddenly there was ground beneath my feet. Not having expected it, naturally I fell over. I landed on soft grass and the air was knocked out of me. I let go of Rennie and Vi and placed my hands on the ground to break my fall. My head spun. I felt like I'd be sick. I coughed, expecting to throw up, but didn't.

I was surprised to notice that my eyes were closed. I opened them, and the world rushed in. I found myself kneeling in deep, lush grass all blown in the same direction by the prevailing wind off the sea. I was right on the edge of land, high above cobalt blue water. A wide bay curved to either side of me, its cliffs exposing strata turned and twisted through the ages so that their rock and mineral stripes stood vertical. My stomach lurched again when I looked downward, and I rolled away from the cliff edge a few feet before I risked standing, just in case I was unsteady on my feet. I rested on my heels. Desperately hoping we hadn't brought anyone else through with us, I looked around. No sign of anyone but the three of us. "Thank fuck for that," I breathed, and placed both hands over my heart.

The sun was high, I guessed late morning or midday, and the air balmy warm. The clifftop was empty but for us and a cottage that stood a short distance away, with some outbuildings clustered around it. Grey smoke rose from behind it somewhere. Beyond that was a dark forest of tall trees that swayed in the wind.

Vi and Rennie stood twenty feet further inland, dusting themselves off.

"You alright, Ernie?" Vi called.

I could hardly hear his voice; it was pushed away from me by the hale sea wind, and only faint threads of sound reached my ears.

I nodded. "I think so."

Smell came to me then. Two smells, actually: ocean air and the forge that was out of sight just beyond the cottage. I heard a hissing sound on a gust of wind that came at me sideways across the clifftop: hot metal plunged into cold water.

Rennie beckoned impatiently. I stood and began my trudge to where she and Vi waited.

"How d'you end up over there?" said Vi. "We both had hold of you."

I shrugged. "Dunno. Everything started spinning and didn't stop for a while."

He nodded. "It can happen if you're not completely sure of where you're going."

"I had no bloody idea of where I was going."

"Quite," said Rennie.

"How could I have?"

"You didn't trust the Path enough," she replied, as though this was the most obvious thing ever. "It's alright. Could've been worse, eh?" she added, inclining her head towards the cliff edge. "That was pretty close. Perhaps we should have practised a bit of dimension-shifting before we set off."

"There wasn't really time for that, to be fair," I sighed, frustrated by her patronising tone. "And I think I saw—"

Rennie clapped me on the shoulder, cutting me off. I was really beginning to dislike this gesture; it had never been a habit of hers before. I wondered where — or who — she'd picked it up from.

"Ah, good! He's here," she announced, and she turned and began marching towards the cottage.

"Right-o," said Vi, and followed a step behind her.

I watched them for a few paces then fell in behind, following their footsteps through the thick, tall grass. I had about thirty feet of thinking time in which to reflect on whatever feelings I had about the situation, before we met with the Sunmaker.

As Rennie and Vi strode on, I hung back, checking over my shoulder every few seconds for any sign that we'd been followed. After about fifteen checks, still seeing nothing, I decided to focus on what lay ahead: the Sunmaker himself. I felt anxious in a way that's actually quite rational before encountering a being of his stature. I was sure these fancy Makers both had some kind of spiel they'd trot out when meeting friends or foes or, as in our case, trios of assorted Elemental Mages come to ask favours of them. I felt the sting of Impostor Syndrome: what if he deemed me unworthy to approach his forge? I felt, in magical terms, like someone who had spent the past decade eating junk food and doing no exercise barring the shamble to the fridge or the toilet, and who decides all of a sudden: ah! I know! I shall run a marathon! Terribly unprepared for this malarkey, in other words.

Rennie looked over her shoulder. "Come on, Ernie," she called. Some of the sound of her voice was snatched away by the wind, but enough reached my ears for me to comprehend that she was tired of my dithering.

I picked up my pace. Blades of long grass slapped against my shins and I dragged myself forward.

I'd never met either of the Makers in person before; never had any need to deal with them. We'd always had plenty of inter-Elemental liaisons who were willing to make connections, and I'd never been that into travelling, really. I'd always preferred the warm fire of home, the material comforts of my own hearth and larder, and knowing where the nearest decent pub was. And I had my dealer on speed-dial. I could never quite tear myself away from all that. My previous self, I should say, since look, here I was, getting out of the House, travelling.

When Rennie appeared to see something and then broke into a run, I knew that the situation was not as she had hoped to find it. She disappeared around the corner of the cottage and out of sight, and Vi sprinted after her.

I found myself alone. I was on a threshold between an apparently endless expanse of grassland on one side, the ocean far below on the other, and the stone cottage up ahead. I was afraid: I didn't know how I would get back to the House if anything happened. I looked back over my shoulder and could see no sign of the portal we'd come through. No suspended shimmer of air. Perhaps it was disguised against the rippling grasses; they were pretty shimmery on their own without any strange movement hovering above the tips of their blades. An image bubbled up and settled in my mind's eye: me, on my own, a madwoman roaming the fields forever in search of my way home, my cheeks hollowed, eyes staring, and clothes shredded.

I sped up as though merely thinking this thing had made it real and I had to get away from it. I had given it power, but I could also take it away. I ran to the cottage.

I pelted around the corner and stopped when I saw what had happened. The worn soles of my boots skidded on the gravel path.

A mess of what looked like entrails lay scattered across the ground. Short sections of pinkish grey intestine flecked with blood and smeary stains of half-digested matter were arranged over the mown grass as if they had been laid out for display. This was not what I'd expected to find at the House of a Maker.

The Makers were the oldest of us, two ancient Mages so strong they had grown physically taller and broader, their bodies responding to a need for increased storage capacity for all the additional power they had. They had, no doubt, heard every possible configuration of Words, seen — or indeed, Seen — the lines of every possible sigil, and would consider all of these things to be mere trifles, nonsense, far beneath their superior knowledge. After all, they could shape and combine the very Elements themselves, and they alone could forge Weapons that held the power of lives and deaths. Therefore, when I was faced with lengths of gut un-knotted and laid out, my very soul was shaken.

I walked a few paces. Between the lines of entrails, I saw hairs. Long, dark hairs. And some lumps of other stuff. Skin. Fat. The remnants of what was once a glossy coat.

In the forge, Rennie and Vi stood over a crumpled figure. Even though he was curled up on the floor, I could see how huge the Sunmaker was, and how defeated he now lay. He gave deep, bovine sobs as Vi spoke soft, kind words into his great shell of an ear.

The Maker unfolded himself and came to a kneeling position; in this posture he was as tall as me at my fullest height. His face, which sat beneath a shock of flame-red curly hair, was puffy, and tears ran down his freckled cheeks, collecting ash and leaving pink valleys in their wake. He sniffed, and wiped his nose with a cloth he pulled from the pocket on the front of his thick leather apron. I noticed then how oversized everything in the forge was: the mighty anvil, the hammers so huge I could never pick them up, let alone wield them, the bellows like a church organ — every tool scaled up to fit the enormous hands that used them.

"What happened here?" Vi asked, his voice soft.

The Sunmaker shook his massive head and sniffed. "He killed my Fred," and he bent forward, overtaken by great hitching sobs.

I now understood who the entrails belonged to, and the long, dark hairs. Fred was the Maker's Familiar, his horse, who, judging by the extent of the mess, must have been a sizeable fellow himself. To slaughter such a beast was a truly heinous affront, a sundering of one of the strongest of all the bonds in all the worlds.

The Sunmaker once again collapsed into racking sobs as huge and corporeal as he was, and we stood with him as he wept, all grieving with him, though none of us could do a thing to right the wrong that had been done.

"He," he said between rasping breaths, "he wanted me to—"

"To what?" Rennie said.

"Make him a Weapon," the Maker said, and he hung his head. "He hurt Fred and said if I didn't do as he commanded, he'd kill him. I had no choice." He looked at each of us in turn. I could hardly bear the emotion in his eyes, the sky blue of his irises as clear as agony, as sharp as death by the single stroke of a blade.

He wiped his freckled cheeks again and pushed a lock of auburn hair back from his face. "I refused." He sobbed again, and again calmed himself. "We fought, and I bested him. I thought that would be the end of it, but," and here he broke down again, "he killed my Fred out of spite." He let out a great bellow, which echoed into the sky.

My heart broke for him. The cruelty of it was almost beyond belief. Almost. It had Richard's fingerprints all over it.

I looked around, saw the ground festooned with bloody ropes of gut like strings of lights laid out for a party before being hung. Where was the rest of him? I wondered. Where was the rest of Fred?

The answer would have to wait, because striding towards us was a Wood-Mage. The same one I'd spotted in the alleyway and, if I wasn't mistaken, outside Violet-Next-Door's bedroom window. As he strode, he threw out long, narrow branches covered in evil-looking thorns.

Vi and Rennie fanned out to my left and right. None of us had weapons; we'd have to fight with our bare hands. I winced at the thought of all the scratches we'd get, but then, grimly, I remembered the scars I already had, and thought perhaps it wouldn't be the end of the world if I were to get a few more.

From behind me came a roar as the Sunmaker stood. I couldn't help but flinch, which ruined my attempt to intimidate the Wood-Mage. I didn't need to, as it turned out, because the Sunmaker strode the few — for him — paces to where the Wood-Mage had now stopped what he'd been doing and was looking up, wide-eyed, at the giant who approached.

In a very business-like manner, wasting no time on self-indulgent vengeful words, the Sunmaker picked up the Wood-

Mage, carried him to the forge-fire, threw him in, and used an enormous poker to keep him there.

I screwed up my face; the screams were awful. More disturbing, though, was the fragrance of rosewood that drifted my way. It smelled beautiful. That did it; I felt decidedly sick. I bent over, rested my hands on my knees, and took some deep breaths. The screams stopped, and the Sunmaker stood back, satisfied.

"To the forest," he said, again wasting no time. "I buried Fred there, a seed. A tree will grow, and it will be the strongest tree. And its fruit shall live, and be his son, and grow tall. And together we shall avenge my friend." His azure eyes glittered with love and menace.

I nodded, but did not understand. I felt full, and had to spit something out. May Earth forgive me for being such a bloody idiot I thought as I opened my mouth and let the stupid syllables tumble from my lips. I cursed myself for not remembering all my reading on magical trees. It's the sort of thing I, of all Mages, should have been able to remember. "I'm sorry," I said, "but, um, I mean, won't that take a while? We don't have much time left if we're to stop the Grey from getting to the Moonseer. He won't give up; he'll never give up."

The Sunmaker looked at me, still kneeling, his eyes level with mine.

I felt my cheeks flush, but more words jostled each other forward and pressed themselves out into the air as though they were tumbling suicidally down a sheer cliff. "We need to catch up with Richard quickly, and trees, uh, grow slowly. Well, I mean, all the ones I've ever met were pretty slow-growing, in the scheme of things. I'm sure your sense of time is different, though. Longer than mine is." My cheeks burned, and all the bits of my body that could clench did so, firmly.

The Maker smiled and shook his great boulder of a head. "Not this kind," he said in his booming voice. He sounded like an ox. Low, steady, and strong.

I still didn't understand.

"Harken," he said. "Can you not hear it growing?"

I closed my eyes and turned my head to listen. I heard nothing but the wind in the leaves and the crackle of the forge-fire. I felt ashamed, but when I stole sideways glances at Vi and Rennie, their expressions were as bewildered as mine.

The Sunmaker stood then, and towered over us. He smelled of soot and sweat and oil, and the heat of the forge of ages radiated from his skin. Without a word, he marched away in the direction of the forest whose boundary line met the edge of his garden. His long strides had already taken him quite a way, and we hurried to follow him.

The three of us went through the garden, where gigantic pumpkins lay awaiting harvest and fruit trees dripped with the year's bounty. Ahead, and growing quickly closer as we jogged toward it, the border of the forest reared up, a wall of night-time green and black. The Sunmaker was waiting for us at its edge and, as we grew near, he beckoned for us to follow.

As soon as we came under the trees, the light changed. Rather than dark and foreboding, as it had appeared from the outside, this forest was bright, awash with golden light that blazed down between the wide-spaced trees. As we ran, I saw deer bounding away, their tails flicking white as they leapt over the thick undergrowth. The air smelled golden, too, like yellow flowers, like freshly baked bread, like a lover's skin after sunbathing.

We came into a large clearing and stopped running. My moment of understanding had arrived.

Twenty-Five

The four of us stood at the edge of the clearing, side by side, catching our breath. The Sunmaker placed his hands on his broad hips and smiled with glowing pride.

"See?" he boomed.

"I do now," I said.

The tree was growing. And I know that all trees are growing, but they don't tend to grow visibly, in real time, as you watch. I felt like either my time had slowed dramatically so that I could now see such a thing as a tree growing, or the earth's tectonic plates moving, or the seasons changing in seconds, but when I looked away from the tree and saw that the rest of the world moved at the same speed as before, I knew that this *was* normal speed. It was just that this particular tree was growing unusually quickly. It was like watching time-lapse video footage of seedlings reaching for the light while their roots delve downward for water. The branches danced and twisted as they grew up and out and, with a rustling sound, the leaves grew long and flat, into ovals with pointed ends. They began as pale green knots, then darkened as they opened. Some of the knots became buds that then exploded into sprays of dark red flowers. Their fragrance hit me a minute later, and it was the smell of freshly spilled blood.

The Sunmaker laughed to see me so confounded.

"I've never seen anything like this," I said, still breathless. I resolved to work on my fitness, both physical and spiritual, once I was back home.

He smiled, showing teeth that were stained tea-and-tobacco brown, and dipped his head in the smallest of nods. "I imagine you have not," he said. He threw back his head and gave a resounding laugh that echoed among the trees like thunder, then clapped his hands together.

The tree, by now forty feet high at its topmost point, stopped growing. The leaves shivered in unison, as if they were together saying a Word.

The Sunmaker nodded and clapped his palms together again with a sound like a thunderclap.

Rennie drew in a deep breath. Her eyes widened. "I think I know what this is," she said, "though I've never seen one being Made before, only read about it."

The Sunmaker walked to the tree and laid both hands upon its trunk. He murmured some low sounds up into the canopy, and a single leaf fell. He turned to face us and held out his arms with the leaf carried in his open palms. It must have been three feet long, since it covered both of them. And it was growing and changing. As the Sunmaker held it, the leaf grew bigger and bigger, keeping its shape. It changed from a leaf into a bright green shield. He laid it down on the ground, then reached up to one of the tree's lowest hanging branches and snapped it off. He thrust the lower point of the branch into the earth so that it stood upright on its end, beside the shield. It changed too, growing straighter and slimmer. The leaves fell from it, and one end flattened out and tapered to a heinous point. The Sunmaker watched the change, concentrating deeply. His eyes searched the surface of the spear and the shield as if looking for flaws, examining them as he would artefacts he had just forged with his own hands. Which, of course, he had.

He plucked the spear from the ground and scrutinised it more closely. A smile slowly curved his lips, and his eyes glowed with blue fire. He held out the spear in front of him.

"Do you see?" he said.

The three of us nodded in unison.

"Good. Now, learn."

He picked up the shield from the ground. As he lifted it, holding its edge in one hand, he gave a flick of his wrist. The shield changed. Where it had before held a rigid shape, it now looked like silk. It rippled in the air as he brought his arm up over his head and around so that he draped the shield over his shoulders like a cloak. He gave a quick smile, lowered his head, crouched and covered himself.

"Do you see?" he said.

"Yes. Well, no," said Rennie. "You're quite invisible, darling. Bravo!"

A disembodied laugh came from the place where the Sunmaker had until recently been crouching. "We've no time for games now," he said, still invisible, then threw off the cloak, brought it up and over his head and flicked his wrist in the same manner as before, and the soft, flowing fabric became once again a leaf-shaped shield. He plunged its tip into the earth and stood up. "Your turn," he said.

The Sunmaker reached up into the tree and snapped off another branch, then another and another. He gathered them together, held them above his head, and flung them at us.

I felt a flash of terror as I saw the branches separate in mid-air so that they pointed at Rennie, Vi and I respectively. Heading straight for us, they were, on a collision course. A thought of barbeque skewers came into my mind. I stood idiotically for a split second before a force I could not control raised my arm to meet the branch that flew toward me. As soon as I wrapped my fingers around it, I felt the texture of the branch change. It was a spear now, still wooden but reinforced. It felt as hard as pitch-cured pine, and when I brought it down to examine it, I saw that its blade was fashioned from no material I had ever encountered. It was as dark as the long hairs I had seen strewn across the ground at the forge. It had a pattern deep within it that moved like flame fanned by a hot breeze blown from the firmament's vast bellows.

Rennie's spear had a bright red shaft and a flame-orange sheen to the blade, as befitting a Fire-Mage. She gazed at it fiercely, and her eyes glowed like embers.

I looked at Vi. He held in his hands what looked very much like a giant stick. I thought for a moment that perhaps his spear hadn't formed properly, that the magics had for some reason not worked as they were supposed to — but then I realised that this was far from the truth. His spear was *meant* to be a giant stick. It *had* to be. It was the kind of object you've seen a hundred golden Labradors carrying joyfully along forest paths or over beaches, a trophy clamped between grinning canine teeth. This, though, was a deadly weapon. The blade formed an extension of the shaft, a part of it that flattened out and then tapered to a point. It was off-white, like the fang of some huge and ancient wolf. I swelled with pride on Vi's behalf and tightened my grip on my own new Weapon.

Rennie was entranced by the play of blood-red fire along the shaft of her spear. Her eyes mirrored the darkness inside it, pulsing with impassioned flame as she explored every millimetre of its form. "This truly is a thing of wonder," she said.

The Sunmaker looked at her strangely. "It is a thing of grief," he corrected her. "A thing of heartbreak."

Rennie looked at him. Her eyes dulled briefly in a small gesture of contrition.

Vi held his spear to his side. It suited him, added something, perhaps just an intangible air of confidence I didn't usually credit him with. I chided myself internally.

The Sunmaker plucked three leaves from a low branch of the tree and held them in his open palm. He took a great, deep breath, and blew. The leaves tumbled and spiralled through the air and, just as the spears had done, one found its way to each of us.

I rested my spear on the ground — I didn't feel quite comfortable with shoving it into the earth — and caught the leaf, which by now had grown to about four feet in length, in both hands. It kept growing, and I felt its composition change and harden. A few seconds later, I stood with my left forearm threaded through the loops of leathery fibre that had grown on the back of the shield.

The Sunmaker looked at me. "Go on," he said. "Make a cloak."

I quailed at the thought of it. "Why me?"

"Because I say so."

I looked at Rennie and Vi. They held their shields as though they had carried these weapons for years and been saved by them in many battles. Neither of the bastards offered words of help, or stepped forward — which I desperately hoped at least Rennie would, show-off that she was — to do it in my stead. They just stood there, looking at me, and was that the tiniest smirk I saw at the corner of Vi's mouth?

I snorted in disapproval at being made an example of like this. Most unfair. Hesitantly, I un-hooked my arm from the fibrous loops and took the edge of the shield in my right hand. I was amazed by how lightweight it was. I took a deep breath and threw the shield up into the air above my head, trying to do my best version of the wrist-flick the Sunmaker had demonstrated. Instead of spinning and changing in the air, the shield simply hung there for a breath, then fell back to earth, hitting me square on the top of the head with a *clunk* before toppling off to one side and falling to the ground as lightly as spring blossom.

Everybody laughed.

Tears of embarrassment welled up in my eyes, but I didn't want to give up. I picked up the shield from where it lay at my feet and tried again. As it left my hand, I looked up. It began to change in the air above my head. The edges softened and furled inwards and the fabric rippled. I reached up and plucked the cloak from mid-air, took it in both hands, crouched, and covered myself.

Rennie squealed in delight. "You've *vanished*, darling!" she exclaimed.

"Really?"

"You're just a voice," said Vi. "It worked. Well done."

"Great!" I threw off the cloak, came to standing, and changed it back to a shield with the same flick of the wrist. It was easy now I'd done it once. Second nature. I practised the technique once more while Vi and Rennie had a go with theirs under the Sunmaker's supervision.

"Now we must go on," he said. The smiles faded from our faces as we remembered why we were doing all this.

The four of us gathered up our spears and shields and joined him at the edge of the clearing.

"I will come with you to the water," he said.

I was so relieved we had another joining our team, and one so strong, that I almost burst into tears. For the first time, I felt we had a real chance against the Mage-Killer: us lot with the Sunmaker, and the Council Mages together with the Moonseer. We needed all the might we could muster to be sure we would well and truly win this fight.

"Thank you," was all I could say.

TWENTY-SIX

The wind rose. Leaves whispered secrets to the branches, and the branches creaked in response. I looked up through a gap in the canopy: mottled clouds raced across the sky, heading inland. They strung grey banners that hung low over the treetops, announcing that rain would come. I couldn't have predicted when: the sky between them was bright — for now - and I was no diviner of Water weather.

I shivered. "We should get going. We need to catch up with Richard before he can do any more harm."

"A solid plan," said Vi, "assuming we can make up the distance. He'll be quite a way ahead of us by now."

"There's no point in hanging about here staying still and not chasing him then, is there?" I said, intending my voice to be softer and kinder than it came out. It was as soft and kind as a blow to the temple. Vi looked hurt. I sighed and shook my head. "Sorry, mate. We're on the same side; there was no need for me to speak to you that way." I took a breath and made sure to acknowledge the stillness after I exhaled. I felt calmer. "He is fast, but that's no reason to get discouraged."

"Mm," Rennie nodded in agreement. "My gut tells me that, rather than backtrack to the portal we all arrived through and risk the time it'd take him plus the likelihood of him bumping into us, he's heading for the quickest way to the Unseen Paths to force his way in somewhere along their line, which means he'll be paddling out into the bay as we speak."

"A fair assumption," said Vi, *"but make a new portal? I didn't* think that was possible."

"Well, it kind of is," Rennie said. "The Unseen Paths cannot be changed, and the existing portals are at the ends of them, like doors that lead to tunnels that cut through invisible mountains. But if one has the power and the know-how — which any fully-trained Mage most definitely does — one can create a new, temporary door. It's sort of like blasting a hole in a tunnel wall, if you catch my meaning. Or even blasting an entirely new tunnel — being careful, of course, that you don't blow up the whole mountain," she added. For the briefest of moments, she looked like she was tempted to do just that: make a nice big Fire-y explosion.

Vi nodded calmly, thinking it over. I still wasn't quite convinced and, narrowing my eyes, I felt my lips purse just the slightest bit.

"Oh, don't look so *depressed* about it, Ernie. Trust you to be a misery-guts!" Rennie laughed. She pushed unruly locks of hair back from her face, adopted her most faux-tolerant facial expression, and gave a nonchalant wave of her new spear that made it look like she'd had it for ages, like a pair of worn-out old shoes, and had grown weary of carrying it about with her, cramping her style. "Ouch!" she snapped, and glared at it. "If I'm not mistaken it just bit me."

"What did?" Vi said.

"This damned thing," Rennie said, looking sulkily at her Weapon. She shook it a couple of times.

I felt the cold glow of Schadenfreude and enjoyed it as covertly as I could manage.

"Fred did not like to be mocked or belittled," said the Sunmaker. "Nor do these Weapons. Be kind to them and they shall treat you in the same regard. Disrespect, too, shall be repaid in kind."

This was brilliant. Rennie looked suspiciously at her spear and shield. Unease tensed her features.

"Let's get to the beach then, in that case," I said, inexplicably keen to get soaked to the skin all of a sudden. Not at all because I just wanted to see Rennie get told off again, of course.

"This way," the Sunmaker said, pointing across the clearing in the direction of the bay. "There is a path. Steep, yes, dangerous, yes, but we may walk it." He beckoned with the arm holding his Weapon and made off at a pace the rest of us would be hard pressed to match. As he turned away from the new-grown tree, he spoke some Words to it and underlined them with a click of his fingers. The tree burst into flames.

Fortunately, considering the suddenness of the eruption, the rest of us were not within range. I felt the red-orange surge in both my physical and non-physical bodies and was sure I'd have been history on all planes had I been any nearer.

I gave the burning tree a respectably wide berth. As I passed, I saw a horse's head rear up in the smoke as it rose into the air, dark and terrible. An eye opened and held me for a moment, and I felt a strange pull backward at the same time as I walked on. I shook my head, returned my gaze to the direction my feet were going, and carried on across the clearing and into the trees on the other side, following the Sunmaker's veering path to the cliff's edge.

He was striding ahead of us, already some distance away. I ran in his wake, with Vi and then Rennie to the rear of me. I felt afraid to be at the front of our little crew, but the Maker's power exhilarated me. I gained courage from seeing his great strides forward and feeling the earth tremble beneath the soles of his boots. He did not look back to gauge our positions or examine our faces for hints of emotion, but I could sense that he knew where we were and what we were feeling. Perhaps I was merely projecting, but I, too, felt the keen stab and the ensnaring embrace of grief. I felt a connection to the Sunmaker that I did not share with the others, who had not lost on the same level as he or I had. Neither Vi nor Rennie had chanced to have such closeness with another being that to lose it could make you wish for death, Vi because of his shyness and Rennie due to her incapacity for deep feeling about anything or anyone much besides herself. I let this sensation, the gorgeous intimacy of loss, spur me onward. Long grasses brushed across the leather of my boots, dappled light touched my skin for tiny moments, and my spear felt strong and lethal in my hand.

After a while, the land began to dip downward. The edge of the forest, and therefore also the cliff, felt close.

When I got there, I saw that the path had not yet lost us much height. We stood high above the sea, and the waves had that innocuous, miniature look they do from a vantage point.

The Sunmaker stood just behind the final row of trees before the land fell away, scanning the horizon. The ribbons of cloud that moved overhead while we stood by the glade had passed inland and out of sight, and now high puffs of white floated far above, moving on a slow wind. Beyond and below, the marigold disc of sun lowered to meet the steel grey sea. I was not heartened; it felt like the lull before a great tempest that boils up out of nowhere, or perhaps rises from the water itself.

Standing at the Sunmaker's side, I drank in this false tranquillity.

"There," he said, pointing.

I looked out over the ocean, into the glow of the lowering sun. I squinted, and raised my free hand to shield my eyes while I searched the dark water for any sign of what he had seen. "I can't see anything," I said, blinking at the sun's glare.

"Follow the line of my arm exactly."

I stood on tiptoes to try and match the line as closely as my stature would allow. My calf and shin muscles protested, and I stood down flat again, frustrated at how unfit I was. I rubbed my eyes and looked once more.

My eyes were watering, and the sunlight was still too bright, but I could see something. In the far distance, it looked like the water itself was afire.

"That it? I can see a kind of glow over there, but it could just be the light of the sun on the water. It looks like it's burning, but it's probably just a reflection." I shook my head and blinked the glare away again. "Like a mirage, or something. It's just a trick of the light."

"No," the Sunmaker said. "You are correct. Something is happening over there."

I took my attention back to that bright place far out. My eyes streamed. I wiped them dry. I looked again. The weird glow seemed, if anything, to have spread. I hoped I didn't have a migraine coming on, but knew, no sooner had I entertained this thought, that I wouldn't have to worry about that. I had far, far more to worry about.

"Oh shit, is that *him?*" The pit of my stomach sank as it churned. "Is he through?"

"Run to the water," the Sunmaker urged and launched himself along the path that went tumbling over the edge and down.

I leapt and skidded down the zigzagging path with all the energy I could summon. Every few seconds, I glanced out at the water, but could not see anything because the sun still shone into my face. I was glad of it, in the end, as it forced me to keep my eyes on the path.

The path itself was no more than a rough line of bare patches strung together by fortunate accident rather than by dint of any planning, its edges picked out with occasional clumps of sea-grass that anchored the loose sand in place. It was dotted with worn, ancient shells belonging to a cornucopia of sea-dwelling creatures, some of which I recognised and many I did not. Spikes of sun-bleached antler, presumably from the more adventurous of the forest deer, jutted upward from buried skulls, hard white branches that threatened to snag my clothing and trip me up. I managed to jump over them, only once clipping the toe of my boot on a protruding spur and almost falling forward.

We reached the bottom of the cliff and gathered there in the shade, letting the breeze dry the sweat from our foreheads. A long, dark cloud had momentarily covered the sun, so I could look more easily out to sea. I saw it then. Or, I should say, I saw them. Flashes of light on the water. The bad feeling that had lurked in my lower belly most of the time over the past few days, the part of me that did not adapt well to rapid change, reasserted itself with vigour. I rested my shield and spear on the ground, gave my abdomen a rub and my arms a stretch. It felt good. This prompted the others to do the same and we spent a moment tending to our aches and twinges. I then felt self-conscious as I saw the scene from the outside. I imagined we'd win a competition for most bizarre workout video, should such a thing exist, and couldn't resist a half-smile.

The ground shuddered. I looked out over the water and saw a great plume rise from its surface.

"He is fighting the Sea," said the Sunmaker.

"Arrogant wanker," I said.

"He must be trying to create a portal under the water," Rennie said. "He won't manage it, especially since he failed to get the Sunmaker to help him." She sniffed in derision at the exact moment another explosion rocked the land and sent a column of water skyward. It was a long way off, but I could have sworn I heard the individual droplets splashing back down into their Element again.

I raised one eyebrow. "You sure about that?" I said as I picked up my spear and shield.

"Come on, Ern," she said, giving me a clap on the shoulder. It was the shoulder of my right arm, the one whose hand held the spear, which growled at her, channelling my irritation. She recoiled, looking suitably affronted.

I looked back out to sea and grinned for a microsecond, keeping my face turned away from her, then reinstalled my studied scowl as I turned back and met her gaze levelly.

She muttered to herself, then said something under her breath. I presumed it was a swear word, since she yelped in pain and threw her spear onto the beach.

"That thing doesn't like me," she said, rubbing the palm of her hand.

"No harm done, mate," I said. "It didn't draw blood, look. Just apologise and pick it up again."

She looked at the spear, which I'd have sworn would be flicking her a V sign if it had fingers. She gave a sigh that any sulky teenager would have envied, and rolled her eyes. "Sorry, spear," she said and bent to pick it up again, her hand hesitating over it before she closed her grip. "I didn't mean it." I hoped the spear did not have a keen ear for insincerity.

The Sunmaker broke away from us and walked down to the top of the last ridge of sand before the land yielded to water. The rest of us followed and the four of us stood in a row on the beach, holding our shiny new Weapons, waiting for something to happen.

The ground gave another, even more momentous shudder, hurling yet more of the ocean upward about a mile offshore. Dark shapes rose inside the plume of water, ethereal forms coalescing into tentacles and fins and then melting away into formlessness. A rising wail spiralled up and then reverberated, lowering, into a deep vibration. It felt as though something was being mustered, drawn together. Then, with a great bang like a door being slammed shut, it was over. The sky lightened and the sea felt less turbulent, though to our physical eyes it had not changed. The wind cut across its surface, whipping up sharp waves flecked with white foam.

We stood and listened to the sounds of air and water for a while. I held my breath, willing the waves to keep gently crashing, a spell against further signs of Richard's attempt to wrestle the Sea into submission. I started breathing again and waited a little longer, until I was sure-ish that he had not managed to pierce his way through. He'd always enjoyed weakening the strong. He was just a bully, when all was said and done.

"I don't think he made it through," I said. "It'd not be this quiet otherwise. He must be off to try somewhere else."

"Where does that leave us?" said Vi.

"At an advantage," the Sunmaker said. "He is out there on the water and will be weakened by his failure. This is the perfect time for you to hunt him."

Hunt? Oh, shit. Here it was. My time of reckoning. And I don't mind admitting I was absolutely bloody petrified. "Right now?" I said.

"Yes."

"Are you sure that's wise? I mean, do we *have* to go all the way out there where it's so wet and chilly?" I said, inclining my head towards the water, which looked more ominous to me by the second.

The Sunmaker turned and pointed to a place on the cliffs. "Look there," he said.

He was pointing at a spot that I judged to be a hundred feet or so past the forge. He drew a line in the air with his fingertip. "Do you see that dark stripe in the rocks?"

I did. There was an interruption in the strata, as though someone had sliced through layers of sponge cake and icing and slid one side of the cut so that the layers no longer matched. "Ah, a fault."

"Indeed," he said. "It is rare that the line of an Unseen Path is visible in the material world, but there we are. The portal you came through is directly above it, on top of the cliff, and if you look—" he traced the line of the fault down to the foot of the cliff, along the steep, narrow strip of beach that clung to its base and out into the water.

I was dismayed to see that he was pointing to precisely where plumes of water had been sent up a few moments earlier. He paused there and then continued to move his finger in a diagonal line across the water and to the headland on the other side of the bay.

"The quickest way to the Path is over water," the Maker said. "By land would take three times longer."

"I see," Vi said. "That's why he's gone that way, I suppose. But how are we going to follow him? We don't have a boat and not even I am a particularly strong distance swimmer."

The Sunmaker laughed and the sea and the sky laughed with him. "Yes, you do have a boat," he said. He broke away from us and began to walk down the deep, curved shelf of sand that dropped the land down to the sea.

The three of us watched him go. I observed the way that each step made him sink down into the dry sand, and heard the crunch of desiccated seaweed that marked each of the many high tide points under the soles of his boots as he pressed it deeper into its pale golden bed. He held his arms at his sides, slightly bent at the elbows, muscles flexing as he walked.

Rennie, Vi, and I looked at each other.

"S'pose we should go after him," I said. "He looks serious."

We followed him down the slope like a gaggle of school kids on a day trip, plodding along behind a teacher.

The sea looked wild. It had appeared benign from higher up, above the leavings of even the highest storm-tides, but now, closer, I could see how dangerous it was. The steep incline of the beach meant that the waves reared up suddenly, close to the shoreline. Each breaker made the earth vibrate as it crashed down and surged forward before the foam fizzed like the bubbles in a sparkling wine freed from thick glass, and the brave edge of the water was quickly sucked back to the deep. The waves came up sudden and high, and I saw silhouetted ribbons of seaweed inside them, held up against the sky. The water had the texture of cold liquid metal. In our favour, the steep incline of the beach meant that the calm water just behind where the breakers formed was close — but there was the raw power of the twelve-foot waves to contend with first. I knew to dive straight forward, rather than try to jump and reach the crest, if we had to swim, but I didn't want to get wet again so soon and have to pull myself, heavy with clothing, through deep, indifferent water.

The Sunmaker looked out to sea. "Do you see where the gulls circle, over yonder? That is the direction to which you must hold."

I did. A column of wheeling birds hung over the water about half a mile out into the bay, and the headland lay much further off, directly behind them. It looked an impossible distance to cross wearing boots and leggings and the vaguely sensible jacket I'd picked out before I'd had any inkling about our impending adventures. I felt as though the boundary between myself and what I must do was not a tangible line between possible and impossible, but rather a subtle reconfiguration of the Universe that meant I could neither understand nor speak Her words to ask for safe passage.

"I do, yes," I said, "but how do we get all the way out there? And you said we had a boat. Sorry, but I can't see one anywhere." I looked along the shoreline in both directions again, just to be sure, and saw no tell-tale humps of green tarpaulin.

"Fear not," the Maker said. He knelt down on the sand, bringing his face level with mine. He laid his spear on the beach and took up his shield in both hands, holding it flat. He closed his eyes and hummed low notes that stayed in the air, stretching and intertwining into a deep song. The shield began to grow, lengthening and broadening, until it got too big for him to hold above the ground, and he placed it down.

Thirty seconds later, I was looking at a green, spearhead-shaped boat. It had the same elongated oval shape, but the line of the leaf's central vein had deepened into an inverted ridge. I walked along its length, admiring it, then touched the outside of the hull. It had the warmth of wood and the coldness of iron. A gust of wind blew, and it trembled like a silver birch leaf, but did not tip over.

The Maker looked on proudly while I examined the vessel. He nodded. "Are you ready?"

I nodded back.

"Then get in."

TWENTY-SEVEN

The boat sat high in the water, light as air and quivering with energy. For the first time in as long as I could remember, I found myself filled with courage and looking forward to the fight that awaited me. I don't think I had been this brave even before I'd lost most of what I valued and thrown away the rest. Coming back to a new house that was starting to feel like mine, to a group that I could belong to, I felt a new trust, the trust that comes from liking oneself enough to heal.

I climbed in and took a place at the bow. Holding my spear in my left hand and the shield hooked over my forearm, I gripped the edge of the boat with my right hand and ran my thumb tip along the surface just below the gunwale on the inside. I had no idea what the thing was Made of. I shrugged; it didn't matter.

Vi and Rennie clambered in behind me. Vi, though man-formed, channelled the energy of an exuberant Spaniel. He looked around excitedly and I felt like it was taking him some considerable effort not to bark and howl at the sky. Rennie looked less enthused; she hunkered down and made herself small. Her shield lay at her feet. Her eyes met mine for a moment, and I saw how their flame was dampened. All that water in such a short space of time, and not a drop of Flame of Health for miles around; it must have been exhausting. She held her spear loosely, as though she didn't entirely trust it after their altercations. The feeling was probably mutual.

"When all this is over," she chuntered, "I'm going on holiday somewhere *hot.*"

"You'll have earned it, mate," I said, and smiled at her. I turned to look out to sea, but could not see past the line of breaking waves. On the water they were fearsome, rearing up sharply over the steep beach and towering high before beginning to curl over at the top and press forward toward the land. The sky held a few birds, but their cries were hidden by the sound of the waves forming and crashing, forming and crashing, forming and crashing.

The Sunmaker stood waist-deep in water, holding the boat steady.

"Come on then; there's room," I shouted over the fizz and roar of the breaking waves.

He shook his head.

That comfortable old sick feeling burst through its flimsy curtain of bravery and gripped my guts with bony fingers I knew too well. I could not help but let anguish show in my face. "What? I thought you were coming with us?" I cried, feeling like a naïve little girl who had been manipulated by a promise that was never meant.

"I did," the Sunmaker said. "I am here. But I cannot come any further. Without a familiar, I am too vulnerable."

"Great," I said.

Rennie just glared at him.

He raised his eyebrows and we were duly scolded. He was different. Far removed from an ordinary Mage and more powerful than me and Rennie put together, plus Vi — plus the whole bloody Seven Clans, actually — and we all knew it.

The Sunmaker smiled. "Without the strength of my Fred beside me, I am greatly depleted until his heir grows from the skeleton of the burned tree, as he did years ago, after his father had passed. That will take some time and, until then, I must nurture him without respite. I must stay close to the forge, in any case; it is my home," he said. "And I must see to the Falcons."

"Fair enough," I said. I hadn't noticed any Falcons about, and I keenly regretted not looking harder.

"Now," he said, "hold on, you three little ones."

I felt ridiculous sitting cross-legged at the bow with Vi and Rennie behind me, clinging to the sides of the boat. I'd hoped I wouldn't be messing about in such a vessel again so soon after Wilbur's funeral, but I suspected that this one, though technically a giant leaf, was more sea-worthy than the heap of junk that lazed on the shore near the House and which had carried us just fine.

I laid down my spear and held on as instructed, and the Maker took in a great deep breath and pushed the boat into the water. I felt a thrill of excitement and fear when the water took the weight of the boat and a surge of relief when it didn't immediately fill with water that seeped through the leaf-vein patterned joins between its planks. I prayed to any gods who may have been listening that it would hold far enough to get us where we needed to go, and pushed away questions about exactly how things would work once we got there. A question that did occur to me, perhaps a little too late, was how we'd propel and steer it.

"Hey, did he give either of you any oars?" I said over my shoulder. I tried to keep my tone light, but the horrified look on Rennie's face exploded like a giant firework. "Oh no—" I started to say, then I looked ahead just in time to see a huge wave rear up right in front of me. It seemed to hover, a gigantic, heavy wall of clear, steel-cold water. I just had time to breathe in before the Sunmaker, who had waded out until the water came up to his barrel-like chest, shoved the boat forward again, pushing us right through the wave and clean out the back of it as it pulled away. We even got some air-time over the low water behind it.

We clipped the top of the smaller wave that followed and landed gently down on calmer water. I heard the rush and crash as the waves broke on the shore behind us, understood that we were through that gauntlet and that the boat was not going to get swamped, and I screamed in acknowledgement and release of how afraid I'd been. As the sound faded, it made way for a fresh wave of fear of what now lay ahead and, as if in response, a vibration resonated through the water. I realised that I had been secretly hoping the leaf-boat would sink just offshore, thwarting our mission, so I would not have to face Richard. It was too late now though, for the shore was growing further away by the second.

꙰

The boat continued forward on the energy the Maker's push had given. I expected it to slow at any moment, but it did not; it travelled as though drawing on a reserve of fuel from somewhere invisible. Air from the firmament's bellows, perhaps. The bow cut the water like a honed blade and the vessel skipped over the peaks of the gentle waves that undulated on the surface of the deep, black sea. I peered over the edge. The water was inscrutable.

I looked behind me: Vi and Rennie had regained their composure and looked, though not keen, at least resigned to what was happening. As the boat slid along in a perfectly straight line, the three of us looked at each other, lost for words.

"Guess we didn't need oars after all," I said, shrugging.

"Guess not," said Rennie. She placed her spear gently, respectfully, in the bottom of the boat and rubbed her palms together. I noticed that the ends of her fingers had gone pale. That was funny; I'd never thought of her as one for sluggish circulation. Then, I wondered, how often must she get cold?

Under different circumstances, I'd have admired the beauty of this landscape: the curve of the bay, shaped like a crescent moon; the vast pale sky; the light that sprinkled everything it touched with golden dust. I cast my gaze around to take in the wide sweep of the bay. On the side we had launched from, the cliffs were high and forest-topped. Their sheer grey walls scooped a perfect curve that cupped the bay, giving the Sunmaker's cottage and forge their superior vantage point. The cliffs stayed high most of the way round, until, approaching the headland, they slowly shallowed their incline and gave way to lower, grassy hills dotted with a few stands of deciduous trees. I so wanted to roam the fields and the woodland, study the earth there and look for mushrooms and rare meadow flowers. I looked up at the sky where the sinking sun hung like a great lantern, illuminating the cloud in rainbow streamers.

Rennie pointed ahead of us with a quivering, bloodless fingertip. "Look."

I peered over the side of the boat. "What in all the Elements is this?"

It had been impossible to see from the shore, or else the tide was going out very quickly indeed, but the water beneath was paling as land rose beneath it.

"Is that a sandbank?"

"What?" said Vi, crawling forward to join me at the bow.

Rennie braced herself and stood up.

"Yeah," she said. "It is, and if we don't watch out, we're going to—"

As the prow of the boat nudged sand, she toppled forward and landed on top of Vi and I.

"Ooof!" she said. "Sorry."

"It's alright," I said. "We broke your fall. You're welcome."

The three of us sat there for a few moments before Vi pierced our stupor. "Should we maybe, er, you know—"

"What?"

"Do something to avoid getting beached? I wouldn't be surprised if this were another trap."

The three of us picked up our spears. "On three," Vi said. "One, two, three! Push!"

We pushed. Far from simply plunging into the soft sand, our spears held against its surface as though it were stone or wood and succeeded in pushing the prow of the boat off the sandbank's shallow slope. We began to move again immediately, still under the influence of the Sunmaker's immense magic.

I kept an eye out to make sure we were staying far enough away to avoid running aground again. When I was satisfied we were clear, I looked ahead to where a tiny figure in a tiny boat was advancing landward.

"We're closing on him," announced Vi, his voice grim. "I just hope we're not too late."

We were about two hundred yards from the shore. I could see Richard's boat pulled up onto the sand and his trail of boot-prints leading off up the beach towards the shallow cliff that loomed over it. Leaving my spear and shield in the bottom of the boat, I began to stand so I could get a better look, but was glad to still be crouching when the leaf-boat was rocked by an explosion.

"Bloody hell, he's at it again," I sighed as a huge amount of sand was thrown into the air from a spot at the base of the cliff. I quickly checked the location of the Path by tracking the fault line from the cliffs beneath the Maker's cottage in a straight di-agonal through the bay and past the sandbank. There was an-other blast, big enough to shower us with wet sand, and this time we were close enough to hear the rage-fuelled Words he was using in his attempt.

"He doesn't seem to be getting far," Vi observed drily before he Changed, ready for the chase.

"Good," huffed Rennie. "He'll be sorry when I catch up with him, that's all I can say. I'm *freezing*."

We hit the beach, jumped out, and pulled the boat far enough up its slope to be sure it wouldn't get pulled back into the water. I spitefully toyed with the idea of pushing Richard's boat out to sea, then realised this would make him more likely to nick ours, and thought better of it. I said a prayer of thanks to the Sunmaker. "See you soon, I hope," I whispered to the leaf-boat. I grabbed my spear and shield and the three of us began to walk towards the cliffs. Here, they were not the rugged wall they were beneath the Sunmaker's cottage, but a shallower incline dotted with scrub and I could see a patch of sparse woodland at the top.

A shudder rocked the ground we stood on and faded to a low rumble.

"We need to move fast," I said.

"Ye—es," said a horribly familiar voice. "You do. What a dreadful choice. To simply await death, or to court it, knowing its inevitability?"

I spun around.

All I saw were the beach, the boats a little way off and, beyond, the sea, with the light of the late afternoon sun glittering on its surface. Nobody was there. Clearly, I'd lost it. I could have sworn I'd heard Richard's voice, but he was over by the cliff, wasn't he? I shook my head, wiped sweat from my forehead and swept loose strands of hair from my face.

"Did you hear that?" I waited a few seconds for a reply, but received none. "Guys?" I turned back to my companions.

Vi and Rennie were frozen, statue-like. Their facial expressions were caught mid-way to surprise: mouths slightly open, eyes widening, whatever words or sounds they had thought up not yet formed.

"Rens? Vi?" I touched Rennie's sleeve and squeezed the arm beneath it. Nothing. I bent and touched Vi's head and prodded his nose, which I knew he hated. Nothing there either.

I heard that voice on the air again as a laugh that came from far away. Then, as I stared helplessly at my friends while I imagined having to get them into the boat and back to the shore like this, there came a great ripping and tearing sound from behind me. A hand grabbed my arm and pulled.

I was yanked off my feet and flew backwards, but through sheer stubbornness managed to keep hold of my weapons. Vi and Rennie's frozen expressions were pulled away, and suddenly I saw the whole world through a filter. It was as though dusk was suddenly falling, but through the smoky blue-grey I saw that the sun still hovered above the horizon. Sound had gone funny, too; the sea now whispered through a thickness, damped as if by a barrier made from cotton wool.

I understood then. This was what the whole world would look like if he got his way. No light, no shadow, just endless grey. It was horrifyingly familiar, a blanket of depression. My resolve was renewed: I would do anything I could to stop this numbness from smothering the world.

I pulled myself to my feet, and turned. There he was. There the fucker was. Right behind me.

"How—?" I said, the word dribbling out of my gaping mouth like the last drops of blood before death.

Richard grinned. "I simply crept up on you." Cold arrogance strained his voice, made his eyes the hardest blue. "While you indulged in sentimentality"—he gestured with the sweep of an arm at the bay, the sky, the sea — "I merely availed myself of your distraction. Really, Earthfield, I am *shocked* at your lack of attentiveness. You're not the Mage I once so respected."

"Oh, save it for someone who gives a shit." I had to try not to let him rile me or I'd be at even more of a disadvantage. But I was riled. Oh, I was riled.

Richard smiled through perfect teeth. A fake smile beneath malicious eyes. He raised his left arm in front of him and held it out at chest height. Wrapped around his hand and wrist was what looked like a bunch of metallic ribbons. They moved as satin would in a breeze, rippling like pennants hung to welcome a victorious warrior home. Blood dripped from their bladed tips onto the sand, and was that horse-hair I saw tangled up in the metal in places? My stomach lurched.

I braced myself: if this was going to be it, I didn't want to go out unaware of what was happening.

Richard laughed, a thin, high sound. He leapt into the air. I barely had time to raise my shield and spear before he bore down on me. The metallic ribbons had turned to thrashing blade-tipped arms, and now they sought me.

I ducked down behind the shield, keeping the spear by my side. I wanted to jab out with it, stab him, stab anything, but was reduced to cowering beneath my gifted shell. Five years without combat training came to a humiliating climax in that moment. Furious with myself, I spat onto the sand, braced my legs, and pushed myself to standing, keeping the shield in place as protective cover but reaching the spear around to thrust it forward. Unexpectedly, it made skinfall, causing Richard to yelp in surprise. I sensed him jump backward out of my reach, and I retracted the spear.

He screamed a command. The shield was wrenched away from me so powerfully I felt it might take my arm along with it. My forearm slid from the straps, and I watched as my protector was flung, spinning, through the air. It landed on the sand some way off, hard to see in the grey murk and impossible for me to retrieve.

The bladed thing, moving without need of instruction from its master, scuttled towards me across the sand like a murderous octopus with additional limbs. Richard stood back, watching, a malevolent grin broadening across his face.

Keeping my eyes on the silvery abomination, I stepped backward down the slope of the beach until my feet splashed into the water. I felt my boots begin to sink. Down they went, about four inches into the wet sand.

Richard clicked his fingers, and the many-armed beast became limp and hung in the air, its knife-blades gently swaying.

"I think I shall finish you off with my own hands. It is the honourable way, after all," he said as he strode towards me.

Despite my fear, I scoffed. What did he know about honour?

He ran at me then, punched me square on the bridge of the nose with a *crack*, and spun away and back up the incline. This was embarrassing more than anything, though an inconvenient spot to be hit. My eyes watered, and I wiped tears away as he laughed at me from his vantage point on the drier sand. He then took off, running up the beach in the direction of the shallow-sloped cliffs.

I still had hold of my spear and gripped it tightly for reassurance. "Can I count on you, mate?" I muttered under my breath, and energy pulsed from my Weapon into my hand. I glanced at where the frozen Vi and Rennie still stood on the beach, at the high tide line, just visible through the grey fog Richard had created. I wondered how I'd get back to them if I made it through this — which was looking increasingly unlikely. And, if I did, how the bloody hell I'd un-freeze them I had no idea. I'd have to deal with that when — if — I got back in one piece.

I took a deep breath, let it out, and ran.

Through the grey, I saw that Richard hadn't stopped at the foot of the cliff, as I'd expected, to continue his attempts to break into the Path. He was scrambling upward, I assumed to try a new place to enter, perhaps even by drilling down from above. I had no choice but to follow him, so I willed my aching legs to carry on, and put all my energy into the pursuit. I held the spear in my right hand. It turned out to be a very effective clambering aid, and I was able to take long strides and haul myself up the scrub-covered slope without falling so much as once. I hoped my Weapon wasn't offended to be temporarily repurposed as a hiking pole. I wanted badly to glance back and check on my friends, but could neither spare the seconds it would take to do so, nor risk turning my attention away from the chase. I continued my ascent of the crumbling cliff held together by strong-rooted bushes, breathing hard.

I reached the top, stumbling onto a springy bed of long grasses. Keeping hold of the spear, I tumbled forward, once, then pushed myself upright.

Richard left me no time to prepare a defence and ran at me again across the green clifftop, this time jumping into a flying kick.

He imagined me an easy target, no doubt, but I used my feet as roots to support me while I crouched, aimed and stabbed the spear in the direction of his groin. I thrust forward then pulled back, and his shriek told me I'd made contact. He fell to the side, rolled over the soft ground, and leapt up again. Just a surface wound.

"Bollocks," I said to myself, then couldn't resist a snigger. I then realised I'd sent root energy through my feet on purpose for the first time in years, quite easily in fact. I felt dizzy at this revelation, and swayed.

Richard stood and raised his arms to shoulder height. He spoke a Word then — I should have expected it, really.

The knife-armed metal monster, which was wrapped around his forearm like a collection of lethally unpleasant bangles, came back to life and scurried my way. I had a brief vision of my own shredded face, but the thing curled into a tight ball and hit me in the solar plexus. The force of the blow made me somersault backward, and I was momentarily taken back to that afternoon in the pub when a kind, gentle friend had jumped, dog-formed, up onto the chair beside mine, as though the important bits of my life were about to flash before my eyes.

I landed on my feet on the edge of the clifftop, the blow cushioned by the earth and vegetation, but one gust of wind could knock me backwards and send me tumbling all the way down to the beach. Miraculously, I was still holding the spear. I glanced down at the frozen, shadowy Vi and Rennie, wishing they'd been able to see me execute that back-flip. Now who was the show-off?

Richard spoke another Word, but this time I was prepared. At the moment his mouth opened, I spoke one of my own. The two clashed in mid-air, causing an explosion that startled some of the gulls circling overhead — though most of them were un-perturbed, the hard bastards.

We ran at each other, jumped, and locked in mid-air, each screaming a mix of expletives and Words. Crashing back down onto the ground, we wrestled to an audience of crickets, rolling through long grass and to the edge of a patch of hardy clifftop trees. I lost my spear somewhere along the way and only real-ised this when Richard was above me and I felt his hands around my neck.

My hair was matted and tangled across my face, threatening to help my enemy in his task, but I was glad because it stopped me from seeing him, stopped me from being able to look into his eyes. I felt my strength begin to ebb away and, with one last desperate effort, I prised his fingers from my throat, let go with my right hand — the stronger one — and punched upward, try-ing to hook my thumb into his left eye socket. I dug in, but he pulled his head away. This movement allowed me to twist so I could push him off me, and I rolled away from him and jumped to my feet.

He wiped the trickle of blood from the small wound my thumbnail had made to the skin on the inside corner of his left eye, and held up his fingers to show it to me. "Nice try," he said, shaking his head slowly in feigned disappointment, and grinned horribly before advancing upon me again.

I made to punch him in the head, but changed stance at the last split second so I could instead land a blow to his throat. He let out a weird, strangulated cry and staggered backwards a couple of paces, allowing me to repay him the punch he'd ad-ministered to my nose. Still bloody sore, that was.

My pettiness proved costly. He took hold of my wrist and twisted my arm up behind my back so painfully that I had to drop to my knees on the ground.

"You fucking bastard!" I screamed up into his bloodied face as he loomed over me, still grinning that horrible grin that didn't reach his cold eyes. He kept twisting my arm up and back, forcing me fully down. I lay on my front, trying to press myself up with my free arm, but he bore down on me with all his strength, and it was too much. He placed a knee in the small of my back, still twisting my arm so hard I thought he might dislocate my shoulder. I cried out in pain through gritted teeth, and he placed his free hand on the side of my head and pushed down, and down, and down into the yielding earth. By the Makers, did he mean to bury me alive?

"Your time has come, Earthfield," he said softly. "Give up this fight. You're better off dead, eh? Reunited with those you miss. Elias, for example."

At the sound of Elias's name from his murderer's lips, something happened. Something that hadn't happened in an awfully long time. I felt the merest whisper of a tingle at the base of my spine: I was Changing, and I knew I wouldn't be able to stop it.

It had been so long that a part of me didn't recognise the sensation at first, but then a deep understanding rippled through me. I started to panic, which didn't help as I was fearing for my life. For a few seconds, as I lay there close to asphyxiation and partial dismemberment, a part of me actually *resisted*. It wanted to go back to the partial life I had been living: a life without risk, a life without vulnerability, a life chopped and sawn and pollarded, but it was soon overtaken by the simple desire to accept life, in all its nuance.

A wave of energy shot all the way up my spine, and it felt so beautifully, openly tree-ish that, against my fear, I opened up to it. And, after that first surge, I chose to shape this sensation into something I could use.

Richard sensed it begin, and his grip loosened involuntarily. "No," he spat, pressing down again. "No, you are *weak*. You are *afraid*. You are *nothing*," grimacing as he emphasised these words.

But the ripple spread and grew. Exhilaration overtook anxiety; the joy of being whole again overtook the grief of past losses, and then my body began to Change. My strength was enough now to push myself up onto my knees and then stand.

Richard's eyes widened. "No!" he protested, and his hands looked for purchase on my shoulders, then around my neck, then, pointlessly, he tried to pull at my hair as I grew taller. But my mind and body were working together, and they were unstoppable. I sensed lengthening as my hair twisted and sought the sun. My body broadened and toughened, becoming stout, upright. Roots grew from the soles of my feet and quested downward.

Richard Grey shrieked at me to stop, stop this, and he clung to me in desperation, digging the tips of his fingers into my hardening skin as his feet left the ground. I felt him as no more than a mild irritation: a weevil; a waspling. My roots pushed down and down, working ways between the long roots of coastal grass and scrub. When they found the deep, dark Earth beneath, I spoke Words to draw its power upward, all the way through my body. When it reached my fingertips, leaves sprouted along every strand of what had been my hair. I laughed, and it was a quivering of green that elevated to a bellow.

Richard's fingers were struggling to maintain purchase, and he screamed, his face contorted in denial. My arms, then, I gathered at my chest, my fingers I splayed, and, at the last moment before my skin turned to beech bark and my bones became Mineral-hard, I pushed forward and out, shredding my adversary's body. Pieces of him flew in all directions and, his spell broken, the grey haze dissipated and was blown away on the sea breeze. The light was clear and bright.

It was only a matter of seconds before the first gulls were on the scene to enjoy this unexpected feast. I was glad; it saved me needing to do any tidying. I simply stood, enjoying the feel of the wind through my branches and the sun on my bark and leaves.

A few minutes later, Rennie and a man-formed Vi appeared at the clifftop. They ran to me, breathless from the climb, their faces lit up with happiness only mildly spoiled by the grisly scene that met them, and threw their arms around me.

"Magnificent, darling!" Rennie exclaimed between breaths, looking up into my canopy, her tears of joy evaporating as they ran onto her cheeks. "You did it!"

Vi simply held me. I felt his breath as he said something, but he spoke so quietly I didn't catch the words.

"Ta," I said in a rustling of leaves. I thought perhaps I should be making a speech or something at this momentous juncture, but when it came to it, that one word was all I could manage.

I was tired; it would take me a while to get used to my Change-Form after so long, but the feeling was so overwhelmingly good that I kept it going a while longer. I knew I'd have to heal my wounded body, but I could do that back at the House.

My House. I was keen to know how the cat was recovering and to help Eric with his studies. From the Hearth room, I could work my way through the ale stores, plan one of my legendary Yule parties, find my own little patch in the garden where I could go and be a tree any time I wanted — but all that could wait, for now.

It was enough, right then, just to be my full self again.

Acknowledgements

Here I give profound and joyful gratitude to all who have supported this journey.

In terms of two-legged beings, thank you so much Marc, Auds and Andy for reading various drafts and holding space for my frequent existential crises, and Chris, KeiKei and Nina for being very patient friends indeed. Thank you also to my tutors on the Creative Writing MA, for their feedback on the opening of this book and on other projects. Having flawed work taken seriously through the stages of its development is important.

Many four-legged beings have also been involved, principally my cats Merlin (not very smart, but miles of emotional depth and healing ginger boi energy) and Willow (smartest lady, full of grey tortitude, also an interdimensional traveller whose organisational prowess I marvel at daily and which I drew upon for the character of the cat).

Much love also to the many trees of this city, and to my favourite pubs, in whose corners I sat with my laptop and a pint (or two) those many afternoons.

About the Author

Jools Warner is a tarot nerd from Saturn, and author of *Ernie and the Mage-Killer*. Starting out her current incarnation in a succession of unassuming English towns, early creative experiments fell by the wayside when the depression kicked in and refused to budge for quite some time. Story-writing was forsaken altogether, which was a bit silly, to be honest; it could have been rather helpful. Academic successes led to a PhD in Death Studies (yes, really) and a career in said field. Realising later, however, as a person sometimes does, that this was not what she really wanted to do, and wondering whatever happened to that whole writing thing, she took decisive steps. Wrestling with self-doubt, Jools wrote words, and then more words, qualified as a yoga instructor, left academia, did an MA in Creative Writing, turned professional with the tarot thing, and wrote even more words. She lives atop a hill in Sheffield, UK, sharing her home with two cats, one of whom is really bureaucratic.

Sphinx and Sul Books

Sphinx is the fiction imprint of Sul Books.

Born from a collaboration of two long-time independent esoteric publishers, and named to honor the Suleviae — the sisterhood of goddesses revered at springs throughout Europe — Sul Books is dedicated to publishing works that manifest aspects of the sacred sight that heals what humans have harmed.

Each of our imprints is guided by a commitment to pluralism, dissent, and the autonomy of humans, with a core focus on the importance of indigenous, animist, and non-industrial ways of being in the world.

Find out more at Sulbooks.com